tHE Last Knight

The Last Knight

A Knight and Rogue Novel

HILARI BELL

An Imprint of HarperCollins *Publishers*

Eos is an imprint of HarperCollins Publishers.

The Last Knight
Copyright © 2007 by Hilari Bell

Library of Congress Cataloging-in-Publication Data
Bell, Hilari.
    The last knight / Hilari Bell. — 1st ed.
        p.   cm. — (Knight and rogue)
    Summary: In alternate chapters, eighteen-year-old Sir Michael Sevenson, an
anachronistic knight errant, and seventeen-year-old Fisk, his street-wise squire,
tell of their noble quest to bring Lady Ceciel to justice while trying to solve her
husband's murder.
    ISBN 978-0-06-082503-4 (trade bdg.)
    ISBN 978-0-06-082504-1 (lib. bdg.)
    [1. Knights and knighthood—Fiction. 2. Fantasy.] I. Title.
PZ7.B38894Las 2007   2006036427
[Fic]—dc22   CIP
                                                       AC

Typography by Joel Tippie
1 2 3 4 5 6 7 8 9 10
❖
First Edition

To Aunt Temple and Uncle Bill,
who've supported my books from the start

The Last Knight

CHAPTER 1

Fisk

To say it was a dark and stormy night would be a gross understatement. It was colder than a witch's kiss, wetter than a spring swamp, and blacker than a tax collector's heart. A sane man would have been curled up in front of a fire with a cup of mulled wine and a good boo—, ah, a willing wench. But not me. I was out in it. I'm squire to a hero.

At least the downpour that had drenched us all afternoon was now beginning to slacken. The Green Moon hadn't risen, but the Creature Moon was high enough to glow dimly through the churning clouds, shedding just enough light for me to watch the damsel being lowered from the tower. Not that I could see her well, with the rain splattering into my eyes whenever I looked up; she was only a dim shape of swirling skirts and hair, dangling from a knotted rope.

Sir Michael, my employer, had tied those knots to make handholds for the climb down. He was inside the tower now, slowly releasing the rope. The woman bounced when the knots slid over the windowsill, but the lady had the sense to brace her feet against the tower. She was doing all right.

But if she slipped and set up a screech, or if anything alerted the guards, who were currently dicing on the tower's ground floor, I was going to take Tipple and ride off as fast as I could. Tipple was the faster and sounder of the two horses I was "guarding," and even she wouldn't be able to move quickly in this much mud. I had seen enough of my employer, in the one week we'd known each other, to be certain he'd put up a good enough fight to delay them while I escaped.

I had suggested hiring a nice dry carriage . . . but even if he'd agreed, Sir Michael would have expected me to drive it.

When Sir Michael first told me he'd take me as his squire (this was after he'd told me he was a knight errant, and I'd asked if his keepers knew he was out), he said that all proper knights errant had trusty squires behind them.

Shaken as I was at the time, I still had the sense to refrain from saying that "behind him" was where I intended to stay. Looking after lunatics isn't a job I fancy—but then, I didn't have much choice in the matter.

This is the modern age. Knights errant have been extinct for over two hundred years, and even when they existed, errantry wasn't what you'd call a practical profession. I'd outgrown that kind of romantic idiocy before I was ten, but looking at his calm face, I realized that Sir Michael—a full year older than my own seventeen—was perfectly serious.

He'd done a better job getting into the tower than I had expected—crazy people must have an advantage when it comes to doing crazy things. The rain-slick ruins of the keep provided a treacherous but manageable staircase that stopped just short of the third-floor window where Sir Michael had entered the tower. The only tricky part was climbing the last ten feet of sheer stone to the third floor. It took him four tries. A woman climbing down never could have done it.

The tower's upper windows were dark, which meant there were probably no guards on the upper floors. The lady's steward had warned us, several times, what would happen if the guards caught us.

But the lady was now only twenty feet from the ground and no alarm had sounded.

Who had bothered to maintain this old tower, and why? It had no use that I could see, except as a prison.

Even if the noble who owned the manor at the foot of the hill was trying to wed a spectacularly Gifted young widow by force, he still wouldn't need a prison often enough to make preserving the tower worthwhile.

Gifts may pass from a woman to her children of either sex, but no man, no matter how great his own Gifts, will pass them on to his descendants. Because of this, Gifted women are sometimes forced into marriage—though these days the force usually consists of gold roundels applied to the pockets of the woman's male relations. But the ragged old man with the missing foot had sworn that he was steward to a lady who was being held prisoner in the tower, and here she was, coming down on the rope.

Sir Michael had worried that she might have been dosed with aquilas, which is frequently used to subdue abducted damsels. That could have slowed down our escape, but nothing had hindered matters so far.

She was less than ten feet from the ground now, so it was time for me to do something.

I checked Chanticleer's and Tipple's tethers—though being bright beasts they showed no sign of wanting to leave the shelter of the crumbling wall—and walked carefully through the slippery mud to the tower's base.

The lady's long, dark hair no longer swirled, but

clung to her head in much the same way the bodice of her dress clung to her figure. An admirable figure, but it didn't keep me from noticing that she had pulled back one dainty foot to kick me in the face. Her expression was a mixture of fear, determination, and misery, but determination came out on top.

I stopped, well out of range, and murmured, "It's me, Fisk, his squire. So don't kick me, all right?"

"His *what* ?" she whispered. The rope jerked and she bounced downward. Her descent had looked smoother from a distance. Or perhaps Sir Michael was getting tired.

I stepped forward warily, and caught her in my arms as the rope slackened. "It's a long story."

Her amused, rain-wet face was attractive, if you like strong, even features better than soft prettiness. Me, I like both, but the willful glint in her eyes was enough to warn any sensible man.

I set her down and began untying the harness knotted around her waist and thighs.

She tried to help, but her hands were too cold. She was soaked to the skin, so offering my cloak—which was almost soaked through—would have been stupid, if chivalrous. I *was* going to offer her a blanket from our pack, but the moment the knots came loose, she grabbed my hand and pulled me toward the horses.

"Come on! We've got to get out of here."

Sheer surprise froze me in my tracks. *I* had been willing to desert Sir Michael at the first sign of trouble, but I hadn't expected the damsel we were rescuing to share that attitude. Maybe she was too frightened to think clearly.

When I didn't move, she dropped my arm and squished toward the horses by herself. I got there first.

"We have to wait for him," I hissed.

She didn't look frightened. She glared at me.

I glared back, glad that I was bigger and stronger than she was. Well, stronger anyway—she was a tallish woman and I am only of middle height. She certainly hadn't been dosed with aquilas, or anything else. I was beginning to regret that.

She saw that I wasn't backing down and turned away, folding her arms around herself. She was shivering. I didn't offer her a blanket.

We both looked up.

Sir Michael was only a third of the way down. Like the lady, he used his feet against the tower, but then the wind caught his cloak and spun him into the wall with a smack that made me flinch. Dice games tend to be noisy, thank goodness, and the tower walls were thick, but even so . . .

Sir Michael wrapped his feet around the rope and stood on one of the knots. It occurred to me, as I watched him sway, that if he was hurt it was all over, because I was *not* going to try to climb that rope.

Maybe he was resting his arms. He had already climbed a tower wall and lowered a woman. Then his cloak swirled out, and I saw he had unfastened the clasp. He flung it away, and the wind carried it over the wall into darkness. It couldn't have fallen far—if his cloak was as wet as mine it must weigh half a stone—but I wasn't about to go after it.

Chanticleer looked up too, nostrils flaring as he caught his master's scent. My heart lurched, for there was a reason Sir Michael had named his big gray gelding after a rooster. "A neigh that would rouse the dead" was how he phrased it. It would certainly rouse the tower guard.

The lady's eyes widened in alarm, but she didn't seem to have any bright ideas either. If it had been day I would have slapped the horse's muzzle. Chant wasn't magica—both the Green and the Furred Gods be thanked. But with the small, tan Creature Moon glinting through the clouds, striking any animal was a bad idea. Riding after dark, on a mud-slick road, all kinds of things could go wrong.

Instead, I wrapped the corner of my cloak around

Chanticleer's nose. I was only trying to muffle the sound, but my cloak distracted the beast from any thought of calling to his master as he tried to unwrap himself. By the time we finished wrestling, Sir Michael was halfway down the rope.

He descended slowly now, stopping to rest several times. He tried, once, to use his legs on the rope, but the wind thumped him against the wall so hard he almost lost his grip. So he had to go down hand over hand, and he almost made it. He was only twelve feet from the ground when his grip gave out, and he fell into the mud with a liquid splat.

Fortunately, the mud was quite deep. I picked my way over to him. "Are you all right, Noble Sir?"

Mud coated his shoulder-length, light brown hair and splattered his mildly handsome face. He blinked dazedly. Then sense returned to his eyes and with it a blazing excitement.

"Fi," he gasped. "Um fi." Sir Michael lifted a filthy hand and I hauled him to his feet. Grabbing my arm, he staggered toward the horses. About halfway there he quit leaning on me and his breathing steadied.

The woman had untethered both beasts, but she had waited for us instead of mounting and galloping off, as I'd half expected. It hadn't worried me—I'd figured she'd take Chanticleer, who was bigger and better-looking than Tipple, and we'd catch her easily when he came up lame.

As it was, no one went galloping off. Sir Michael, after a glance at the quiet tower, took the time to drag a couple of blankets out of our packs—one for her, one for him. I winced when the blanket fell over his filthy shoulders, since the job of washing it would no doubt fall to me.

He mounted Chanticleer, and I assisted the lady into the saddle in front of him with an inelegant, but effective, boost to the buttocks. Then I mounted Tipple and we set off at a brisk walk, which was the fastest pace practical in the dark and mud.

The rain had stopped, but the skittering breeze found every gap in my damp clothing, making me grateful for Tipple's neck, where I warmed first one hand and then the other.

The grayish globe of the Green Moon had now risen and we could see the road well enough to avoid the rocks, though some of the potholes still surprised us. Sir Michael might have been right not to rent a carriage, but the sharp wind was sufficiently annoying to keep me from admitting it.

He was explaining to the lady that we couldn't go faster because Chanticleer had a bad leg.

". . . not truly bad, but he'll come up lame if I ride

him too hard. And with the Creature Moon showing that wouldn't be advisable, would it?"

If I read him right, Sir Michael wouldn't override a horse even if the Furred God had never existed.

The lady frowned. "Why ride such a poor beast at all?"

"He wishes it," Sir Michael told her. "He'd been put out to pasture and was pining to go. Every time another horse went out he'd neigh most pathetically. So when I set off on my errantry I took him, and he's been a true and faithful companion."

"I'd have thought a . . . a knight errant would have a magic horse." The lady spoke cautiously, like someone humoring a lunatic.

Sir Michael was sane enough to understand how crazy he appeared to others. He grinned and replied practically, "If I'd taken one of the magica, my father would have taken it back. Don't worry, Chant will get us there."

"And where is 'there' ?" the lady asked. "I'm grateful for my rescue, but I'd like to know where we're going." She was trying to sound soft and damsel-like, but there was a distinct edge in her voice.

"We're taking you to your steward," Sir Michael told her. "He's the one who told us of your plight."

Every muscle in the lady's body relaxed. "Hackle."

She was smiling—the first genuine smile I'd seen on her face.

"Hackle?" asked Sir Michael.

"My steward. And a true friend. Just as your squire"— her lips twitched—"must be to you."

Sir Michael glanced at me, and I tried to look loyal and true. It's not an expression with which I've had much practice.

"Perhaps. Someday," he murmured.

Over my corpse. I might be trapped in this mess now, but I planned to take my leave of this mad "knight errant"—at the first moment I could manage it without getting every sheriff in the realm on my tail.

Sir Michael and the lady had gone on to talk about horses. I've noticed that nobles use the topic of horses the way farmers use weather or townsmen taxes—an instant common interest.

Having no interest in the subject myself, I concentrated on finding the shallower stretches of mud. Tipple may be spotted like a jester's britches, but she's a sensible beast and was happy to cooperate. Sir Michael had rescued her from a drunken carter, who was beating her for putting him into a ditch. She was drunk too at the time, a habit Sir Michael blames on the carter. Having known the little mare a week, I believe she has a natural inclination toward the vice.

She's fine as long as you keep her away from beer. Sir Michael was using her as a packhorse until he needed a mount for me.

As we neared the Halloway River the woods gave way to fallow fields, so it was surprising when a quiet voice hailed us from a thicket beside the road.

The lady started, but relaxed again when her steward rode out of the brush.

Eight hard-faced men followed him. Their cloaks didn't match, which was odd for men in the same service. If they were trying to disguise themselves, they were doing a good job of it—their armor didn't match either. Most men-at-arms wore breastplates, bracers, light helms, and maybe some chain mail over their joints. These men all had helms, but some wore plain leather bracers, while some were studded with metal, and their breastplates had the same random look about them. What's the difference between a bandit and a man-at-arms? Men-at-arms get paid on Skinday—bandits get paid every day.

Under his cloak, the steward wore the same ragged doublet in which he'd first approached us.

"My lady." His voice held warm relief and an affection that couldn't have been faked. "Are you all right?"

"I'm fine, Hackle. Thanks to you."

Hackle dropped his reins to take her hand, and laid

his forehead against it in the old ceremonial gesture of fealty.

Sir Michael was visibly moved. Me, I felt some thanks were due to us—or at least to him. But if he had no complaints, who was I to quibble?

Hackle straightened and called for one of the men to lead up a spare horse—already wearing a sidesaddle. There was a bit of commotion about getting the lady from one horse to the other. To do her justice, she was perfectly willing to dismount into the mud and mount again, and Hackle, with his peg leg, could hardly assist her. It was Sir Michael who won the honor of stepping down and splashing around Chanticleer's nose to lift the lady from one horse to the next—which was doubly absurd, since she was as muddy as he was. Well, almost as muddy.

"Where do you go now?" he asked, as she struggled to arrange her damp skirts.

She looked at Hackle, who replied, "To her brother. He'll be able to keep her safe from that scoundrel, I promise you."

The back of my neck prickled. "Where is this brother?" I asked. "Why didn't *he* rescue her?"

"He was away on business," Hackle said smoothly. "I feared it would take several days to track him down, and that the lady might be wed before he could reach her."

It must have taken him several days to find us—knights errant don't exactly litter the countryside—but Sir Michael accepted the story.

The lady thanked Sir Michael. He said it was his privilege. I wished they'd finish so we could leave.

Evidently Hackle felt the same. "My lady, we must go."

"Do you want Fisk and me to accompany you?" Sir Michael asked helpfully.

"No!" The lady and Hackle spoke together. Only a split second of self-control kept me from joining in.

"You have done your part, Sir Michael," the lady went on. "You have my gratitude."

"May I also have your name?" Sir Michael asked.

Why hadn't I wondered about that? Damsels in ballads weren't required to give names, but really . . . I'd better get away from Sir Michael soon. All this chivalry was turning my brain to mush.

The lady knew her ballads too. "Perhaps. Someday." She smiled mysteriously and rode off, her men following.

Sir Michael stood in the mud and watched them go, wearing the satisfied expression of someone who has fulfilled his knightly duty. I wished I could whack him.

"Can we go now?" I asked instead. "And find a dry place to spend what little is left of the night?"

"Certainly!" Sir Michael sprang into the saddle like

the youth he was. Mind you, I was a youth too, but the shining enthusiasm on his face made me feel like a gaffer.

"I noticed a farmhouse back down the road," he continued. "We'll sleep in their barn. Most folks don't mind, as long as you pay in the morning. So, Fisk, what do you think of your first adventure?"

In truth, it wasn't my first adventure—not by any means. But it was my first good deed, so I thought about it. And what I thought was . . .

"It was too easy."

"Too . . . You weren't the one climbing that cursed rope!"

"I don't mean that. It went off too well. Nothing went wrong. Nothing disrupted the plan. When a con goes that smoothly, it's usually because someone is setting *you* up."

Much too easy. I was beginning to get nervous.

Sir Michael laughed. "This isn't a con, Fisk, 'tis an adventure! A glorious one."

A glorious adventure. In other words, a disaster in the making.

"You're the knight, Noble Sir."

We slept in the barn loft, snuggled deep in piles of straw. The dogs had put up quite a racket, until Sir

Michael made friends with them. I've noticed that a lot of nobles have the Gift of animal handling.

Getting warm relaxed me. When I heard footsteps and jingling metal in the barn below, I pulled my blanket over my head and went back to sleep—until rough hands grabbed my ankles and dragged me out of the straw.

I sleep on my stomach, so my chin hit the wooden floor with a painful thud. By the time I recovered, the hands had pinned my arms behind my back, holding me against the floor. Another set of hands ran along my sides, like someone was looking for a purse—or a weapon.

"We don't have any money," I muttered, twisting my head and blinking the straw out of my eyelashes. In truth we hadn't much, but I'd have said the same no matter how much coin we carried.

The morning light, glowing dimly through the big hatch in the floor, was bright enough to show the triumph on the faces of five men-at-arms—with *matching* cloaks and armor.

They hauled Sir Michael to his feet. He wasn't very impressive, with rumpled, straw-filled hair, and his shirt hanging loose over his britches. But the length of his hair identified him as noble—and therefore the boss. Two men were holding his arms.

"Is this your cloak?" The fifth man, who had patrol leader written all over him, held out a dirty, dark brown cloak. The seven oaks with intertwined branches embroidered on the corners were clearly visible. But Sir Michael's saddle, which had the same device embossed on the skirt, was down below with the horses. There was a chance, a bare chance—

"Yes, 'tis mine," said my idiot employer. He was trying to stand straight and proud, which is hard when someone is twisting your arms behind your back. "What is the meaning of this?"

This was no time to call attention to myself. Maybe, just maybe, they wouldn't recognize me. Though if they didn't, I was sure Sir Michael would truthfully remind them.

"If this is your cloak then you know what it means, you son of a mongrel cur," said the patrol leader pleasantly. "You're under arrest, on the authority of Lord Dorian."

"On what charge?" Sir Michael demanded. I was curious myself, in a sick, stomach-knotted way.

"On the charge of helping a murderess escape the liege's justice."

"What!" Sir Michael beat me to it, but not by much. Our shrieks blended perfectly.

The leader grinned. "Well played, scum. But this

cloak, which matches the saddle down below, was found at the foot of Sorrowston Tower. And the rope that was hanging from the window of Ceciel Mallory's cell matches the tether ropes in your pack, so playing innocent isn't going to save you."

I kept my mouth shut as they tied our hands and prepared to haul us off to jail—probably the same tower we'd just broken that lying, murderous bitch out of.

No matter what happened, I wanted a few words alone with my employer—but not yet. There wasn't a wisecrack in the world that was worth the risk of hanging for it.

CHAPTER 2
Michael

Fisk clanked into the cell and flashed a sharp look about. Seeing that I was the only other occupant, he stalked over and sat on the second small cot, arranging his manacled wrists in his lap. His expression was angry and sullen, as it had been since our arrest, but now there was strain around the edges. If the judicars had interrogated him as fiercely as they had me, 'twas no wonder.

The guard stepped into the cramped, stone-walled room to make certain that nothing was amiss. The late-afternoon light streaming through the high, barred window showed all there was to see, but they took no chances with the "daring villains" who had broken a murderess out of Sorrowston Tower. A final hard look assured the guard I was lying on my cot, staring gloomily up at the ceiling, so he departed.

The click of the lock still echoed when my squire spoke. "I thought you planned to *save* me from a life of crime. What does a knight errant do now, Noble Sir?"

I sighed. Fisk only calls me Noble Sir when he's being sarcastic—a thing he thinks I haven't noticed, though I'd have to be stone stupid to have missed it. I've invited him to call me Michael, for I know that the philosophers are right when they say a man's birth rank is no measure of his worth. Fisk hasn't yet called me anything but Sir, or Noble Sir. Mayhap he'll come to it, someday. In the meantime, however, I should like it if he called me Noble Sir less frequently.

When I didn't reply, Fisk went on bitterly, "Though knight *erring* would be more like it. Of all the stupid, lamebrained, half-assed stunts . . ."

It isn't proper for a squire to scold a knight, but I saw no way to stop him. Besides, being in jail again must have brought back fearful memories of his last imprisonment, which was too recent to be easily forgotten.

When I first encountered Fisk, little more than a week ago, 'twas early in the month of Appleon and the road into Deepbend teemed with carts of apples being carried off to fruit cellars, cider mills, and the larger towns. We'd had several bright days, by the Green God's grace, and the cart wheels raised a fine dust that coated my clothes and the inside of my mouth—but a few fracts tossed to a carter fetched me a crisp apple, which cleared the dusty taste wonderfully.

I was happy that day, as I've been, by and large, since I left my home. The life of a knight errant wasn't quite what I had expected. In the old ballads, errantry entails heroic deeds, terrible risks, and the defeat of great evils. I'd spent more of the last year doing odd jobs than good deeds. But in that year of wandering, first north to the timberlands, then south down the Erran River, I'd had my share of adventure, become proficient at all sorts of tasks, and, yes, assisted a few good folk who were in need of an outstretched hand.

Finding myself only a few weeks' travel from home, I thought I should visit my family and assure them of my well-being. When I made this decision it had seemed a good notion, but the closer to home I came, the more my anticipation of a lively argument weighed on my mind. I thought I'd spent the last year right worthily—but I knew my father would not agree. I rode into Deepbend trying to displace my worries with thoughts of a hot noon meal at an inn. Most of my wages from the barge master were still in my purse, and I felt quite rich.

The flowers in the window boxes had faded, but the ivy climbing the dark timbers was red as a cock's wattle and the thatch shone like buffed gold.

When I saw the crowd in the market square, I hoped there might be a tourney in the offing. In centuries past, when knights brought the king's justice to an unruly realm, the tourney was their training ground. Those who lost paid a high penalty, forfeiting their horse and the armor they fought in to the knight who defeated them. And back then, armor was very expensive to replace.

In these times, tourneys are little more than an excuse for a great fair. But a mock battle is still offered and Chant's leg had been holding up well lately. Between us, we might have had a chance at the cash prize that has replaced the horse-and-armor ransom. 'Twould also serve as an excuse to delay my homecoming, but I didn't dwell on that.

Riding farther into the square, I saw a long platform with three black-caped judicars seated at a table upon it, and remembered that in Lord Malcolm's fiefdom the first Hornday of the month was judgment day. The size of the crowd spoke of some crime so terrible it called for redemption in blood. This chilled me, though Father would call me soft for it. I considered traveling on and making my noon meal of apples. But Lord Malcolm is neighbor to my father's liege, and I knew I should stay long enough to discover what the crime had been.

Even as I made my decision, they led out the prisoners. There were three of them, and Chant's high back gave me an excellent view over the crowd. The first was a pinch-faced woman, of middle age, whose cap and apron were so white they glowed in the sun. The next was a man, older, but still hard-muscled, wearing a farmer's rough work shirt, with a black and purple swelling on one cheek. His lip was split as well, and he winced when the sun struck his eyes. As obvious a case of drunken brawling as ever I've seen, and recent enough that he was still hungover. He stumbled mounting the steps to the platform, and the last man in line thrust out a manacled hand to catch him.

The third prisoner was a young man, close to my own age. His short hair was trimmed more neatly than that of most commoners, and he wore a clean shirt and drab doublet, like those of a clerk, or a young merchant. He kept a hand under the older man's elbow until they settled into place before the judicars. His expression was distant and still, and I saw that he had helped the man without thinking about it. His face was so honest that I wondered if the judicars might have erred. He was neither handsome nor homely, the kind of young man mothers pray will come courting their daughters and the daughters dismiss as too dull.

But his place, last in line, indicated that his crime was the most serious—and his pallor that the sentence was likely to be severe.

For someone whose face was green with terror, his composure was admirable.

A clerk read out charges against the woman. She and her husband were bakers, with a habit of sliding their thumbs onto the scales when they weighed the loaves. Their customers complained, and the deputies had caught her at it.

Her husband, who stood at the front of the crowd, obviously considered himself to be on trial with his wife. Judging by the comments I overheard, he deserved to be.

They defended themselves hotly—they had never been accused of such a thing! (The crowd laughed at this.) They couldn't think who'd persecute them so maliciously. The deputies were blind, bought, acting out of spite, idiots . . .

Then the clerk read the sum of the damages claimed by their victims—nearly a hundred gold roundels. The baker and his wife shrieked with outrage.

This time the judicars silenced them. Or rather, the judicar who sat in the middle did. He had a narrow face, a gray-streaked beard, and a personality forceful enough to silence the bakers and the crowd.

He said that the amount claimed seemed excessive. In fact, his clerk estimated that if every man, woman, and child in town had eaten an entire loaf of bread every day for a year, they still couldn't have been cheated out of half that sum.

The townsfolk laughed again, a little sheepishly. 'Tis known that when a criminal is caught, even folk with honest intent tend to imagine that more is owed them than they truly lost. And not everyone is honest.

The judicars conferred, then decreed the baker's wife guilty. She could redeem herself if all the loaves *and* all the flour the couple owned were portioned out to all customers who had accounts at their shop, and that further, she must pay five gold roundels to reimburse the court.

The baker moaned that they were ruined, ruined, and his wife looked even more pinched. But in the opinion of the crowd it was a fair judgment.

The next case up was the older man with the bruised face. The tapster from the inn where the fight took place testified that the old man had indeed started it—this time.

A man of the same age and sort as the prisoner, standing to the right of the platform, said wait till next time and he'd do better. His speech was slurred by a badly swollen lip.

The old man on the platform shouted, "You and what other three men?" then winced as his headache punished him.

The crowd's amusement told me this was an old feud that never caused great trouble. 'Twas the innkeeper who brought charges, and a bill for smashed furniture, a window, and the keg that had been hurled out the window.

The judicars found the damages, thirteen gold roundels and four fracts, reasonable. They added the usual ten percent charge for the nuisance of having to replace everything, and five gold roundels to the court.

The total made the old man flinch. When he protested that it would take him months to work that off, an embarrassed-looking woman in the front of the crowd told her "pa" that he'd no call to complain after the trouble and shame he'd caused his family.

The stout young man beside her paid the fine, remarking cheerfully that he was going to get some help building that fence, after all. The crowd chuckled, and the judicars reminded the man that since he had redeemed his father-in-law, he was responsible for the old man's behavior until he paid his debt.

Then a deputy pushed the third prisoner, the young man, forward, and the crowd's mood changed as if a cloud had swept over the sun.

The young man was identified as most often calling himself Fisk—and it appeared that he had good reason for using several names.

He had convinced a rug merchant in Meeton to invest in an undiscovered tin mine—which didn't exist except in Fisk's counterfeit samples. He had sold a woman who ran a dress shop a potion guaranteed to restore her lost youth and beauty. He had convinced a young spice merchant to finance an expedition to find the fabled cities of gold that belonged to the savages who dwelt in the desert. He had . . .

The young man denied none of the charges, though his lips clamped tighter and tighter.

Opinion in the crowd was mixed—there was little doubt of the man's guilt, but his victims were not popular.

Indeed, when the elderly seamstress confessed her shame, a young woman in front of me muttered, "Serves her right, the nasty old hag." She then told the man beside her that one of her cousins had sewed for the woman, who worked her girls hard, paid them little, and slapped them if a customer was displeased.

As the list went on and comments rumbled around me, I gathered that the spice merchant, who was rumored to drive a ruthless bargain, was the strong-willed judicar's nephew.

I began to feel uneasy. The judicar had been admirably impartial so far, but men can act outside their natures when family is involved. The sums this young man had taken were large, but the people he'd gulled were rich—and though all were angry, none claimed to have been impoverished.

Fisk *did* protest some of the sums, but he, understandably, had kept no records.

The plump judicar seated on the left appeared to share my disquiet—his eyes were downcast, and his fingers drummed on the table.

The charges were finally finished. I'm not good with sums, but I knew the total would be large.

The leading judicar leaned forward and spoke: "There is no doubt of this man's guilt. Nor can anyone doubt that he has befooled and robbed others. For their sakes, I am levying a nuisance charge of thirty percent on the total fine."

The crowd gasped—ten percent was standard, twenty might be levied if the crime was unusually vicious, but thirty percent was unheard of. A sick feeling took possession of my stomach—this was injustice! It could be appealed to the liege, but unless the liege showed up in the next ten minutes, appeals would be too late to help Fisk.

Neither of the other judicars protested. The one in charge continued, "The addition of five gold roundels to pay the court raises the total fine to nine hundred and fifteen roundels. Master Fisk, can you pay this sum and redeem yourself?"

Fisk's face was taut, but he answered boldly, "You know perfectly well I can't. In fact, since I'm sure you know how much I have to the last brass fract, why don't you tell me? How much am I short?"

A shocked murmur rippled through the crowd and the judicar turned an ugly shade of red, but he spoke coolly.

"The amount in your possession, Master Fisk, falls fifty-two gold roundels short of the court's demand."

Only fifty-two? He must be a very successful rogue! But short was short, and a fine not redeemed in gold must be redeemed in labor—or blood. In cases of non-violent crime judicars almost always ask for labor, but the sinking in my heart, and the ill-concealed fear on Fisk's face, proclaimed that this judicar was going to demand blood. Fisk must have known it from the start.

"So, Master Fisk, since you can't redeem yourself . . ."

Knowing he faced flogging, perhaps even maiming, Fisk had still helped the old man on the steps.

". . . unless someone else puts forward the rest of the sum . . ."

Fifty-two gold roundels would buy a fat pig. The crowd might have some pity for the rogue, but no one can spare that much money for a stranger. A criminal stranger, for whom *they* would be responsible until he paid them back.

I had fifty gold roundels in my purse.

".‌ . . I must demand your restitution in . . ."

I don't know who was more astonished when I called out that I would redeem him. The judicar was furious, but having set the terms himself, there was nothing he could do. Fisk's expression was a treat. The speed with which his astonished relief changed to suspicion told me much about how the world had treated him thus far.

I had to make up the last few roundels in silver and brass, but a light purse doesn't worry me. Though I did wonder, with some trepidation, what Father would think of him.

Fisk thought that I was crazy when I told him I was a knight errant—I have learned to say it straight out, and let folk laugh as they will. When I said I'd take him as my squire, and let him redeem himself in that capacity, he made no protest—until I refused to set a time limit on his service. I could have done so, but I was afraid that if I loosed him in the world he'd get into trouble again. And that would be a pity, for I believed there was a good man under his cynical manner.

The true problem was that he resented having to be grateful to me. I understood that.

Listening now to the tramp of many horses arriving outside our cell—knowing who it must be, curse it—I feared I was about to find myself in the same position.

Fisk heard them too, and fell silent.

"'Tis all right," I assured him, trying to steel, or at least conceal, my quaking nerves. "They're coming for me, but they'll bring you along."

"That makes it all right? Who's coming? Murder is redeemed in blood, if not in life! I don't know the penalty for helping a murderess escape, but—"

"Don't worry," I told him. "This price is mine alone to pay—which is fair, since the error was mine. I only wish it was to be paid in blood. It would hurt less."

Fisk opened his mouth to call me a lunatic—and not for the first time—but the lock clicked, the door opened, and in he came. He looked well, though he must have ridden the night through to get here from Seven Oaks so quickly.

"Hello, Michael. I see I needn't ask how your career as a knight errant is progressing."

I remembered how Fisk had stood up to the judicars in the marketplace, straight and calm. When your fate is upon you, 'tis best to face it boldly. Especially when fate is blocking the only exit.

"Hello, Father."

CHAPTER 3

Fisk

Father? *You poor bastard.* Needless to say, I didn't speak the thought aloud.

There are two kinds of noblemen. (Actually there are probably twenty or thirty kinds, as there are within any subset of humanity, but still . . .) The first kind are men who, if they hadn't been high-born, would have been perfectly ordinary shepherds or shopkeepers or whatever. They make wonderful gulls. The second kind are men who would have clawed their way to the top no matter what they were born. And as a man whose name wasn't Jack Bannister used to say, you don't even want to think about gulling them.

Baron Seven Oaks was obviously one of the latter. His dark wool doublet and britches looked plain, until you saw how well they were made. Good fabric, well cut, needs no other ornament, and Baron Seven

Oaks evidently knew it—or maybe he just didn't care. His iron-gray hair was cut shorter than most nobles', though not quite peasant short. He could have shaved it to his scalp—no one who saw the straightness of his back, and the arrogant way he held his head, would ever mistake him for anything but what he was.

I began to feel more hopeful. With this man on our side, we might keep our hides intact after all. *But was he on our side?* My father had his faults, but he'd never looked at me as if he was dispassionately considering whether or not to eviscerate me.

Sir Michael stood up under that look better than I would have. Perhaps he was accustomed to it.

The old man's keen eyes took in the scruffy wool and leather, the shaggy, too-long hair, the small scar that marked one side of Sir Michael's jaw. My employer looked more like a down-on-his-luck bandit than a noble's son—until you saw his eyes.

Sir Michael let his father finish his examination and then asked him straight out, "Have you redeemed me, Sir?"

"Yes," said his father, with equal bluntness.

"And my squire as well?"

The old man turned that eviscerating look on me—I sat up straighter. The baron sighed.

"There was no need. Your testimony cleared him of everything but serving an idiot."

Sir Michael drew a deep, bracing breath. "How much?"

Was there a trace of pity in the baron's gaze? His face and voice were neutral. "Five thousand gold roundels."

Sir Michael paled. "Sir . . . can you afford that?"

"Can I *afford* it? Not easily. Can I pay it? Yes. I already have."

Some of the stiffness went out of Sir Michael's back. His voice was rough with relief and pain as he asked, "And how am I to repay so great a sum?"

His father considered him. "I'm not sure. I'm still thinking about it."

A flicker of surprise crossed Sir Michael's face, and I guessed that the baron was seldom unsure about anything.

"You'll let me know when you make up your mind?" Had it been anyone but Sir Michael, I'd have sworn I heard sarcasm in his voice.

The baron heard it too and smiled—a rather grim smile. "Oh, I'll let you know. Meanwhile, we might as well go home." He cast a distasteful look around the cell, turned, and went out.

Taking another deep breath, Sir Michael started after him and I followed.

Sir Michael soon caught up with the old man. "My horses? My gear?"

"I brought the horses. There's gear on their saddles, so I assume 'tis yours."

We clattered up the rickety wooden steps and into the sunlight. I hadn't been out of the prison since yesterday, and the air, still fresh from last night's shower, smelled wonderful: clear, crisp, and lightly scented with woodsmoke from the nearby village and the spicy smell of wet fallen leaves.

Two men-at-arms, whose pine-green cloaks bore the Seven Oaks badge, were waiting for us, holding Chanticleer, Tipple, and a big, roman-nosed, dun stallion that was so ugly most nobles wouldn't have been caught dead on him.

Tipple looked like a midget jester between two knights, and the baron winced at the sight. He looked more displeased about Tipple than he had about me, which I took as a hopeful sign.

Sir Michael noticed his father's expression. "You were the one who taught me that a horse's color is irrelevant, Sir. She's sound and well-mannered."

The baron sighed again, and I made a mental note to keep Tipple *far* away from beer. Then his face softened.

"At least you've taken good care of this fellow." He stroked Chanticleer's nose and the horse snuffled at him. "How's that injured leg of his doing?"

That topic got us mounted and onto the road. It was almost dry now, with only intermittent mudholes remaining from the last big rain.

The prison where we'd been held was in an abandoned mill on the outskirts of Willowere, a village nearly large enough to be called a town. It was very late in the afternoon, and I had hopes of a bath and bed at an inn, not to mention a better meal than the thin stew that had served as prison fare. So I was disappointed when we took the road away from Willowere.

At this time of day sensible people were heading into the village, so we passed a steady stream of returning plow horses, with a handful of carts and carriages, a tinker, a traveling bookseller, and a wandering beggar thrown in for good measure. The beggar hauled out his cup and called for alms as we rode by.

Sir Michael reached for his purse but the sheriff had taken it. It was probably in the pack on Chanticleer's rump.

The baron tossed a handful of fracts into the cup.

"Thank you, Noble Sir!" the beggar cried, rattling the coins with a vigor that made Tipple shy. I barely managed to keep my seat. Not being a nobleman, I wasn't thrown onto a horse's back before I could walk, and I'm not ashamed of it.

The baron scowled. "Horn and hoof! Son, if you had to have a . . . squire, why couldn't you take one of the men-at-arms instead of a town-bred gutterling with 'knave' written all over him?"

I was too surprised to take offense, for most people don't see past my honest face. The baron obviously had the Gift of reading people—it's common among nobles. A pity his son didn't have it. He might have seen through Lady Ceciel.

"Fisk *was* a knave," said Sir Michael. "But now he is a squire. Mayhap the writing you see will change, in time."

The baron looked exasperated, an attitude with which I could sympathize.

Sir Michael asked, rather hastily, how someone named Benton was doing.

Benton was at university and had started his master's work. I forgot that I was trying to avoid notice and asked what his subject was. The baron looked surprised at such a knowledgeable question. He replied that it had to do with a new way to learn about the lives of the ancients by digging up their ruins, though that was as much as he could figure out from Benton's letters.

It sounded like a promising thesis, but I'd gone back to avoiding attention, so I just nodded. If the baron could pay five thousand gold roundels to redeem Sir Michael, he could buy his other son a place at university whether his master's work was judged worthy or not.

For Benton, I learned, was a son, as were Justin (who was doing well at the High Liege's court, and might find himself in the treasury) and Rupert (who had probably returned home by now from looking at some new breeding stock).

They all appeared to be older than Sir Michael, which gave me my first clue as to why a noble's son was wandering the countryside as a knight errant. A wife's dowry usually provides for the second son, but any others have to find their own place. Of course, there are better places than knight errant—in fact, almost any job would be better, an opinion I suspect the baron shared.

Sir Michael's mother and his sister, Kathryn, were also fine, and some of the neighbors with sons of the right age were beginning to talk of marriage. Old Nan had finally died, but Merriot was . . .

Family gossip is boring if you aren't part of the family, but I did glean a few interesting bits. The number of neighbors who wanted to marry Kathryn told me that Sir Michael's sister was as Gifted as his father was rich.

The magic-sensing Gift is the most important, and

since most nobles select their wives for it, most nobles have it. But the sensing Gift brings with it a host of lesser abilities, which vary widely in type and strength. Some scholars hold that these other gifts aren't true magic. When a magica rabbit freezes to hide itself, it literally becomes invisible—you can look right through it and see the grass it rests on. But the odd talents with which some humans are Gifted consist more of an exaggerated knack for something anyone might do. As the baron recently demonstrated, when he looked at me and saw past the outward indicators to the person I really am, though he had no way to deduce that with the senses granted most folk.

Admittedly, some commoners have Gifts too; a knack for growing plants to sizes, or in places, that no one else can is the most common. And I once lost a considerable sum to a man who could sense the cards that were about to be dealt to him—not often the exact card, as he reluctantly explained to the skeptical judicars, just whether it would be good or bad for his hand. Like most of the lesser Gifts it worked erratically, and sometimes not at all, but he still found it very useful.

Considering the wealth and power they control, it seems unfair that nobles should be blessed with these inborn talents so much more often than the rest of us.

Of course, the possession of Gifts is one of the reasons they gain wealth and power, so I long ago decided to relieve them of a little of that wealth. After all, fair's fair.

Half an hour west of town we turned north on a road that skirted the Derens River. The Derens was too small for shipping, which made it a pretty good bet that we wouldn't encounter any more towns—and villages large enough to support an inn are rare. The temperature sank along with the sun. I huddled in my cloak, trying to resign myself to sleeping in another barn. But just as the dusk was fading we rode into a good-sized village and up to the gate of an inn called the Pig and Briar.

I can't speak for the briar part, but the pig made itself evident the moment we rode through the gate. A servant had opened its pen to feed it and, for reasons known only to the porcine mind, it dashed out and ran across the yard, right behind the heels of a pair of oxen, which were yoked to a cart from which the carter was pulling a keg.

I'm told oxen are placid creatures, but few animals are that placid. The pig was between the oxen and the cart and they couldn't see what it was. They kicked, and one heavy hoof connected. Rolled under the cart by the force of the blow, the pig screamed, and that finished the matter as far as the oxen were concerned.

The wagon's brake snapped like a twig—only much louder—as two determined oxen headed away from the monster behind them and toward the gate, where we were. I've also been told oxen are slow, but you couldn't prove it by this pair.

There was barely time to react. The men-at-arms and I were riding in the rear. Man and horse in complete agreement, Tipple and I veered off to the side. Sir Michael and his father were already in the gate— too late to go back, too narrow to turn. With a shout, Sir Michael clapped his heels against Chanticleer's gray hide. The gelding leapt forward and right, with so little space to spare that his tail swept over the ox's back.

The baron was trapped. Without a flicker of doubt in his face, he sent his ugly dun stallion straight toward the charging oxen. The dun sank on its haunches, gathered itself, and leapt, right over the length of oxen and cart. It landed neatly and pranced, snorting.

The pig rose to its feet and limped off. The servant ran after the pig and the carter ran after his oxen, swearing. The baron controlled his horse, and Sir Michael slid from the saddle and walked Chanticleer back and forth, looking for any sign of injury. The men-at-arms rode past me through the gate, one of them pausing to give my shoulder a brisk punch.

"What's the matter?" he asked. "You never seen magica before?"

As a matter of fact, I hadn't. I closed my hanging jaw and kicked Tipple forward. It's one thing to hear about horses that can outrun the wind and leap six times their length, but it was different to actually see that great body floating through the air.

No wonder no one cared that the dun was ugly.

The citybred have little contact with magic since it belongs to the realm of plants, animals, and those few humans whose minds are not strong enough to suppress their instincts. The philosophers say that intelligence and magic are antithetical, and can't exist in the same body. The old myths say that when First Man grew more intelligent than the gods, they took away his magic out of jealousy. The Savants, who are the only ones likely to know, have said nothing about why some plants and animals are born with magic that enhances their natural properties. No one really knows. Just as no one knows why men can inherit the Gift for sensing magic but only women can pass it on to their children.

I have no sensing Gift, and might not even have believed in magic if it weren't for Potter's house.

Potter lived about five streets from the small, ram-shackle house where I grew up. City born and bred, he didn't believe in magic. So when he bought a load of lumber to replace the decaying floor in his work-room, he scoffed at the herbalist's warning that there were boards from a magica oak in the load. "The stouter to build with if they are," he said. He wasn't the one who'd cut the tree. The Green God was a moon myth, Potter said . . . until the plants began to grow.

They were ordinary plants, grass and weeds, and they grew at a normal rate. But they grew between the new-laid floorboards of Potter's workroom and pulled them apart. They grew in his foundation, tearing jagged cracks in the brick walls. They grew despite all the pulling, burning, and poisoning Potter and his wife could do. Finally, with their house falling around their ears, Potter and his wife moved out.

Today a thriving meadow grows over the ruins of Potter's house, with a young oak in its center that the herbalists say is magica. No one dares build on that lot, although Potter would sell it for a few brass fracts if he could find anyone fool enough to buy.

The commotion in the inn yard settled down, eventually. It turned out that the baron had ordered rooms and dinner when he left the inn this morning, and the apologetic innkeeper assured us that all was in readiness. My only regret was that we weren't going to eat the pig.

Tipple stretched her neck toward the taproom window, nostrils wide. I reined her in sharply, dismounted, and told the groom to keep her on a tight lead and double-check the catch on her stall. The groom gave me an odd look since she couldn't stray far once the gate was closed for the night, but it was all I could do. I followed the others into the inn.

The smell of cooking drifting down the long hall between the taproom and the private dining rooms made my mouth water, but I didn't mind learning we were to bathe before dinner.

One of the men-at-arms brought a pack of clothing up to the room Michael and I shared, and a serving girl took my clothes away to see what could be done with them.

The clean shirts in the pack were cut to Sir Michael's size—he's taller, I'm stockier—but since shirts are loose they didn't fit me too badly. My doublet and britches were returned, looking remarkably good considering they'd only been brushed off and sponged down.

Sir Michael pulled on the first garment to hand, a fine wool doublet embroidered with a leafy pattern in dark brown thread. I considered helping him—was a squire supposed to? Or was that only with armor?—but he didn't appear to expect it. The clothes had obviously been his before he left home, and I noted that the doublet's shoulders were a little too tight, and the britches' waistband a little too loose. In clean, expensive clothes, Sir Michael *looked* like a noble. Or was it his silence, and the frown lines between his brows, that made him seem so distant?

He caught me staring at him. I don't know what showed in my expression, but his own softened into a smile.

"We may as well go down to dinner. Don't worry, he never eats people. Well, hardly ever."

"Eating your guests would be bad manners," I agreed tartly.

But while the baron might not eat strangers, I wouldn't bet a brass fract that he didn't sometimes chew up his sons and spit out the bones. It was in Sir Michael's eyes.

When we walked into the private dining room, I realized that a squire would be expected to serve—at least, they did back in the time when knights and squires existed. I had never served a meal, but I'd been served. I could probably handle it, but that meant I wouldn't be able to eat till after the meal was over, and that was a really dismaying thought.

Sir Michael saw my hesitation and waved me to the

third place at the table, set a little down from the other two. What was a squire's social rank these days? Probably no one knew. As high or low as I cared to make it . . . which introduced some interesting possibilities.

Dinner was excellent, with a creamy chicken and potato soup, followed by goose with some sort of cider sauce and a tender saddle of roast mutton, several dishes of vegetables, and finally a pastry stuffed with minced apples, raisins, and whatnot.

The baron and I ate heartily, while Sir Michael picked at his food. The gleam of candles and firelight on polished wood made the silence less cold than it might have been.

The servants cleared away the dishes and brought in a heavy, sweet wine.

Testing my theory that I could make my job whatever I willed, I got up and took the tray from the maidservant and poured for the baron and Sir Michael. I had no particular desire to become a servant, but I hoped they'd be less likely to dismiss me if I was being useful. I could see that something was about to happen.

The baron saw what I was doing—he gave me a sardonic look, but he didn't throw me out. I served them both and then settled in a chair by the door. The baron sipped his wine and set the goblet on the table.

Sir Michael hadn't touched his—neither of them wanted to be drunk. The wind rattled the casements, but the candles never wavered.

"Michael?"

"Yes, Sir. Have you decided what to do with me yet?"

"Not quite. But I think you should understand some of the factors I'm considering."

"I set a killer free and it cost you five thousand gold roundels! There's something else you have to consider?"

"I'm afraid so." The baron leaned back in his chair, his ease a sharp contrast to Sir Michael's stiffness.

"Ceciel Mallory, the woman you freed, poisoned her husband, Baron Herbert Mallory, in his home—Craggan Keep, which is on the coast. That's where the new Mallorian Barony is."

Sir Michael frowned. "The *new* Mallorian Barony? I thought . . . wait. Why was she under arrest in Lord Dorian's fiefdom?"

"That's part of the story. Mallorian, as you no doubt remember, is a smallish barony held from Lord Dorian.

"Many years ago, the old Baron Mallory quarreled with his elder son, Herbert. I never knew what it was about, and it no longer matters. Their enmity resulted in Sir Herbert's swearing his fealty to Lord Gerald, instead of Lord Dorian."

Sir Michael began to look interested. "Horn and hoof, that must have caused a furor! I can't see Lord Dorian letting a barony, even a small one, slide out of his fiefdom that easily. Why didn't I ever hear about this?"

" 'Twas over before you were born. And you've never had much interest in local affairs, have you?"

There was a bite in those last words, and Sir Michael winced.

"In any event," Baron Seven Oaks went on, "the old baron disowned Herbert, so his second son, Bertram, inherited Mallorian. Lord Gerald granted Sir Herbert a small barony—just a keep and the town it wards. Sir Herbert married Mistress Ceciel many years later. I understand she's peasant stock, of a very Gifted line. But unfortunately for Sir Herbert, she had no children."

I felt a reluctant flash of pity for the murderous Ceciel; a woman who couldn't pass on her Gifts had a hard lot in life. Perhaps she had some excuse for doing Sir Herbert in, though poison . . .

"Sir Herbert and Sir Bertram remained friends. After their father's death, Sir Herbert told his brother he wished to be buried in their family's ancestral grove. So when he died, his wife shipped his body home—her first and only mistake. Sir Herbert was in his early sixties . . ."

I sat up straighter—the woman we'd rescued couldn't have been more than forty.

". . . and in excellent health. Sir Bertram asked an herbalist to examine his brother's body, and she found traces of not only poison, but *magica* poison. The Lady Ceciel is an expert herbalist, so when she came to attend her husband's interment, Baron Mallory had her arrested."

Sir Michael frowned. "Then she was never tried?"

"No—though I believe her flight confirms her guilt. Lord Dorian forbade any man of hers or Lord Gerald's to set foot in his fiefdom on pain of death, and set guards on the main roads to enforce it."

Which accounted for her man Hackle's ragged clothes. He was in disguise.

"He also imprisoned her in Sorrowston Tower, because it was more defensible than Willowere's jail. He hadn't reckoned on knights errant." The baron's mouth twitched wryly. "So you see, 'tis a matter of honor with Lord Dorian now."

Sir Michael froze as the implications crashed home. No wonder it had cost the baron five thousand gold roundels to redeem his son. Sir Michael had offended Lord Dorian . . . who was also his father's liege lord.

Poor Sir Michael.

Early the next afternoon we rode into Seven Oaks. Sir Michael was sunk in gloom, but the baron looked far too cheerful for someone whose son had cost him five thousand gold roundels, and displeased his liege lord.

The house was ten minutes' ride from the river. I had expected one of those impressive, but hideously uncomfortable, stone keeps—the kind almost everyone abandoned the moment they realized their neighbors were no longer likely to attack them. But most nobles are still holding on to their dark, damp fortresses, generations after the first High Liege put a stop to such nonsense. Perhaps they liked to fight with their neighbors more than the rest of us.

Someone in the Sevenson line had been smarter than that. I guessed the manor to be about a hundred years old, with a stone foundation and upper floors of plastered timber. The ivy growing up the walls was stout enough for a burglar to reach any window he chose, but ivy is noisy to climb. Give me a lock pick or a glass cutter any day.

The seven oaks, which made the estate's name inevitable, stood three on each side of the house, with one massive ancient in the front. Oaks lose their leaves later than most trees, and these glowed wine red in the sunlight.

Someone must have spotted us shortly after we left the river road, for servants scurried about and grooms came out to take our horses. As we rode up to the manor, two nobles, a man and a woman, emerged from the door at the top of the short flight of steps. The woman was middle-aged, but she had Sir Michael's light brown hair and even features.

The young man beside her—Rupert, no doubt—was a scaled-down version of the baron, shorter, stockier, the hatchet face blunted. Unfortunately, he hadn't inherited the baron's good taste—the old-style slashed doublet was too fancy for the country, and someone should have told him that high-complexioned men shouldn't wear red.

Mother and son both stared down at Sir Michael with cool disapproval. This didn't surprise my employer; his expression was resigned as he dismounted and started up the steps. He'd only climbed two of them when the big carved door burst open and a girl hurtled out and tumbled down to throw her arms around him. Sir Michael grabbed her and staggered back down the stairs.

"Michael, Michael, Michael!" Her voice was muffled by his doublet.

"Kathy, Kathy, Kathy!" Sir Michael replied, laughing, as he regained his balance. "Let me look at you."

He had to hold her away to do so, and I saw that she was at the hobbledehoy stage, thirteen or fourteen, all knees and elbows. Her tangled hair was darker than Sir Michael's, which made it mouse brown, and gold spectacles slid down a long, thin nose. But the shining joy on her face made up for any amount of plainness—and the right Gifts and dowry can make the downright ugly attractive, much less the merely plain.

Sir Michael hugged his sister again and climbed the steps with an arm around her shoulders. His mother took his free hand and tipped up one cheek for his kiss, carefully keeping her wide skirts uncrushed. Rupert relented enough to clasp his brother's shoulders and look him over, rather anxiously, for damage.

I followed the family into the entryway. It was pretty much as I'd expected, except that the inlaid wood of the floor was unusually fine. The gold leaf running down the roof beams was patterned in a chain of oak leaves. Several of the plastered walls held faded tapestries, which probably came from the old keep.

The baron led Sir Michael and Rupert off in one direction, and the baroness summoned Kathryn with an imperious wave of her hand and set off toward the back of the house. An elderly manservant showed me to my room and told me, politely, that I would like to rest after my journey.

It was one of the lesser guest rooms, holding a bed, a chest, and a wardrobe cupboard. The pitcher and basin on a table beside the bed and the discreetly covered chamber pot were the only other amenities. But it was clean and snug, and the bed was canopied with a patterned linen that must have cost quite a bit for a lesser guest room.

I lay on the bed for ten minutes before I became bored with resting, and set out to explore the house. If anyone asked, I planned to say I was looking for Sir Michael—but I hoped I wouldn't find him.

Most of the rooms on this floor were bedrooms, though I found a sewing room with two embroidery frames in a sunny corner chamber. The presence of a clock on the mantel indicated that someone spent a lot of time here, and also confirmed that the household was rich—you seldom find clocks in women's rooms. The work in one frame was impeccable; the work in the other showed signs of being picked out and redone several times.

Behind the next door I found the library. It was large enough, as private collections go, but the selection was uninspired. Only two sections held books that had been used—the first contained a well-chosen, and surprisingly varied, collection of history books that probably belonged to the absent Benton. The other held books of ballads and legends, usually the most popular section in any library. Sir Michael had obviously read them.

Besides books, and a row of windows that looked out over the gardens, orchards, and stables, the room contained a long table and a desk with a tapestry behind it. The tapestry caught my eye, for the colors were bright. Instead of one great scene from some ancient legend, it displayed many small scenes, which chased each other around the edges, then inward in a spiral that ended in the center. Drawing closer, I saw it told the story of a group of adventurers on some quest. I was snickering over the first scene, which showed a farmer with many daughters dragging a startled soldier toward his house, when a soft voice spoke behind me.

"Delightful, isn't it?"

I jumped, but I'd already recognized Lady Kathryn's voice before I turned.

"It's better than that. If your mother made this, she is very talented indeed."

Even as I spoke, I knew the cool woman I'd seen on the steps couldn't have created this. Perfect embroidery, yes, but not the joyous laughter that began this tale.

Kathryn shook her head. "I'm afraid not. It was woven by a woman called Mistress Kara, who lives down the coast in Granbor. Her tapestries are very popular, despite the unusual style."

My eyes went back to the tapestry. "I don't recognize the story."

"You wouldn't." Kathryn pushed up her spectacles. "Mistress Kara doesn't use the old legends, she makes up her own."

"Really? I've never heard of a weaver doing that."

Kathryn took a deep breath. "They asked me to look for you. Well, Michael did. Father's holding court tonight. He sent off riders, inviting every neighbor who could arrive by evening."

"How many is that?" I asked, wondering why she looked so glum.

"Only five," she said. "But they all have *big* families."

I smiled despite myself. My youngest sister would now be very close to Kathryn's age.

Kathryn visibly gathered her courage. "Anyway, there's going to be a feast and then Father's going to . . . to pronounce on Michael, with witnesses, you see? 'Twill all be desperately uncomfortable, but you're to come, and Michael told me you haven't any other clothes so I'm to lend you some of Benton's because he won't mind."

Her face was scarlet by the time she finished, but her embarrassment was for my pride rather than hers.

"Thank you," I said. "That's very kind."

She nodded and went over to the window to let her cheeks cool, but when she looked out her back stiffened.

I went to stand beside her. My employer walked through the fallow gardens toward the orchard, a lady's hand resting on his arm. From where we stood I could see only her hair, which was red-gold, and her dress, which was the color of wild roses.

Then she turned, laughing at something Sir Michael had said, and my breath caught at the perfection of her features. Her face was so lovely, I didn't even glance at her figure.

"That's my cousin, Rosamund." Kathryn's voice was colorless. "She's an orphan, in Father's ward, but she's very well dowered. She's . . ." Her stiff shoulders slumped. "She's all right, in spite of her looks. A little silly."

Why would that depress the girl? Then I saw Sir Michael's expression and my heart chilled.

Worship. The pure, stupid devotion of a knight for a fair lady—as chaste as calf love, and every bit as painful. Beautiful, rich, and probably Gifted, she would never be given to a fourth son. And judging by her unconcerned expression, she probably wouldn't want to marry him even if it had been possible.

Sir Michael and his lady vanished under the orchard's boughs, and Kathryn and I regarded each other in perfect, grim understanding.

"Master Fisk, I don't know what father's going to say tonight, but . . . you're my brother's friend. Watch over him. I'm afraid he's going to need it."

This didn't seem the right moment to mention that I intended to get free of Sir Michael at the first opportunity.

Mistress Kathryn and I spent the rest of the afternoon going through the absent Benton's wardrobe. I chose a good doublet of heavy, dark brown linen to wear that evening, and with Kathryn's cheerful permission, pinched several of his older, rougher outfits as well.

The neighbors began arriving shortly before sunset—and they did have large families. The table in the cavernous dining hall was set for almost fifty.

There were enough candles to heat the room, even without the hearth fires that crackled at both ends of the hall. The neighboring families had dressed up for the occasion—glowing velvets, damask, and brocade—and their avid gossip rang from the stone floor to the rafters. Moving among them, I learned that Sir Michael was well liked, even if they did think this "knight errant business" was insane and "look where it *got* him, my dear." I heard one man offer the opinion that no good came from putting too tight a rein on your sons, but most people felt that no father deserved *this*.

The feast was lavish, eight full courses, and my respect for the baroness's ability grew. The neighbors ate heartily, but after the third course my appetite deserted me. Sir Michael, seated on his father's right, ate less than he had the night before, and even the baron dined lightly, though he drank more than I'd expected.

The baroness, seated on her husband's left, ate well, spoke politely, and never showed a scrap of emotion, either then or through what followed. Rupert sat at the foot of the table, looking important. Kathryn was evidently too young to attend.

The meal wore on, and as the final course (a plum custard cake coated with honey and powdered sugar) was served, the expectation that had hovered over the room all evening settled like a soaked blanket. Pockets of silence formed, and when people spoke their voices were too loud, their laughter too shrill.

When the baron pushed back his chair and stood, the conversation died as if its throat had been cut.

"Michael Sevenson, come thou and stand before me."

A chill passed over my skin at the sound of the old, high speech. It still flavored the vocabulary of the nobility, but these days it was used only for legal decrees. The baron's use of it now made whatever he said a legal requirement, and neither argument nor appeal was accepted when high speech was used. Which was doubtless why the baron used it—before witnesses.

"All gathered herein know what thou hast done. All gathered know that I have redeemed thee, and at what price. 'Tis the price of thy redemption to me that I now decree and declare."

Sir Michael nodded, his face sober and self-contained in the flickering light. His hands were clasped behind his back. Were they as cold as mine? Probably colder.

"The terms are these. First, thou shalt pursue Ceciel Mallory, capture her, and return her to Lord Dorian's justice. Thus thou shalt right the wrong thou hast done, both to the law and to the dead. I am certain"—irony glinted in the baron's voice—"that this will be within the power of the 'knight' who was able to free her under the noses of the sheriff's men."

I was by no means certain of this. Depending on how far she fled, and how well she covered her tracks, we could spend years just trying to find the accursed wench!

But the neighbors nodded approvingly. Sir Michael showed no surprise, though his lips flattened at his father's ridicule.

"The second term of thy redemption is that thou shalt go to the kinsmen of the murdered man, and offer them apology."

Sir Michael grimaced at that. Facing the man whose brother's killer we'd set free wouldn't be pleasant, but I had to admit it was fair. The neighbors were nodding like silly sheep.

"The third and final term is this: When the first two tasks are accomplished, thou shalt return to this house and take up the position of estate steward of Seven Oaks, under the governance of Baron Seven Oaks, whoever he may be. Thou shalt serve him for as long as he wills, even to the end of thy days."

This, Sir Michael had not expected. "Father, please!" he protested, despite the high speech.

The baron talked right over him, setting the official seal on his fate. "These are the terms of thy repayment. Until and unless the terms are met, thou art an indebted man, honorless in the eyes of thy fellows, rightless in the eyes of the law. If any hand be turned against thee, thou mayst claim no redress. If thou shouldst fail to meet these terms, thou shalt be declared an unredeemed man, cast off from thy family, from honor, from the law, and from men's aid, forever. These are my words, this is my will, let it be thus."

"Let it be thus," the witnesses rumbled.

I didn't join in.

Sir Michael swayed as if he'd been struck. For a moment I thought he was going to fall to his knees at the baron's feet, not to beg for mercy, but because his legs had failed him. Then he bowed in submission, turned, and walked out.

The gossip around me resumed with a rush, but I paid no heed, intent on getting out of the room as soon as I could.

I looked in his room first, then started opening each door in the hall, methodically, though I wasn't certain he was even in the house. The vibrant wails of viol and flute drifted up the staircase, so I probably had an hour before people began coming upstairs—and found me peeking into their rooms. It was probably just as well that Kathryn ambushed me and dragged me into the dark sewing room.

It felt different, lit by nothing but the pale light from the hall candles . . . emptier.

In a sibilant whisper, she demanded to know the worst. I told her what her father had said, watching her expression change as I spoke.

"What I don't understand," I finished, "is what's so terrible about the last part. Your father said he had to be estate steward, and he looked as if he'd received a death sentence!"

Kathryn drew a shaky breath. "'Tis not that bad, though it may feel that way to Michael. That's what he and Father were fighting about last year. Didn't you know?"

I remembered some of the neighbors' gossip, but I wanted to know a lot more. "I've only been with Sir Michael a little over a week," I explained, hoping this would make my ignorance more understandable.

Evidently it did, for she nodded and went on. "When Michael came home from university last year, Father had decided that he was going to become Rupert's estate steward. 'Tis a good job, for a fourth son, and 'tis not as if Michael wanted to do anything else. It wasn't an unreasonable idea, but Michael refused. He said he wanted to travel. To do more with his life than bury himself on the same estate where he'd been born.

"Father asked how he intended to support himself on these travels—which I must say was unfair, for Michael isn't a wastrel. If he wanted to travel for a while, Father could easily have staked him, but . . . Father doesn't like to be thwarted."

Her voice trailed off and I nodded encouragingly. "I can see that."

"Yes, well, they had a huge argument, with Father nagging Michael to say what, exactly, he hoped to accomplish in this *travel* of his. I don't think Michael really knew, but finally he said that he might just do some good in the world, and Father accused him of wanting to be 'some kind of fool knight errant' and . . ." A hint of mischief brightened her expression. ". . . I'm afraid the idea took root. Michael left home the next morning, and from his letters it sounds like that's exactly what he's done. Which *I* think is no small accomplishment, starting out with only one lame horse and a handful of fracts."

"Quite," I said. This explained a great deal about Michael. "So tonight . . ."

The animation left her face. "Father won the argument, at last. But 'tis not so bad being an estate steward. Lots of people would *want* the job."

But not Sir Michael. The thought hung, unspoken, between us.

I decided that sometimes it was a squire's duty to leave his employer alone, and went to bed.

We left before dawn the next morning. The mist off the river swirled around our legs as we walked out to the stables. Our footsteps sounded both loud and muffled at the same time.

The baron and baroness weren't there, and Kathryn was probably asleep, but Rupert showed up to see his brother off.

Sir Michael appeared more cheerful than he had for the last few days. Which seemed strange, until I realized that we were setting out on a quest. Another glorious adventure, no doubt.

"I had old Eldridge check your gear." Rupert sounded as if he wanted to apologize, but wasn't quite sure what for. "Some of your tack was pretty worn, so he replaced it. And you've got food for several weeks."

"Thank you, brother," said Sir Michael. "That was a kindly tho . . . Eldridge? I thought he planned to retire—last year."

Rupert's eyes dropped. "He did. But Father didn't think 'twould be worth the trouble to train a new man for only a few months, so he persuaded Eldridge to stay on . . . for a while."

"I see." The adventuring light left Sir Michael's eyes, and his mouth was tight.

I saw, too. Old Eldridge must be the current steward, and "a few months" was the amount of time the baron had believed it would take Sir Michael to fail at knight errantry and come crawling home. He had succeeded for a full year, but now he had to fail . . . or be dishonored and leave a murderess at large.

Poor Michael.

CHAPTER 4
Michael

So my career as a knight errant was to come to an end, and one so ignoble it made my heart ache. I suppose it really was a foolish notion, as my father said, but there were one or two who had cause to be grateful for it, which is more than most can say of their dreams.

And it wasn't over yet, not quite. Instead of waking to a morning bent over cramped columns of farm accounts, I rode with my squire beside a rushing river, with the sun beginning to burn off the mist. The only sound that rose above the river's chuckle was the waking clarion of the blackbirds.

One last heroic deed—the most desperate, the most heroic of them all—undertaken in the cause of honor and justice. Even if it was my error that made it necessary.

I mentioned as much to my squire, who had been uncharacteristically silent, though that might be because he dislikes rising early.

Fisk gave me a sour look. "In my opinion, Noble Sir, heroism is vastly overrated. It was *heroism* that got us into this mess . . . perhaps you haven't noticed?"

His irony was so sharp that I smiled despite myself, and he glared at me.

"That wasn't heroism, 'twas my foolishness in permitting Hackle to gull me."

Fisk snorted. "It was your . . . heroism that made the foolishness possible. That's how con artists work. We talk to a gull, find out what he dreams of, what he wants so badly he'd leap at the chance to make a fool of himself. Then we offer him that. It works every time."

I decided to let this pass; that was Fisk's past, and I meant to give him a chance for a different future. But . . .

"I take your point, but I can't see heroism as a weakness. Without aspirations men would still be dwelling in caves, killing with stones and clubs like the desert savages. And this last quest isn't a matter of heroism, but of righting a wrong and redeeming our honor."

A chance to argue lightened Fisk's mood.

"It's also about every bully and brigand who wants

an easy target and knows an indebted man can't go to the law. Not to mention your father cutting you off without a fract. Ah, speaking of which, Sir?"

"Yes?" I spoke a bit curtly. Fisk's last speech had some sting in it, though it wasn't true.

"When this is over . . . Well, an estate steward won't need a squire."

"Not a squire, mayhap, but an estate steward could certainly use a trusty clerk to keep his ledgers."

When he isn't lying, Fisk's face is very candid. His downcast expression was almost comical, but there was something under the simple disappointment akin to pain, or even fear, that made me add, "Don't worry. When the time is right, I'll end your indebtedness. I swear it on my honor."

Fisk's expression turned wry. "I knew a man once whose name was not Jack Bannister. He broke his oaths regularly, and got quite rich doing it."

I almost said, rather hotly, that I was not this Jack. But this time 'twas definitely pain I heard under Fisk's sardonic tone. I saw that Jack Bannister (or whatever his name really was) had also broken his word to Fisk, and Fisk's trust with it. The silence stretched. The growing light warmed my shoulders.

"I suppose," I said finally, "that a man's word is as good as his own regard for it. This Jack of yours saw his oath as worthless, and his oaths were just that. For myself, an oath is as binding as an iron chain. No, more binding, for a chain may be sawed through, or twisted apart, or the lock picked. But from an oath, or any debt of honor, there's no escape."

I decided that we would first confront Baron Bertram Mallory, the kinsman to whom my apology was owed—a thing I had intended to do anyway, though I knew how painful and embarrassing it would be. Being ordered to do something you have already resolved on doing is a frustrating and humiliating experience. Mayhap 'twas fortunate that the Mallorian Barony was a full day's ride to the northwest. For the sake of Chant's leg I planned to make a day and a half of it, which would give me time to recover from the blow Father had struck my pride. Injured pride is not conducive to apologies.

We forded the river in midafternoon, and made camp a few hours later in a cave beside the road. The early stop gave me time to string my short bow and shoot a few partridges, stretching our supplies.

I tramped back to camp with the birds dangling from my hands, heavy as feathered stone shot, for game is fat in the fall.

The cave was not a hole in the earth, but a triangular

wedge beneath a big stone bank, cut by the stream in flood years. Travelers' fires had blackened the overhanging rock, and Fisk had gathered wood and started a fire while I was gone.

This was a pleasant change, for when he first joined me, city-bred Fisk had no more notion of how to set up camp than . . . well, than a townsman. He grimaced when he saw the birds in my hand, for I had declared I would teach him to clean game the next time I shot something.

I smashed an oatcake into crumbs and scattered them for the other birds, appeasing the Furred God by assisting life, since I had taken it.

Fisk did fairly well, for he is deft with a knife, though a little squeamish. I cooked the partridges, however. My first taste of Fisk's camp cooking had been more than enough.

I've wondered a lot about Fisk, in the short time he's been with me. He tries to act like the gutterling my father proclaimed him, but he knows full well the use of both handkerchief and napkin. His personal habits are cleanly, and his manners very good—even when his attention is clearly on something else. This may be something a con artist would cultivate, but still . . .

Fisk seldom speaks of his past and he eludes my

questions, so I've stopped asking. He'll talk when he trusts me, and not before.

Having risen early, we were more than ready for sleep once we'd eaten. Fisk laid out the bedrolls on piles of leaves, and I complimented him on the softness of the bed.

"It's all right." He yawned. "As long as nothing crawls in and joins us during the night. Unless of course it's human, female, and preferably good-looking."

I smiled at his jest, but replied, "I don't know. If such a thing happened to me, I fear I'd be too startled to enjoy it."

"You'd get over that," Fisk said dryly. "Trust me."

"Would you?" The darkness beneath the overhang lent itself to intimate questions. "Not get over being startled, I know that would pass. But would you lie with a stranger, if she offered herself?"

"I guess it depends on the stranger," said Fisk. "If she was clean and willing, and there wasn't so much in my purse that I'd mind when she stole it, why not? Not," he added, "that the situation is likely to arise. Especially in the middle of the howling wilderness."

The howling wilderness is seldom covered with cultivated fields and traversed by good roads. But I didn't tell him this, for with moonlight silvering the uplifted branches, and night birds crying warnings to the small creatures that rustled through the leaves, the night did have a wild sort of beauty.

"But what about love?" I asked instead. "Or at least, affection. Bedding a woman without friendship would be . . . I wouldn't care for it! All folk seek love with their beddings. Surely you must too."

I thrust the painful thought of Rosamund aside, for I knew she didn't think of me that way. But someday, if my quest succeeded. If—

"Oh, I'd like to be loved—who wouldn't?" Fisk's voice interrupted my thoughts. "But I'd settle for lust. Not that I get that, either. Well, not often."

I laughed at his exaggerated gloom and heard him chuckle too, but something in his voice made me add, "If that's true, then you're settling for too little."

The leaves rustled as he turned his back on me. His voice was muffled when he replied, "Sometimes, Noble Sir, you have to settle for what you can get."

Despite the craven slowness with which we traveled, we reached Baron Mallory's keep by midmorning.

'Twas of the old style: four square towers, with high walls between them. A stone bridge spanned an old moat, dry now, with grass overgrowing its banks and a cow grazing in the bottom.

We rode across the bridge, one behind the other, as

its narrowness dictated. This would have been an excellent defense in olden times, but now it must prove a fearful inconvenience whenever someone delivered a cartload of supplies. Baron Mallory could have replaced it with a wider one, but there was an air of shabbiness about the old walls that made me wonder about the baron's finances. Though when we clattered under the portcullis (rusted into place, thank goodness) the grooms who came out to take our horses were well clothed and well ordered.

A manservant escorted us to the baron. The windows were paned in diamonds of clear, modern glass instead of the old thick circles, and the tapestries that covered the walls could have sold for much, so perhaps Sir Bertram was tradition-minded, not impoverished.

Whichever it was, the old man had a strong sense of the dramatic. The manservant opened great double doors, revealing a long, empty hall, its rafters hung with banners. Baron Mallory sat in a carved chair on a dais at the far end.

Walking down the length of the floor toward him, my footfalls ringing in the silence, I felt smaller with each step—doubtless, I was meant to. My embarrassment faded and resentment replaced it—I dislike being deliberately humbled. Fisk crept softly behind me, doing his best to become invisible, as is his habit when he wants to make certain I take all the blame. In this case, I had to admit I deserved it.

I halted at the foot of the dais, for to climb it would have left me standing on the baron's toes, and looked up at him. "I am Sir Michael Sevenson, and I have come to apologize for my error in setting Ceciel Mallory free."

"I know who you are, young man. And why you're here. I expected you yesterday." Fisk stirred behind me, but I wasn't surprised that he knew we were coming.

Sir Bertram looked me over like a curious crow, an impression that was reinforced by the black clothes of mourning. His hair, which grew in a neat fringe around his bald head, just touched his collar, and while he was thin, he still seemed hardy. Father had said Sir Herbert was in his early sixties, and this man was his younger brother, but his face was deeply lined, like that of a man a decade older, and the eyes that regarded me so intently were red and swollen.

I forgot that he had made me walk the length of the hall, and even the humiliation of confessing my own error. "I am truly sorry, Sir, for what happened to your brother. I'm going to bring Ceciel Mallory back. If she poisoned him, you'll have justice."

"Justice?" His face twisted. "What good will justice do my brother now?" Then he sagged in the great chair. "I suppose justice is all that's left," he said wearily. "Come with me, Michael Sevenson, freer of poisoners. I want you to see something."

He stepped down from the dais and strode off. We followed, of course, though I was anxious about our destination. The baron was clearly grieved by his brother's death, and keeps this old held dungeons, or even worse places.

But we passed out through a postern door, and set off briskly through the kitchen garden and up the wooded hill behind the keep.

Fisk stared when we came over the hill's crown, and saw the size of the blood oak grove stretching down its slopes. I knew enough of country life to understand that all the nearby villages would bring their dead here as well.

Blood oak leaves die in autumn, as other leaves do, but for some reason they cling to the branches even in death, only falling when the spring growth comes. There are several myths to account for this, but no one really knows why. Whatever the reason, walking through the blood oak grove was an uneasy experience, even on a sunlit autumn morning. The dry leaves rustled and whispered together, as if the dead buried beneath their roots were gossiping back and forth.

As we went downhill, the trees became smaller and

younger. Soon we reached the recent part of the burying grove and a grave into which the earth had barely
settled. The sapling planted there had only five leaves,
still turning to the deep russet of dried blood. 'Twas
the wrong time of year to transplant, but a blood oak
planted over a corpse always thrives. Scientists say 'tis
because they draw nourishment from a body's decay,
but the old tradition that a good man's soul sustains
them appeals more to the heart. If that was true, Sir
Herbert must have been a good man, for this tree was
perfect. In fact . . . I bent to look closer.

Saplings are often unmarked, for insects and animals have had fewer chances at them, but something
about this plant pricked at my sensing Gift. I knelt and
held out my hand toward the sapling, not quite touching it, and felt the unmistakable prickle of its energy
against my palm. The sensing Gift is the only human
Gift that is always reliable, even if you have to touch a
thing to be certain whether it holds magic or not.
Every village has access to someone with the sensing
Gift, so no one would ever be fool enough to cut this
tree. Sir Herbert's grave would be marked for decades,
even centuries. I wondered what sacrifice Sir Bertram
had made to get this plant. He must have loved his
brother very much.

"I know that all men end as food for plants," the

baron said. "But that woman put my brother here before his time, and I want her dead for it."

For all the conscious drama of the setting, his voice was rough with real grief. I stayed on my knees beside the grave and spoke gently.

"You must have known Ceciel Mallory well. Can you tell us where she might have gone?"

The old man snorted. "If I knew where she was I'd go after her myself—your redemption be hanged! I've no idea where she would go. I warned Herbert not to marry her, but he'd a stubborn streak and paid no heed. He never did, the old fool." He sat beside the grave and patted the soft earth.

"Why didn't you want them to marry? I'd heard she was from a Gifted line."

"Oh yes," said Sir Bertram bitterly. "Gifted with greed, deceit, and evil!" Then the passion deserted him, and his shoulders slumped. "I shouldn't speak of the whole family thus, for the sister is our local herbalist, both mixer and talker, and a good woman. And the brother is an honest woodworker, with his own shop. In fact, 'twas Agnes, the sister, who confirmed that my brother had been poisoned—although she didn't know whom I suspected when I asked her to examine his body."

A path wound up the slope to the burying grove. A

party of mourners emerged upon it as we spoke, four men carrying the shrouded corpse in its sling. The widow, a black shawl covering her head and shoulders, walked behind. Glancing about, I saw a fresh pile of earth with four shovels in it, and a sapling in a bucket beside. They were far enough off that we shouldn't intrude on each other.

"I did oppose the marriage," Sir Bertram continued. "Though I foresaw no tragedy such as this. 'Twas just . . . I thought him unwise to marry a woman so much younger than he, who must care only for his rank and wealth. My own Margery is dead five years." He reached out and touched a tall sapling a few feet away. "But she gave me two fine sons, a daughter to gladden my heart, and many happy years. I miss her, always, but I've had more joy than most. Unlike poor Herbert. But as he said, if he wanted children he had to marry a younger woman. Mistress Ceciel was in her twenties, well old enough to know what she did."

The mourners moved up the hill; the corpse carriers staggering as the path steepened.

"When was this, Sir? How long had they been married?"

"Hmm, let me think. It must be over eighteen years now, for Father had just died. Herbert sought out Mistress Agnes for some petty complaint and met her sister there. He praised her only moderately, but I knew his attraction, for every week he returned to the herbalist's house. When he left for Craggan Keep, he took Ceciel with him, as his wife."

"But why would she kill him after eighteen years of marriage?" Astonishment lifted my voice. It sounded loud in the quiet grove, and Sir Bertram glared at me.

"I know not, and neither do I care; all I want is to see the bitch pay for it. For years I begged him to put her off. He said they did well enough, but I could see there was no love between them."

The mourners came toward us. They were close enough that I could see the widow now, fair and delicate, with a handkerchief pressed to her eyes. I felt a surge of anger at the woman who had forced that kind of grief on Sir Bertram.

"'Tis sad that no love came to them," I agreed. "But surely that's no cause to put off a wife of eighteen yea—"

"'Twas not for that," Sir Bertram said indignantly. "I realize that few marriages are blessed as mine was. I told him to put her off when we discovered her lie— when Herbert told me she was Giftless and barren."

CHAPTER 5
Fisk

"Giftless and barren?" Sir Michael repeated.

Once again I felt an unwilling sympathy for Lady Ceciel. No wonder she'd been unwed in her twenties. It's terrible when the Gift dies out of a line, as I should know—if my mother hadn't been the Giftless daughter of another Giftless daughter, I might be Sir Michael's equal instead of . . . well, what I am.

But inability to provide an heir for a man's land is the ultimate curse among noblewomen. Even a commoner can put off his wife for it, if it's proved the fault is in her and not him. Lady Ceciel could have been thrown out of her fancy keep with nothing but the dowry she'd brought to the marriage—motive enough for murder, and yet . . .

Sir Michael had seen it too. "Yet you say Sir Herbert

refused to put her off?"

"Year after year." Sir Bertram nodded. "Despite all my admonitions. I never understood it. And now he can't explain."

I listened to Sir Michael repeat his promise that he would bring Lady Ceciel back to justice. Though how he intended to go about it I couldn't think; she could be anywhere by now.

The mourning party reached the grave and lowered the corpse. Two of the carriers wore black capes that marked them as the dead man's sons, but the widow was young enough to be their sister—their younger sister. I could see why the old man had been tempted into a second marriage, for she'd a fine figure under all that black. I couldn't make out much of her face, though. She kept patting a lacy handkerchief against her bone-dry eyes. Her gaze was appreciatively fixed on the back of one of the corpse carriers, now wielding a shovel. His doublet was short, his britches were tight, and he was not, thankfully, one of the stepsons— though he might have been one of their friends.

I smiled and wished the hussy luck. She'd probably earned it, and judging by the ages of her husband's sons, nature had done her work instead of poison.

My attention came back to the conversation at hand when Sir Michael asked how he could find Mistress

Agnes, the herbalist. The old man gave directions will-ingly—she lived just over the border of the next baron's fief, half a day's ride west.

I waited, in proper squirely silence, until we were riding away from Sir Bertram's keep before I spoke. "You're not, you *can't* be, thinking of going there next?"

"Why not? Lady Ceciel's family are the most likely to know where she might be."

"And the least likely to tell you! What under two moons makes you think her own family is going to give her up?"

"I don't say they'd reveal her hiding place, but they sound like honest folk, and they may speak of her nature and habits. If we learn these things, we may guess where she might have flown. Besides, Mistress Agnes is the one who found Sir Herbert had been poi-soned, and I wish to learn more of this."

I listened to this naive speech with growing irrita-tion. Why should I have to instruct this noble fool in facts any city street urchin knows by the time he's weaned? Because I'd been fool enough to get caught, that's why. And until a chance to seize my freedom came along, I was stuck with him.

"Sir, no one is going to tell the man who wants to hang their sister *anything*. They're not going to like you, no matter how nice you are. Sir Bertram was hard enough to face." (Though I would remember how Sir Michael's honest contrition had disarmed him, if I ever got myself caught again.) "These people are going to hate you. Unless . . ."

"Unless what?"

"Well, if you told them Lord Dorian sent you to investigate because he has doubts about her guilt, then they might be willing to talk."

Sir Michael hesitated for all of three seconds before declaring, "No, that would be dishonorable."

"But it might succeed! Which might help us find Lady Ceciel, which would get you out of trouble with the law—not to mention your father."

Sir Michael sighed. "My father would be the first to say I shouldn't lie. In fact, that's the only thing I ever did . . . Never mind. Truth always serves best in the long run."

The only thing I ever did right? That lived up to his standards?

"All the more reason to thwart the old tyrant," I told him.

The journey would have been tedious if we hadn't spent most of it arguing.

Over an early dinner at a small tavern only ten minutes' ride from Mistress Agnes's home, we reached a compromise of sorts. Sir Michael agreed to refrain from telling her the whole truth the moment he introduced himself, though he refused to lie if she asked him. I figured "Why do you want to know?" would be the first question she asked, but it was his redemption. I was just along for the ride.

Mistress Agnes's house was an overgrown cottage, timbered and thatched, with windows made of the old glass rounds that are impossible to cut and nearly impossible to break. They gleamed like gems in the afternoon light, making the cottage look quite appealing until you remembered that mice and rats adore thatched roofs. Perhaps she kept cats.

Mistress Agnes came to the door when she heard our horses, wiping her hands on her apron as if we'd interrupted her preparation of dinner, or perhaps some more arcane brewing. Plump and still pretty, she looked like a woman who might keep cats. The soft curls beneath her cap were threaded with gray. She examined us with a critical, healer's eye, and something in the directness of her gaze told me not to underestimate the woman, for all her warm, feather-bolster appearance.

"Good afternoon, good sirs. What may I do for you?"

Sir Michael dismounted. "We do not seek your services, Mistress. I'm here in search of information."

Mistress Agnes smiled. "I welcome a chance to share my craft lore. If you ask more than a few questions, I'll have to charge for lessons, though I keep the price as low as I can."

It was a simple mistake, and possibly a useful one. If Sir Michael would spend twenty minutes asking about herbal mixtures, he could then steer the topic to Sir Herbert's poisoning and all manner of information might slip out. So I was exasperated, if not surprised, when Sir Michael said, "I'm sorry, Mistress, but I haven't come to ask about your craft. I need to learn more of your sister."

Mistress Agnes's face turned hostile faster than flipping a griddle cake. "Why do you want to know about Ceciel?"

See, Michael, I told you. Perhaps he'd paid more attention than I thought, for he hesitated a moment.

"I need to know more of your sister, because I'm interested in justice."

"Justice for her?" Mistress Agnes asked shrewdly. "Or for old Herbert?"

"Justice for whoever deserves it," said Sir Michael. "I only want the truth."

Honesty shone from him like a cursed lamp. Only the truly sincere or the very best con artists could pull off that look, and I felt a sting of jealousy as I watched Mistress Agnes crumble before it.

She summoned a boy to take our horses and here was the first surprise, for even without the flattish face, the blank, constant smile would have proclaimed him one of the simple ones. Most people avoid them, though they're usually gentle, because their foolishness makes them difficult to deal with. And those who are magica can be dangerous if they're thwarted.

In humans magic takes unpredictable forms, and the simple ones are too slow-witted to understand what they do when, in fear or temper, they destroy or maim or kill. It's not their fault that they're born thus, and while many people loathe them, I feel an uncomfortable mixture of wariness and pity. Pity generally wins out, for their lives are often miserable, and those who are magica never live long.

So I smiled at the boy when he took Tipple's reins, and he beamed back at me. It was good of Mistress Agnes to take him in. Man must look after man since no god watches out for us—and that includes the simple ones.

Mistress Agnes led us into the cottage. The scent of roasting goose and onions fought with medicinal herbs and lost. The big front room was the herbarium— every rafter hung with bunches of leaves. Pots and bottles filled the shelves and tables, jostling against mortars, braziers, cooling jars, and page after page of notes and recipes, both loose and bound. There was even a distillery in one corner.

Mistress Agnes swept notes, pots, and the wired-together bones of a human hand off three stools and seated herself.

"I don't believe for one minute that my sister killed her husband," she announced. "He was a stuffy old goat, but he'd kept their bargain and she was content with it. She had no reason! None! But Sir Bertram *insists* that she was the only one who could have, because she's a skilled herb-mixer. Well, sirs, so am I and so are many others—that isn't enough to condemn her!"

"Yet you were the one who examined Sir Herbert. Is it certain, Mistress, that he died of poison?"

Mistress Agnes gnawed her lower lip, desire to defend her sister warring visibly with her habit of telling the truth.

"It's certain," she admitted. "And poisoned with magic too. You know that usually all magic does is increase the natural effects of healing herbs? It can be sensed, faintly, for a few hours to a few days, depending on the herb, the dosage, and, oh, all manner of things. And it doesn't linger in the body except under very unusual circumstances."

This was a point in Ceciel's favor. Anyone who can read or memorize the formulas can mix herbs into potions, but an herb-talker, who locates and deals with magica plants, *must* have the sensing Gift. And according to Sir Bertram, Ceciel didn't. She could have purchased magica herbs, but then there would be a witness.

Sir Michael was frowning. "I understood that you examined him many days after his death and still sensed magic."

She nodded grimly. "In his liver, his kidneys, his teeth, and his genitals, so intense there it felt like it would burn the skin from my palm. I've never seen anything like that—especially not in a human body."

Sir Michael was nodding, as if this told him something, but I was grateful when she went on, "It was the magic built up in his kidneys that killed him, for they were . . . deforming. The only way to get such a concentration of magic in particular organs would be to take magica potions—regularly, often, and for a long period of time." Her hands twisted in her apron, but her voice was steady. "I know that makes it look like Cece, but why would she do such a thing? She and Sir Herbert had struck a bargain and she was content with it. She would *never*—"

"Forgive me, Mistress, but can you say for certain what she might do if her husband thought to put her off? I've heard—"

"Faugh! You've been listening to that old goat Bertram. They were as content together as most, and he'd no wish to put her aside."

There was a moment of silence while Sir Michael frowned over the conflicting stories. He and Mistress Agnes were so intent on each other that the sound of horses coming into the yard disturbed neither of them. I looked out the window, but the glass was so thickly distorted that all I could see was that four men had ridden into the yard and dismounted.

"But suppose, Mistress, that his anger at your sister's deceit had grown over the years. Suppose he—"

Mistress Agnes's brows snapped together. "What deceit?" she demanded, in a voice that would have warned a sensible man.

Sir Michael continued, "I refer to her not telling Sir Herbert that she was Giftless and—"

"Be hanged to Sir Bertram if he told you that!" Mistress Agnes rose to her feet, hissing like a boiling kettle. "I know Bertram didn't like her, but I never thought he'd *lie*. It was in this very room, in my presence, that she told Sir Herbert that her line was Gifted, but that she wasn't. And why not? Gifts have been known to skip a generation and go on strong as before. Sir Herbert had no—"

The hall door slammed open with a force that made the bottles rattle, and all three of us jumped.

One of the four stocky men who entered bore a strong resemblance to Mistress Agnes, except for his furious glower.

"Don't you say one more word to this bastard, Aggie. He's going to bring Cece back to be hanged!"

Rumor travels amazingly fast in the countryside. In the city, I've seen it leap from house to house like a wildfire, but in the country villages are hours, even days, apart, so how—

"Not to be hanged." Sir Michael rose to his feet. "To be tried by the law and assigned whatever redemption the judicars deem fit. If she killed her husband, she has to answer for it—surely you understand that. If she's innocent—"

I didn't think they had to understand anything of the kind and neither did they. The brother's face was red with anger and pain . . . mostly anger.

"She'd not have a chance in Lord Dorian's court if she was innocent as a babe!" The brother—a wood-worker, I recalled—stalked around the table, and even Sir Michael had sufficient sense to back away. His arms were as big as most men's thighs.

"Lord Dorian's rule is just, and I should know. My father is his liegeman, and I was raised—"

"Yeah, we know all about him and your father and you. Do you get shares in the money he's going to make off Cory Port if he hangs my sister?"

"What!" Sir Michael stopped backing away. I could have told him this was a mistake, but I was hiding behind the distillery in the corner. In a four-on-one fight, I *never* bet against the odds.

"What port? What are you—"

The brother pushed Sir Michael into the wall. It didn't look like he was trying very hard, but the bottles rattled again and Sir Michael had to shake his head to clear it.

"Cory Port—as if you didn't know." The hulk grabbed Sir Michael's collar and pitched him out of the herbarium into the hall, where he hit another wall. This time Sir Michael came up fighting. Unfortunately, the three journeymen who'd ridden in with the brother were ready to grab him.

Perhaps out of consideration for his sister's furniture, they took the brawl into the yard, but they bounced off the wall a few times on the way out, and one journeyman's head connected loudly with a tall oak chest.

Mistress Agnes followed, arms crossed under her breasts and lips pressed tight. I drifted inconspicuously after her.

At first it took all four of them to hold Sir Michael. He not only swung his fists whenever his arms were free, but also kicked with a vigor and accuracy that was almost ungentlemanly. He'd picked up a few unknightly tricks in his wandering.

The uncluttered yard made a good arena, although at one point the flailing tangle of limbs, fists, and boots collided with the horse trough pump. I'm happy to say it was the brother who sank to his knees, clutching his elbow and swearing.

That left three of them on Michael—two clutching his arms. He stamped on the toes of the third and then kicked him in the chest, sending him staggering to the foot of the steps, where Mistress Agnes and I stood. The man looked around wildly and grabbed me.

I stood quite still in his grasp. "I'm just his squire. I only take orders, and I'm not going to fight. So don't hit me."

He glared at me. One of his eyes was puffing up. Then he turned and went back to the brawl.

I saw with regret that the other two journeymen had gotten a firm grip on Sir Michael's arms, holding him despite his struggles. His nose was bleeding.

The brother rose, stalked over to them, and punched Sir Michael in the stomach. I winced.

He followed that with a nasty blow to the jaw and another to the stomach, the soft thuds almost lost in the gasps and grunts of the participants.

Sir Michael managed to hook one of the journeyman's feet from under him, but it was clear that the ensuing scramble only delayed the inevitable.

Mistress Agnes chewed her lower lip, the anger in her face giving way to concern. She turned and hurried off.

Sir Michael's face was now dark with bruising, and his struggles were weaker. I judged that it would soon be over, since no one spends time and effort beating on someone who can't feel it. If Sir Michael had any sense, he'd go limp and fake his way out of the rest. But going limp under those circumstances is a hard act to pull off, and I doubt the thought even crossed my employer's mind—good sense not being a part of his character.

"What under the two moons is going on here!"

The enraged bellow made me jump, and the leather-aproned man who jogged around the house looked so angry, and so ready to do something about it, that I took a step back even though he wasn't looking at me.

"Of all the idiotic, assinine . . . Let go of that man!"

The journeymen were already backing off, and at his words they released Sir Michael as if he'd suddenly grown hot. He dropped like a stone and lay limply on his back, blood from his nose running into the dirt.

Mistress Agnes's husband, for such he was, proceeded to bawl out his brother-in-law for beating up a baron's son in his sister's own house. I couldn't tell if it was the act or the choice of location that enraged him most. The brother recovered enough composure to bellow back.

Mistress Agnes had followed her husband around the side of the house and now came to stand beside me. The simple boy peered around the corner with wide, frightened eyes.

Mistress Agnes looked at Sir Michael's fallen body. He was beginning to twitch. Her lips firmed.

"No. He tried to get me to betray Cece. Let him bleed." She turned toward the house.

"Ah, Mistress?" I said. "Before you go, may I ask you something? About that port . . ."

Her answer depressed me.

Her husband finished shouting down his brother-in-law, while the journeymen went for their horses. They mounted and rode off, sullen and, I was pleased to note, well bruised.

The husband watched them go and then glanced down at Sir Michael. His brows lifted when he saw his wife had gone, and I guessed that Mistress Agnes had to be very angry indeed if she refused to heal.

He looked again at Sir Michael, who stirred and muttered; then he shrugged and returned to his work.

I strolled across the silent, trampled yard to my

employer. His nose had almost stopped bleeding and didn't appear to be broken, but the whole left side of his face was purple, and the flesh around his left eye was swelling.

His eyes opened suddenly and he blinked up at the sky. His gaze wandered, found me, and focused, very slowly.

"That was not," I told him, "a smart thing to do."

Chapter 6

Michael

I have never believed it honorable to strike a servant, or anyone who can't hit back. But at that moment I would have tried to cuff Fisk into next week had I only been able to stand unassisted.

As it was, I attempted to sit up, but my stomach muscles were so battered that I'd not have succeeded if Fisk hadn't knelt to help me.

I leaned against him and assessed the damage—almost everything hurt, but nothing seemed to be broken. Even my nose, which felt like it was. I eyed Fisk's clean, unmarked face. "You might have lent a hand, squire."

"I might have tried, but it wouldn't have done any good. I don't know how to fight." Fisk's eyes were downcast in shame.

"There's no reason you should know how," I told him firmly. Fisk talked so rough (when he didn't sound like a university scholar) that I had simply assumed he could fight. I'd never thought to ask him.

With Fisk's hand under my arm I rose slowly to my knees, then, staggering, to my feet. Fisk helped me walk to the horse trough and went to fetch the horses while I splashed cold water over my face and head. My bruises throbbed, but the coolness cleared my mind.

I didn't wish to parade my battered state before the townsfolk, whose gossip might reach my father's ears, or risk encountering Lady Ceciel's brother again. There was no reason to go back to Thorbury and several reasons not to. Mistress Agnes's door remained shut, so I would have to manage my own healing, but with Fisk's assistance I should do well enough. I told him as much when he returned, and he didn't protest— I think he had no more desire to encounter Lady Ceciel's brother than I did.

Mounting was awkward and painful, despite Fisk's help, but eventually I was seated in Chant's high saddle— even if I was doubled over the pommel, gasping.

Fisk eyed me dourly. "This is your own fault, you know. You could have gotten out of this with a whole skin if you'd told a few lies, Noble Sir."

"You're wrong, Fisk. The fault lay in deceiving them.

Had I told the truth when we first met, neither Mistress Agnes nor her brother would have been provoked to violence."

Fisk opened his mouth to scold me further, looked me over, and gave it up as a hopeless task. His resigned sigh made me smile, despite the painful protest of my bruised face.

As we rode, I recovered somewhat and was able to instruct Fisk as to what herbs to seek out when we made camp.

"'Twould be best if you could find magica," I told him. "All herbs' properties are stronger when they're magical, especially the healing ones. And this time of year even those without the sensing Gift can find them, for magica greens earliest and dies latest. If 'tis still green in Appleon, there's a very good chance 'tis magica."

"Like that?" Fisk asked, pointing to a clump of glossy green leaves.

"No, that's holly, which stays green all year and has no healing properties. But look here." I urged Chant close to one of the clumps and reached cautiously into the prickly leaves. "See how this leaf is deformed? Insects don't like holly much, but something has nibbled this leaf and the stem is scuffed."

"I see." Fisk eyed the thorns. "So what?"

"Magica is always undamaged, for insects won't go near it, and even hail doesn't crush or scar it."

"And if *I* go picking it I'll break out in a rash, or trip on a root and crack my skull, or—"

"Not if you pick it correctly and offer the proper sacrifice—which for plants is usually to water them, and even a townsman should be able to manage that!"

As the afternoon wore on and I lectured further about how you picked the sprigs of one plant close to the ground and stripped the leaves off another, how you can take every fifth stem of a mint clump, but from willow can take all the wands you want as long as you cut only the lower ones, I began to think I was asking a lot of a city-bred man.

My mother is a skilled herb-talker, who supplies mixers all through Seven Oaks and beyond—I hadn't realized how much she'd taught me until I had to impart the knowledge to someone else.

We made camp in a meadow where a stream joined the road. Or rather Fisk made camp while I sat on a rock, wearily wondering if I should have gone back to town and risked meeting the brother after all.

I crumbled into my bedroll as soon as Fisk laid it out, and sent him downstream to look for the plants I wanted—one of which was willow.

To my delight he did find one that was magica.

Willows grow in damp places, so the sacrifice includes more than water, but the road provided dried dung, and there were dead leaves aplenty to mix in for a good mulch. Fisk must have done a passable job of digging the mulch around the roots, for no ill befell him as he stripped bark from the wands and brewed the bitter tea. By the time he finished making hot ribban-root poultices, 'twas long since dark. He ate dry journeybread and cheese and crawled into his blankets with a martyred sigh. That irritated me, for if he couldn't fight, healing was something he could and should do.

But in the morning I was forced to revise my opinion once again. The poultices on my bruised face and hands were still damp, which meant that Fisk must have wakened and changed them in the night—mayhap several times. A complex man, my squire.

Between the magica willow tea and the poultices, I felt so much improved that I let Fisk sleep while I fixed breakfast—or rather caught and fixed it. Tickling for trout can be quick, if you've a Gift for animals. The fire's smoke drifted on the breeze, the cloudless sky gave promise of a fine day, and with adventure in the offing, I was content as may be.

As Fisk deftly pulled the spine and rib bones from his roasted trout, I caught him looking at me in the manner of a man with something on his mind. I lifted my brows, and he sighed again.

"Do you remember that Mistress Agnes's brother came in ranting about Cory Port?"

"Just before he pounded me to a pulp," I said dryly. But memory stirred—it had seemed awfully important to him. "Go on," I told my squire.

"Well, I asked Mistress Agnes about it, and she said that Craggan Keep, which now belongs to Mistress Ceciel, governs Cory Port. It's a deepwater harbor, a few days' travel north of Uddersfield."

A chill far deeper than I'd felt in the stream this morning seized me. I hardly needed Fisk to continue— Father had often complained about Uddersfield's harbor fees, and we ship very little. Lord Dorian owns several mines. He ships a lot.

"Mistress Agnes said that if her sister dies, the estate, including the port, goes to Sir Bertram."

"And hence to Lord Dorian," I finished. And my father knew it. Knew it, and sent me to fetch her without even deigning to tell me what was going on. As if I were a child . . . or a fool. I took a deep breath, struggling to keep my emotions off my face. Though he is my squire, Fisk is scarcely more than a stranger, and there are things you don't reveal to strangers. There are some things you don't reveal to anyone you don't trust, but my father could have told *me*. I took another deep breath and went on, "No wonder they thought she'd get no justice from Lord Dorian's court. Although . . . I don't think he'd condemn an innocent woman. He's ambitious, but not without honor."

As is my father. He might not trust me with the truth, but he'd never send an innocent woman to her death.

Fisk eyed me curiously, but his words were neutral. "Agnes also said that if Ceciel married one of Lord Gerald's men she'd be safe, for the castle would go to her husband if she died. Would Lady Ceciel go to Lord Gerald for protection?"

"She might, but surely that's the first thing Lord Dorian and my father would think of. If she was there, they'd have found her already and complained to the High Liege that Lord Gerald was sheltering a criminal. Or they'd have asked Lord Leopold for permission to take troops across his land—either way, they wouldn't need us. But instead, Father ordered me to track her down, which means they don't know where she is."

Fisk thought this over. "How would they know if she went to Lord Gerald? He wouldn't want to advertise it until she was married, and maybe not then. All he'd have to do is dose her with aquilas and she'd cooperate."

I sighed. 'Twas legal, once, for nobles to use the

magic of aquilas to subvert the will of a reluctant woman. That was a *long* time ago, but no one seems able to forget it. The formula for the potion is still known, however. . . .

"That would be *illegal,* Fisk. Any marriage, any sort of agreement she made under those conditions, would be invalid."

Fisk looked stubborn. "Your father told us Lord Dorian set guards on his borders with orders to keep any of Lord Gerald's men from entering. That's why Hackle had to hire bandits to escort her—neither her men nor Lord Gerald's could get to her without starting a war. That's why he . . ."

"Hired us," I finished grimly.

"Look, are you *sure* Lord Gerald doesn't have her?" Fisk asked. "He could be keeping her in secret, somewhere safe."

"No place is secret or safe from servants' gossip. Lord Dorian is bound to have . . . informants on his neighbors' staffs. And if *he* knew, he'd act. No, she's hidden herself somewhere, and 'tis up to us to find her."

Unfortunately, I had no further ideas as to how to go about this, and my last hadn't been notably successful. I feared Fisk would comment on this, but he was still thinking.

"You know, I'm not sure she knows either."

"What?"

"Think back to the night we rescued her. Remember? When you asked where she was going?"

The rain-damp wind whirled through my memory. "And she looked at Hackle, and he said, 'To her brother.' But I can't believe she was there. He and Mistress Agnes were too open in their anger. If they'd had her, they'd have been quieter, and more suspicious."

"True," said Fisk, with an irritating smirk. "But not relevant. You asked her where she was going, and *Hackle* answered. She didn't know his plan. I bet that evil old fox has her tucked somewhere *he* thinks is safe."

"Then we're no better off than we were before, with no idea where she might be and no way—"

"But there is a way!" Fisk leaned forward, eyes alight. "At least, there might be. Hackle is trying to hide *her*, not himself. He may not have covered his own tracks. And I'll stake my last fract that if we find him, we'll find her."

After further discussion we decided to return to Willowere, where we first encountered Hackle, and try to trace him from there.

The stark branches above us webbed the road with sun and shadow, and I found the soft creak of saddle leather conducive to thought. The more I thought, the more I agreed with Fisk's conclusions, yet one question kept nagging me until finally I spoke it aloud.

"Why did she do it?"

"Huh?"

"Why did she do it? According to Mistress Agnes the poison was given to him over a long period, so the poisoner had to be someone in the baron's household. And 'twould require a skilled herb-mixer to create the potion, so it seems Lady Ceciel must be guilty, but why? Even Sir Bertram said his brother had no intention of putting her off. Mistress Agnes never claimed he was unkind to her—much less so savage she'd wish to kill him. So why?"

"Maybe she found he was bedding another woman—or maybe he fell in love with another woman and did decide to put her off."

"In his sixties?"

Fisk looked defensive. "It can happen."

But it wasn't likely.

"If she's guilty, it doesn't matter why," Fisk continued. "And if she isn't, it's the judicar's problem, not yours. All you have to worry about is fetching her back."

"Someone could have bought the poison *from* an herbalist," I said. Yet no reputable herbalist would sell large amounts of poison to anyone, herbalists seldom even made magica poison, and altogether 'twas as unlikely as Fisk's mythical other woman.

I waited for him to point this out, but his gaze was fixed ahead. We were nearing the village now, and farmhouses appeared frequently by the roadside. The one coming up on our left was so old that the roof sagged like a swaybacked horse, though the thatch was in good repair. The stables and sheds of the outbuildings were old, too, and well maintained . . . all but the chicken coop, where a woman was vigorously wielding a shovel.

Riding nearer, the problem was plain to see—something heavy had gone off the road and through the chicken coop's flimsy fence, smashing three woven wicker panels. The panels are easy to replace, but two of the posts they were nailed to had been snapped off near the ground.

The woman had dug down about a foot around the first post. As we watched, she bent to grasp the remains of the post, rocking it back and forth, then tried to wrench it up. The earth refused to yield its grip and she straightened up, rubbing her hands before reaching once more for the shovel.

Her back was turned to us and her hair was hidden under her cap, but the arms revealed by her rolled-up sleeves showed plenty of muscle under the wrinkled, sagging skin of old age.

"That's a hard job for an old woman." Fisk was trying to sound indifferent, but his eyes slid toward me. "I wonder if she has a room for rent."

What had so shaped Fisk that he couldn't simply say, "Let's help her"?

Getting no response from me, he went on. "You know, we were in jail in this town just a few days ago. It might be a good idea to get a room outside it . . . just in case someone was fond of Sir Herbert."

I smiled at this, for 'twas unlikely anyone would be so passionate about a man who hadn't lived in the area for forty years—and Fisk knew it. His cheeks reddened.

"It's also possible that one of the men who guarded Sorrowston Tower lives in this backward cow sty," he said hotly. "They certainly aren't pleased with us. It's only sensible to find a place to sleep where everyone in town doesn't know where we are!"

I grinned, and he glared at me. "You don't have to work so hard for it," I told him, and guided Chant over to the woman. "Good morning, Mistress."

She stuck the shovel into the earth before turning, revealing a face as wrinkled and homely as an old apple.

"Good mor . . ." Her eyes widened. Most of the swelling had gone, but I knew my bruises were fearsome. I smiled reassuringly and went on. "I'm Sir Michael, a knight errant in search of adventure and good deeds, and this is my squire, Fisk. You seem to be in need of younger hands, and 'twould be our honor to assist you."

Her eyes widened further at this speech—a reaction to which I've grown accustomed. I waited for her to recover and either say *"What?"* or burst out laughing.

When I first became a knight errant, it bothered me when people laughed, though I could scarce blame them. In a child, playing knights and quests is cute. For a youth my age . . . But I made up my mind that I'd not quit, no matter how I was mocked. Yes, at first their amusement stung my pride. But as time passed, it stung less. The pride I took in my ability to earn a place in the world, despite the opinion of others, was greater than the injury of laughter.

But instead of the reaction I expected, she turned to Fisk, who looked far more respectable than I did.

"Yes, he means it," Fisk told her gloomily. "It's a long story."

"Squire?"

Fisk looked even gloomier. "Don't ask."

She did laugh then, but 'twas welcoming, and the eyes she turned on me were bright as a magpie's. "Good deeds, huh? Well, Sir Michael, if that's your way of offering to fix my chicken coop, I won't say no. I'm Miss Edda."

We spent the rest of the morning restoring the chicken coop. I managed to find a winch wheel in the barn. We lashed three posts together, hung the wheel above the broken posts, and ran the rope through it and out to Chant's saddle—a trick of leverage I learned working in the mines in the north. The broken posts popped out like rotten teeth. Sinking the new ones and tacking up the panels was simple, though Fisk had to do the heavy work. He was willing but less practiced with both hammer and shovel than I.

Mistress Edda supervised our work, also making sure we didn't steal anything, but even Fisk forgave her suspicion when she brought out cold apple juice to ease our thirst.

We learned that she was a widow, and her son and their hired man had gone to Uddersfield to sell the excess of their harvest. Which should not have been a problem, except for a hound pack that had escaped its handler, and so startled a pair of oxen that they took an ore cart right through her fence and into the chicken coop.

Fisk exclaimed over the coincidence of her son and hired man being absent when he and I needed a place to stay, and offered to do her a further favor by renting those empty rooms.

Eyes sparking shrewdly, Mistress Edda said she was grateful for his kindly thought, but alas, she wasn't an innkeeper. She and Fisk settled into bargaining, and the price they finally settled on seemed fair enough to me, though it was clear they both thought they'd gotten the better deal.

We washed the sweat from our bodies in the horse trough and were back on the road by midafternoon, with the promise of a meal and warm beds when we returned in the evening.

Willowere was part farming village and part river port, for the barges that traveled the Halloway frequently stopped to off-load timber or wool and take on ore, grain, or ale.

We started at dockside, for Fisk said all the gossip in port towns was heard there first. We talked to the tavern keeper, the crane master, and as many loaders as we could find. But while many men remembered Hackle, none could tell us where he'd come from, where he was going, or anything except that he'd been trying to hire men for some "shady business."

No one seemed to realize that Fisk and I were the men he'd hired; still, we were somewhat discouraged returning to Mistress Edda's house that night.

Next morning we spoke to the keeper of the inn where we'd met with Hackle. He did remember not only Hackle but us, and he knew what had come of that meeting. He tried to keep a courteous face, but laughter leaked out at the corners, and he knew no more of Hackle than anyone else.

Thus it was throughout the day; the smith, the shop-keepers, the ferrymen—none could tell us anything except that some of Hackle's coins had been stamped with Lord Gerald's marks. At Fisk's suggestion, I had offered a gold roundel for any useful information, but no one came forward.

The knowledge of our quest spread rapidly through the town. Fisk is less accustomed to laughter than I, and even I was finding it wearisome by the day's end, when we went to the inn where we'd stabled our horses.

"Nothing," Fisk pronounced. "Near as I can tell, the old man stayed in this town for over a week and didn't speak a casual word to *anyone*. It's inhuman, that's what it is."

"But not so peculiar," I answered, "when you consider he was here to arrange a prison break. Would *you* chat with strangers under such circumstances?"

Fisk scowled, but he couldn't argue. The stableboy who was leading Chant and Tipple out to us caught sight of Fisk's face and approached with more caution. His hair was straight as straw, and one of his front teeth was missing.

"Two days wasted," Fisk grumbled. "We might as

well have asked this boy! You, boy, did old man Hackle tell you secrets?"

"Well, Sir, he—"

"Of course he didn't. Why should he? How should anyone in this rustic backwater know . . ."

Fisk went on, but I'd stopped listening. The boy's eyes flashed when Fisk asked his question, and his face fell when my squire interrupted. I held up a hand to silence Fisk.

"Lad, do you know something?"

"No, Sir. Not really."

This time Fisk caught it too. "What is it that you don't *really* know?" His voice had gentled, but the lad's eyes remained downcast.

"It's nothing, Sir."

Fisk looked urgently at me. I looked back at him blankly, for I had no idea how to get the boy to speak. *The money,* he mouthed silently.

"Of course!" The jingling of coin lifted the boy's eyes.

"Oh no, it's not that. I just don't think what I noticed is worth anything. It was stupid, really. I'm probably wrong."

"Let us be the judges of that," said Fisk, in a voice so persuasive it could have pulled fish from the water. His con artist voice? I held a gold roundel so it flashed in the light.

The boy eyed it. "It's just that I thought I recognized his clothes."

"His clothes?" Fisk and I spoke together.

"I said it was stupid."

"No, go on. This is the best information we've had all day." 'Twas the only information, but Fisk's encouragement served the purpose.

"It was the patches on his tunic," the boy went on more confidently. "Remember how ragged he was? I thought I'd seen that pattern of patches before, on Long Tom's clothes, though Tom's patches were brighter, and these were better fabric. The clothes didn't fit well, so I wondered if he'd stolen Long Tom's clothes and repatched them. But that didn't make sense, and they'd have called me a simp, so I didn't say anything."

"Who's Long Tom?" I asked.

"He's a beggar, sir, comes through here in spring and fall, for he works a regular route. He left a few days before Master Hackle came. He tells me stories of his travels in exchange for what I sneak out of the kitchen, and when I recognized the tunic I worried a bit for Tom," the lad finished in a rush. "But I know it's silly. Who'd want a beggar's clothes?"

Fisk's eyes met mine. *A man who needed a disguise to get past Lord Dorian's border guards.*

"You've won yourself a roundel, lad." He caught it with a joyful squeak. "Just one more thing. You say Long Tom works a regular route. Do you know where he'd be now?"

"Not for certain," the boy admitted. "But he winters in Uddersfield, most times."

Fisk and I passed a second night at Mistress Edda's, much of it spent in argument, though I can't think why we quarreled, for we agreed on everything.

We agreed that Hackle had bought the beggar's clothes to pass Lord Dorian's border. We agreed that he'd then replaced the beggar's gaudy patches with something more respectable, so he could stay in town without exciting comment.

We also agreed that it was cursed unlikely that Hackle, who'd been so closemouthed with the towns-folk, had said more to a chance-met beggar, so pursuing him was a waste of time.

Unfortunately neither of us had any better ideas.

The sun was still bright next morning, but the wind that had come up during the night was rattling the last leaves out of the trees like a housemaid beating dust from a rug. 'Tis fine weather for travel in my opinion, though Fisk pulled his cloak tight and prophesied storms.

For all his pessimism, Fisk was a good companion, able to talk or be silent as the mood took us. 'Twas in one of the silent times that the feeling came upon me, so soft I'd scarce have noticed it had not Fisk said, "That's the fourth time you've looked over your shoulder. Did you forget something?"

"No." I pulled Chant to a stop and turned to look back, watching and listening carefully now.

The road behind us was empty. The woods held only trees, brush, and two squirrels chasing each other through the branches. The wind carried a steady stream of leaves to the forest floor and blew my hair into my eyes. But in the cellars of my mind, where Gifts reside, was a nagging feeling that someone watched me.

The sensing Gift is a steady, reliable thing, for magic is either there or it isn't, and you can tell with a single touch. Other Gifts are more . . . ambiguous. I learned not to ignore them on the day a dog with a happily wagging tail turned and sank its teeth into my wrist. But I'd also learned that this vague disquiet could be caused by many things. Mayhap someone was thinking of me—I've felt such things before, even when the person was half a county distant. At all events, there was nothing to be done about it, though I resolved to sleep in safe shelter tonight if the feeling lingered.

But my uneasiness had passed off long before we made camp that evening, and I had forgotten about it. So I was taken unawares when Fisk, who was unpacking the saddlebags, exclaimed in disgust and dropped something.

"What under the two moons is that?" he asked, wiping his hands on his britches.

The light was dimming. I had to go stand beside him to make out the crumpled dark thing that lay at his feet.

"It looks like hide." A rank stench reached my nose and I grimaced. "Boar's hide, uncured." I dropped to my knees. The moment I touched it I felt the familiar tingling, faint with the death of the beast, but unmistakable. My hand jerked back and I jumped away.

"'Tis magica! Where did you find it?"

The dusk drained everything of color, but Fisk's face was paler than usual.

"In Tipple's pack. But surely . . . I mean, *we* didn't kill it! If whoever did made the appropriate sacrifice, then—"

"Then why place it with us? Unless the proper sacrifice was made, no one who owns this hide will be forgiven. Get Tipple's pack back on her—we've got to get out of here." Chant's pack was still on his saddle—all I had to do was yank the girth taut.

"But we don't *own* it." Fisk was gathering Tipple's pack as he spoke. "We didn't kill it, we didn't buy it, we had nothing to do with it!" He shouted the final words into the empty forest, as if the Furred God might hear and forgive us. But the gods aren't human, and they don't reason as we do.

"We have to find a Savant." I swung into Chant's saddle. "Fast. There's a village about half an hour west of here. We might make it."

Fisk didn't reply.

"Fisk?"

He stood, frozen, with Tipple's pack slung over his shoulder, his gaze on a patch of shadow at the edge of the clearing.

Staring into the shadow, I could just make out the high-peaked shoulders and tiny, pricked ears of the wild boar. Its eyes were fixed on my squire.

It has been several centuries since anyone was insane enough to hunt boar for sport, and when they did they used a spear. A long spear, with a heavy cross guard to keep the boar from running up the spear and savaging the hunter. I decided to remain mounted.

"Don't move," I murmured, my throat so tight 'twas a wonder my voice didn't squeak. The warning was unnecessary—Fisk didn't seem to be breathing. I hoped my squire would know enough to climb a tree, as boars are not equipped for climbing. Meanwhile, I moved my right hand, as slowly as I could, over the pack on Chant's rump in search of my sword hilt.

Heroes in ballads are always wearing their swords when trouble arises, but frankly, wearing a sword is cursed inconvenient. 'Tis always in the way when you try to sit down, or whacking into things when you turn around. So I kept my sword in Chant's pack, but I made one concession to knight errantry and the slim possibility of encountering bandits: I'd left the hilt free, so I could draw it from the pack with a single pull. In a full year's adventuring, I'd never before had cause to use it. Now, unable to take my eyes off the boar, I groped over leather, canvas, and buckle and wished I'd had the sense to practice this a time or two. I couldn't find the cursed hilt!

Without so much as a twitch to warn us, the boar charged. Fisk tried to flee, but it ran right under him and knocked him flat as a ball-struck skaddle pin.

The boar turned, snorting, stamping the ground.

Fisk thrashed back through the drifted leaves, his face twisted with terror. He grabbed Tipple's pack and threw it at the beast.

The unwieldy bundle lurched toward the boar, which, thinking itself attacked, charged the pack.

Fisk scrambled away, as the gleaming tusks slashed through canvas as if 'twas paper.

I tore my gaze from the beast and *looked* for my

sword hilt. How could it have worked its way under there? No matter. The sword rang softly as I pulled it free, and I made a hissing click with my teeth that reminded my half-lame riding horse that he had once been a tourney-trained destrier. He quivered and his ears whipped forward. Tourneys were supposed to be training for war, although generally against taller opponents.

Chant didn't care. His muscles bunched beneath my legs; he planted his back feet, spun, and cantered toward the boar, who was still savaging Tipple's pack. I hoped his weakened leg was up to this.

Mayhap the drumming hooves alerted it, or it may have decided the pack was finally dead. The boar lifted its head and charged.

I leaned out of the saddle and swung down, aiming close to the skull, where the spine wasn't so well pro-tected. But the angle was wrong, and my blade sliced its shoulder. Most creatures would have found this a serious injury; it only made the boar mad. It spun in place, slashing at Chant's hind legs.

Chant's kick, better aimed than my sword stroke, sent the boar tumbling. Unfortunately I hadn't expected it, and since I was still unbalanced it sent me tumbling too.

I hit the ground rolling and came to my feet in one

movement, passionately grateful that nobles' sons were still expected to learn what my scholarly brother, Benton, called "that ridiculously outdated nonsense."

The boar's blank eyes regarded me. I know animals don't think this way, but I swear I saw pleasure in them, satisfaction that he had brought me down where he could reach me.

Before this, events had followed too quickly for fear, but now a chill rose from my heart and spread through my limbs, draining them of speed and strength.

The boar charged, quick, so quick I hadn't time to do more than slash at it as I leapt aside. My sword missed clean, and the boar turned in its tracks, swinging its heavy head to catch my leg with one sharp tusk.

Pain blazed up my leg, but my sword swung in blind, instinctive retaliation, and this time found its mark. I heard the wet crunch of bone as my blade sliced through its spine.

The boar sank to its belly and I fell back against a rock, gritting my teeth. Warm blood flowed down my ankle. I had to assess the wound and bind it, but I didn't want to. Not just yet. I shut my eyes.

"Watch out!" Fisk cried.

My eyes snapped open as the boar lumbered to its feet and charged again.

I wish I could say that I leapt to my feet, full ready

to fight. The truth is that I fell backward over the rock. Had the boar been whole, it would have finished me.

As it was, I had time to struggle to my feet and watch in horror as it stumbled around the rock, seeking me. The great muscles in its neck weren't strong enough to lift its head without the aid of a spine, so its snout dragged in the dirt, but still it came on. The boar should have been dead, long seconds dead, and I realized, with a sinking dread that put my previous fear to shame, that it was magica.

No wonder the beast had been so fast. But a severed spine crippled even a magica boar. It could barely walk, much less slash with its tusks.

I set my teeth, stepped forward, and methodically chopped through its neck. The half dozen blows needed to sever the head from the body seemed to take forever. I could feel the magic now, pulsing and raging as the beast, finally, died.

I watched blood flow from the severed neck and sink into the dark mulch of the forest floor. Everything around us—the leaves, the rock, the boar, and I—was spattered with blood. My whole body shook.

With a great rustling of branches, Fisk climbed down from a nearby tree. I was pleased to see he'd had the sense to climb out of danger, but 'twas a distant feeling. Nothing seemed quite real to me.

"It was d-d-dead." His teeth were chattering. He never took his eyes from the corpse at my feet, as if he expected it to come after us even now. "It was dead, but it went right on attacking you."

"It was magica, Fisk," I explained. "Even a real boar will go on fighting after 'tis sorely wounded, and that property is enhanced by magic. It was magica. And I killed it."

CHAPTER 7

Fisk

On Furred God's Night—
the longest night of the year, when the moons rule the
world—people shut themselves into their homes and
tell stories of how the gods punish those who destroy
magica without sacrifice. As I grew older, I'd discounted
most of those stories, but now every one of them came
rushing back. I wished my memory wasn't quite so good.

Sir Michael just stood there, looking as if he'd mis-
laid a spoon or something. I wanted him on the edge
of hysterics, like me. I opened my mouth to snarl at
him and realized that I was right—he was *too* calm.
Some sort of shock? Something deeper than my jangled
nerves. Something to do with magic?

"Sir?" I laid a hand on his shoulder. His head turned
slowly, and his eyes were as blank as his face. "Sir, I
think we should leave now."

It was easier said than done. Chanticleer, bless his big feet, hadn't strayed. But Tipple, though I couldn't blame her for it, had broken her tether and run off.

I thought about chasing after her, but the last of the sunlight had gone and only the pale glow of the Green Moon wavered between the tree trunks. The stillness had a watchful feel to it, like when you're breaking into a warehouse under the eyes of the city guard and they're just waiting for the right moment to nab you.

Sir Michael felt it too; he shivered as the moonlight touched him and looked up, scanning the sky.

"Only blood redeems blood," he said softly. "The Creature Moon rises late these days—in about two hours, I think. It . . . it might be a good idea to find a Savant before then."

His voice was small and, for the first time since we'd met, unsure. He stood beside the boar's body as if his feet were glued in place.

"Then we'll find one," I said, grateful for the years of practice that let me flood my voice with confidence, no matter what I felt. "Just tell me what to do."

I took a few minutes to bandage the bleeding gash in his calf—it wasn't deep, which was a good thing because Sir Michael was no help. I had to pull him from the clearing bodily, but once away he recovered enough to mount Chanticleer, unstrap and drop his pack, and help me up behind the saddle.

With my arm around his waist, I could feel him shaking, though the night was not yet cold. He looked back at the dead boar.

"So where do we find a Savant?" I demanded. He neither spoke nor moved, so I gave Chanticleer a kick, and the horse lurched into an overburdened stroll.

"Where do we find a Savant?" I repeated. "We don't often see them in the city, and I need to know what to do if you turn into a chipmunk or something."

Sir Michael laughed at that and lifted the reins, urging Chanticleer to a more purposeful walk. I sagged like wet cloth with relief. I'd been afraid something was already working on him, and I'd had no idea what to do about it.

"I'm sure it wouldn't be *that* extreme," he said, though he didn't sound sure. "And we've probably got some time before anything happens."

"Two hours, you said."

"What?" Sir Michael stiffened under my hands.

"Two hours. You said that we had the two hours before the Creature Moon rises to find a Savant."

Sir Michael twisted in the saddle, eyes searching my face. "*I* said that?"

"Just a few minutes ago. Why? Is it coming up sooner?"

"No." Sir Michael turned and urged Chanticleer forward again. "No, the time's about right. I just don't remember saying it."

Sir Michael told me that the villagers would have some way to contact the nearest Savant, though the methods varied widely. The next village was only a twenty-minute ride north of the main road, but it seemed to take far longer. Sir Michael stopped Chanticleer at the gate of the first house. The shuttered windows were dark.

"Fisk, I shouldn't go to that house. Suppose something happens? Suppose they have children?"

Only blood redeemed blood. I wished I could forget the story I'd once heard, about a farm family that inadvertently burned out a nest of magica rats.

Of course, Michael's punishment for killing the boar would be different. Those who destroyed magica always suffered, but one of the things that made it so terrifying was that no one could predict exactly what would happen. Or where. Or when. Or whether an innocent squire might be swept up in it.

"I'll go." I untied his purse strings with a practiced ease that I hoped he didn't notice, and hurried to pound on the door.

It took a while for the householder to come downstairs, for he'd stopped to put on his britches and grab a stout oak staff. His wife, in her night robe, came behind him carrying a lamp.

I saw no need to waste time on courtesies. "My master needs to see a Savant. Fast." I held out two gleaming silver roundels, Sir Michael having given the last of the gold to a stable lad, whom he could have easily dickered down. The householder's gaze went from my tense face to Sir Michael's shadowy form waiting at his gate.

"There's a Savant that lives nearby." He reached out and pocketed the coins. "But I don't know about fast. When we need him, we climb to the top of Lurs Hill, across the stream there, and pound on the hollow log. Three raps, wait, three raps, wait, then three more. He comes, but not always fast."

I looked across the moonlit valley to the hill. It wasn't far off, but neither was the rise of the Creature Moon.

"Three raps, three times. Thanks." I had turned to go when the housewife laid a hand on my arm.

"Don't look so frightened. We've been good to the Savant—he comes as fast as he's needed. Your friend will be all right."

I didn't try to explain that I was worried for myself, not my employer. I'd ridden too close to that hide this afternoon, and the boar had gone for me, not Sir Michael—who had killed it.

Sir Michael *had* killed it, when he could easily have taken Chanticleer and fled, leaving me to fend for myself. It would have been the sensible thing to do. I bet the thought never even crossed his mind.

It would have crossed mine.

The ride up the hill took far too long, for Sir Michael refused to abandon me. I might have been safer away from him, but I didn't argue. Sir Michael's Gifts were speaking to him, and ignoring them just then struck me as a really bad idea.

The hilltop was wooded, like everything else in this forsaken wilderness. It was Chanticleer who found the narrow path that led to an old fallen tree, with all the bark beaten off by the villagers' summonses.

Sir Michael eyed the quiet woods warily, and since he was more likely to recognize an oncoming threat than I, I slid off Chanticleer's rump and fumbled through the leaves for a stone. My hands closed around one, river smooth, likely brought by the villagers for this very purpose.

Thud-thud-thud. I had expected a deep, vibrant drum sound that would travel through the forest for miles, but this was scarcely louder than a carpenter's hammer. *Thud-thud-thud!* I struck harder this time, but the sound was still too soft to carry far.

I looked at Sir Michael, but he sat motionless in

the saddle, his eyes searching the darkness between the trees.

I took the stone in both hands and swung as hard as I could. *THUD*. Louder, but still not loud enough to carry. *THUD*. How could this possibly rouse a Savant, who knows how far off, and probably asleep as well? I raised the stone high, prepared to bring it down with all my might, when a gentle hand reached from behind me and clasped my arm.

"No need to break it."

I yelped, jumped, and dropped the stone, which barely missed my head.

The man who released my arm was small—shorter than I and far thinner. Hair that looked as if it had never been cut fell in mossy locks, and his beard almost reached his belt. His clothes, once sturdy and well made, were now so worn that the cloth around the seams had begun to fray. Hair, beard, and clothes were all clean, however, and I perceived that the housewife had told the truth—the villagers took good care of him.

As a child I knew nothing of Savants, but in several years of roaming from town to town I've learned a thing or two. The country folk don't really take care of their Savants—it's a matter of trade. When you need to be certain there's no magica in the field you want to plow or a stand of timber you want to cut, or if you want to give your spring planting a head start or offer thanks for a good hunt, you find a Savant.

Savants have no magic themselves, of course—no normal humans have magic. But they can tell you what sacrifice to make and they intercede—with nature, magic, or maybe with the gods themselves. No one knows for certain what the Savants serve, except the Savants, and they aren't saying. Then you reward the Savant: food, clothes, blankets, a knife—they have no use for money—and they wander back into the wilderness, where they're said to live more primitively than the desert savages.

They say Savants were perfectly ordinary people until the call came and they took to roaming the woods more and more often—until they abandoned homes, families, sometimes even wealth, and vanished into the forest.

Some say they find other Savants who teach them the lore of wild things. Some say the plants and animals themselves do the teaching. But whatever the truth may be, a Savant is the only one who can determine the proper sacrifice to redeem the destruction of magica.

This one gazed at me mildly; the distance in his eyes made him look a little mad. He turned away, and I saw that he'd brought Tipple with him—her broken halter rope was frayed, but she hadn't come to harm. In fact, something in her spotted clown face made her look quite pleased with herself.

It's quite a trick to lead a horse out of a forest without making a sound.

Sir Michael was surprised, too, but then his startled expression gave way to vast relief. He slid from Chanticleer's back and started to speak, but the Savant held up a hand to stop him and approached Chanticleer instead.

First he stroked the gelding's muzzle, muttering to him, and Chanticleer huffed softly back. He checked the bit, to be sure it wasn't a cruel one, I suppose. Then he spent several moments running his hand over Chanticleer's weak leg, making me very glad Sir Michael hadn't pushed the beast to get us here.

If Sir Michael found anything odd in this performance, he didn't show it, though he was shifting from foot to foot in impatience when the Savant straightened.

"What was it?" he asked Sir Michael calmly.

"A boar. We found a piece of magica hide in our pack. It must have been planted there, for we didn't—"

The Savant cut him off with a gesture, his expression saying clearly that it didn't matter. Unlike man's justice, nature—or magic, or the gods—only cares about results.

"Come." He turned and walked into the forest,

leading us down the hill, away from the village. It wasn't easy to follow him, for we had to lead Chanticleer and Tipple around some of the logs that he stepped over. He never looked back to see if we were able to follow, which annoyed me. But Sir Michael stuck to his heels like a well-trained hound, and I wasn't about to be left alone out there.

I have little sense of direction wandering through trackless woods in the middle of the night, so I didn't realize where we were going until I saw the clearing, the blood-spattered rock, and the boar's body. He had led us across country, straight to the spot. No one had told him where it was.

The back of my neck prickled, and Tipple, sensing my unease, nuzzled my collar.

Then the small, tan disc of the Creature Moon rose and even I, Giftless as I am, felt the change as the golden light flooded down, and a second shadow stretched out from the trees. It's well known that the power of the gods is far stronger when their moons rise in the sky, but on this night, I swear I *felt* that power. And I wasn't the only one.

The Savant stepped forward hastily and knelt by the corpse of the boar, laying one hand on its torso and the other on its head. Sir Michael dropped Chanticleer's reins, wrapping his arms around himself as if he were cold. The wild, sullen, judging tension that had come with the moonrise seemed to ease—not vanish, but withdraw into a waiting, watching stillness.

The Savant sighed and gave the boar's head a pat, as if in apology or farewell. Then he drew his knife, pulled down the boar's lower lip, and slit its gum at the base of one long, curved tusk. Only a small seep of red marked the cut, for the thing was already bled dry. The Savant reversed the knife and smashed its hilt into the boar's jaw, cracking bone, and then snapped the tusk free with a single strong twist.

He stood and offered the tusk to Sir Michael, a six-inch ivory spike with a ragged end. Sir Michael took it, his face filled with questions. The Savant pointed at a nearby bush and said, "Dig."

Sir Michael dug, using the tusk and his hands—bare hands, for the Savant wouldn't let me bring him gloves.

Wild pigs must like the roots of that plant. As soon as Sir Michael chopped out three of the thick, white stems and cast them into the undergrowth, the Savant made him fill in the hole and then led him to another bush, where he repeated the process.

Seeing we were going to be some time at this, I unsaddled the horses and gathered the torn and trampled remains of Tipple's pack. Sir Michael's sword lay by the rock, and I cleaned and sheathed it. I asked the Savant if I should help, for I had ridden nearest the hide and I had been the one the boar attacked, but he just shook his head so I let it go.

He did permit me to bring Sir Michael water, since digging up roots with an ivory spike and your bare hands is cursed hard work. Sir Michael's face gleamed with sweat, even in the moonlight, and his hands left grimy smudges when he wiped it.

"Dig," the Savant told him.

The Creature Moon rose and the night wore on. I watched for a while, then wandered off to find the pack we'd dumped from Chanticleer's saddle. The feeling of danger had faded some time ago; the woods held only the natural eeriness of night. The Creature Moon rose until it shone straight through the trees, frosting the boar's corpse with muted gold.

The Savant went to lay a hand on Sir Michael's shoulder. He had started to dig at the base of yet another bush; the frigid air made his breath visible in steamy puffs.

"Now," the Savant told him, "dig a grave."

Sir Michael dug, choosing a place not far from the boar's body.

I tried to help him, but the Savant stopped me. Eventually I wrapped myself in a blanket, in addition to my cloak, though Sir Michael had thrown his cloak aside. He was working too hard to feel the cold.

The Creature Moon sank, slowly, and the bottom of

the grave sank with it. It was soon so deep that Sir Michael had to crouch inside it, pitching out dark handfuls of earth. The boar's tusk was black with dirt and blood, for Michael's blisters had broken some time ago.

The moon was touching the horizon when the Savant said, "Enough."

Sir Michael climbed out of the hole and rolled onto his back, gasping, staring up at the stars. His hands curled limply.

The Savant grabbed the boar's heels, dragged it to the grave, and dropped the beast in, tossing the head in after with a casualness that astonished me. He picked up the accursed hide that had started the whole thing and stroked it, sighing, before laying it in the grave. The bloodstained tusk followed; then he turned to me.

"Fill it in."

I shoved great mounds of loose dirt into the grave, making the boar's corpse vanish as fast as I could—I've never been so glad to see the last of anything. The earth felt cool, almost silky, for my hands were whole, unlike Sir Michael's.

My employer turned to watch. His ragged breathing had eased, though his face was white with weariness.

When the boar was buried and I had packed down the earth, the Savant gestured to Sir Michael, who came over to us. The Savant took his hands and uncurled them, which made him wince. Then the Savant took his wrists and held his palms flat on the grave, letting his blood soak into the soil.

A bird's sleepy twitter broke the silence, and I realized that the sky in the east had turned a lighter shade of gray.

The Savant released Sir Michael's wrists and stood. "The price is paid." He turned to go.

"Wait!" Sir Michael came stiffly to his feet, and stumbled over to Chanticleer's pack. He fumbled painfully with the buckles, pulled out his sword, and laid it aside. Then he refastened the pack, stood, and offered the pack to the Savant.

I bit down a howl of protest—I know it doesn't do to be stingy with Savants, but half our gear was in there!

The Savant weighed it thoughtfully. Then he knelt and dug through the pack till he found a small jar of salve. He handed it to Sir Michael and smiled.

"You'll need this." He picked up the pack and walked into the forest without looking back.

CHAPTER 8

Michael

Fisk made camp for us that morning, since my hands were too sore. Though *camp* might be too grand a word; the grassy nook, sheltered by an orchard wall, was barely big enough for the bedroll Fisk insisted on laying down for me. He cleaned, salved, and bandaged my hands and the cut on my calf. He also made cheese sandwiches, which is about the limit of his culinary skills.

I lay in the sun and watched him sort through the damaged contents of Tipple's pack, for he insisted I needed to rest. In truth the thought of napping suited me, as I'd been up all night. But so had Fisk, fussing over me with an expression that would have made anyone think I was being tortured instead of digging holes. Which reminded me . . .

"How did they know?"

Coming from nowhere, this question deserved no answer beyond "Huh?" but Fisk replied, "The way rumor spreads around here, the whole western half of the realm's probably heard the story. I'm more curious about who 'they' were—I'll bet she didn't put that hide in Tipple's pack herself. Someone she hired?"

"Probably. We were still in Lord Dorian's fiefdom at the inn . . . Root and branch! That's when they planted it on us."

Fisk took out my small sewing kit—a necessity when you're living on your own, though I don't manage a needle well. He chose one of the thickest needles, cut a length of double-strength thread, and after a bit of fumbling in the bottom of the pack, found a candle stub and ran the thread over it. The unburned candles, and the small lantern that sheltered them, had been in Chant's pack and were with the Savant now.

"The real question," Fisk said steadily, "is whether they were trying to kill us, or only delay us." He spread his pack over his knees and began pulling the tear together with smooth, even stitches.

"Not really," I said. "Why did you wax the thread?"

"Not really? Not *really*? Someone tried to kill us, but that's not really important?"

I had to laugh. "I don't think they were trying to kill us—or if they were, they chose a very . . . uncertain method. But Fisk, how did she know? Oh, not the general story, I'm sure that's spread. How did she know where we were, and what we were doing? They found us in Willowere, and *we* didn't even know we were going there until after we left Mistress Agnes's house."

"They could have figured it out pretty easily," said Fisk. "Since we didn't go back to Thorbury, Willowere's the only direction we could have gone. And Mistress Agnes and her brother would gladly tell their sister's agent all about us . . . or maybe *they* hired whoever it is, though that seems out of character for Mistress Agnes."

"For her brother, too." The tear in the pack closed rapidly under Fisk's agile fingers. The sun was warm in this sheltered place, and I yawned before going on. "Why hire someone when you can do it yourself? If he wanted us stopped, he'd just follow us and wallop me again."

Fisk laid down the neatly mended pack and picked up one of his torn shirts. "It amazes me that you can yawn before saying something like that. Someone is trying to delay, perhaps kill us. We don't know who they are, we don't know how they found us, and we haven't the least idea what they're going to try next. Noble Sir, I don't think we know enough."

"Well, we're new at this," I said. Fisk chose another

needle and waxed a length of white thread. Did he realize he'd said "we"? "We'll probably get better, with practice. Why *do* you wax the thread?"

Fisk was mending the torn shirt, with even smaller, neater stitches than he'd used on the pack.

"Practice," he said mournfully. "You intend to make a habit of this?" He was trying to look martyred, but the corners of his mouth twitched, and when he met my eyes he gave in and laughed. "You wax it to keep the thread from tangling. My mother was a seam-stress."

'Twas the first thing Fisk had told me about himself, and it accounted for the neat stitches, if nothing else.

"That's useful," I said sleepily. "That you can sew. I don't suppose you'd consider giving Kathy lessons?"

"Would she pay me? Considering that you just gave away all your clothes, it's a good thing I can sew."

As Fisk went on grumbling, I wondered why watching me dig holes had turned "you and I" into "we," and dropped off to sleep well pleased with my night's work.

I woke to find Fisk lying with his head on Tipple's pack, snoring. I hesitated to wake him, but judging by the position of the sun 'twas midafternoon—time to move on.

Before we left camp Fisk returned my purse. He told

me that while I slept he'd totaled up the coins—a thing I never bothered to do, for knights errant shouldn't care about money—and the result is generally depressing. Then Fisk told me the total—and it depressed me. There wasn't enough to replace the contents of Chant's pack.

We stayed at an inn that night, since we now had only one bedroll between us and in late Appleon that isn't enough. I was somewhat worried about the depleted state of my purse. Usually when I'm broke I work my way, but with sore hands and a sore leg I couldn't earn my keep.

Thus hope mingled with concern when Fisk wandered over to the table where four well-dressed merchants were playing black dan, and bet them he could cut any card they chose out of the deck if he could sort it into piles four times.

The taproom was bright with lamplight, and the scent of roasting turkey was putting edges on the appetites of half a dozen fellow travelers, and a handful of locals who had decided to dine out.

The four merchants had just finished a hand and were shuffling for a rematch. They gazed at Fisk with astonishment, disapproval, or merriment, according to their natures—which is to say one stared, one scowled, and two of them laughed.

"I'll tell you one thing," said one of the men who'd laughed. "We won't be dealing you into our game—although most sharpers aren't as willing to advertise their skills as you seem to be. Aren't you a bit young for this?" His doublet, of a fine mulberry wool, stretched over his belly; his collar and sleeves were snowy white. His round face was good-natured but shrewd.

If Fisk got arrested for cardsharping, as an indebted man, I'd not be able to help him. In fact, if they arrested Fisk they might arrest me as his partner. I drifted over to the table.

"Fisk, may I speak to you for a moment?"

"It's not sharping," Fisk told Master Mulberry Wool. "It's a wager on my skill—or lack thereof."

Mulberry, still smiling, shook his head. "Sorry, but I know better. I saw a sharper working a tourney once who could cut any card out of the deck after one shuffle. I must admit, it was worth paying to see—but I've already seen it."

"All right," said Fisk. "I'll give myself a handicap. I'll cut the card you choose—and you don't even have to tell me which card it is."

"What?"

"*Squire*, may I speak to you?"

"Squire?" one of the other merchants asked.

"It's a long story," said Fisk.

The serving girl giggled and I saw that everyone was watching the confrontation between Fisk and the merchants. 'Twas too late to stop this thing, for even the scowling merchant was now interested. I only hoped Fisk knew what he was doing, and that, if he didn't, we could escape without violence. My hands were in no shape for brawling . . . but I could run, if I was well motivated.

"Let me get this straight," said Master Mulberry. "I pick a card, and I *don't* tell you what it is?"

"That's right," said Fisk. "Write it down secretly, and don't show anyone. Then I'll sort the deck into three piles. You tell me which pile your card is in. We do that three more times—then I'll cut the card out of the deck for you."

"Ah," said Mulberry. "But if you see the contents of the piles each time, you'd have a good chance of identifying a card that's in all four piles I choose."

"I won't see what cards are in the piles," Fisk told him. "I'll lay them face down. You pick them up, look through them, put them down, and then tell me which pile it's in."

The merchant looked intrigued. "I know there's a trick, but I'd like to see this. How much am I supposed to bet against your skill, young sir?"

Fisk pulled out my purse, which I'd have sworn he returned to me earlier, and dumped the contents onto the table. A good-sized mound, but almost all fracts, and base fracts at that. "You bet two silver roundels, plus anyone else who wants to bet, up to fourteen people. I couldn't pay off more than that."

He couldn't pay off more than that? But the knowledge that only a small number would be allowed to bet—not to mention the clear implication that he might lose—soon had another small pile of coins stacked on the table. The merchants and the other bettors gathered around as Fisk took the deck, shuffled once, and fanned it with a single sweep of his hand.

"Choose a card," he told Mulberry, "and write it down."

The merchant was a careful man. His eyes passed slowly over the deck, lingering on several different cards. I thought I saw him eyeing the ten of daggers, or perhaps the dagger's moon, though in his shoes I wouldn't pick any of the moons or face cards, but would choose something ordinary.

"All right, I've chosen."

"Write it down," said Fisk.

While the merchant pulled a notebook from his doublet and made a few quick marks, Fisk picked up the deck, shuffled again, and dealt the cards into three piles. The green and gold of the suits decorated the backs of the cards as well, and they ran through his hands like a river of turning leaves.

Again, Mulberry was careful. He picked up all the piles, looked through them without pausing, and then pointed to the first. "It's in that one."

They repeated the process thrice. The room grew so still we could hear the crackle of the hearth fire and the dishes clattering in the kitchen.

Fisk stacked the piles and closed his eyes, as if feeling for some invisible sign. He cut the deck and held up the four of leaves.

Mulberry threw back his head and laughed—still laughing, he opened his notebook and showed the marks he'd made: a four and a leaf.

An explosion of comment bounced off the rafters. Some of the bettors slapped Fisk's back and congratulated him. Some scowled and looked askance. All wanted to know how he'd done it. But then the cook came in, with a fat brown gobbler on a platter, and the company deserted cards for turkey without a second thought.

All but Mulberry, who stayed at the table, watching Fisk thoughtfully. "I understand how a sharper, a very skilled one, can pick a card out of the deck by feel. I don't understand how you could cut a card with no way to know what it was."

Fisk smiled. "Showing you the trick is one thing, *revealing* it is something else. That would cost two gold roundels."

Mulberry sighed. "I won't get a sound night's sleep till I know." Two gold coins clinked onto the pile—the much larger pile—that Fisk scooped into my purse.

"It's not a matter of sharping," Fisk told him. "So watching my hands, and all the other precautions you took, were wasted. It's a matter of math." Fisk shuffled and cut the deck, showing the lady of horns. Then he went on, suiting his actions to his words. "Fifty-four cards in the piles—eighteen cards per pile. I'm putting them face up this time, so you can see how this works. All I have to do is pick up the pile you showed me first—which is the most natural thing to do, anyway. Now I know that the card you gave me is going to be one of the top six cards of these next three piles. . . ."

With the cards face up 'twas easy to see how the lady traveled first to the top of the piles, then to the bottom, but always nearer to one end or the other. After the fourth sorting she was the top card of the stack.

"So all I do now," Fisk finished, "is stack the piles loosely enough that I can cut this card. If you count down, it'll be the nineteenth card. Or you can take it off the top, but it's more impressive to pull it out of the

middle of the deck. You could do it with a little practice—but I warn you, most people figure it out about
the third time they see it."

"I suppose they do." Mulberry looked amused. "But
that won't stop me from showing it off to my neighbors. I might even get back some of my money.
Mathematical sharping. I like it." He strolled off,
chuckling, in pursuit of turkey.

I sat down beside my squire and eyed him critically.

"It's not really sharping," said Fisk, handing back my
purse. "It's an honest wager. Well, it's mostly entertainment, like a traveling play."

"Oh, I don't have any moral objections—though I do
call it sharping, mathematical or not. But suppose
someone else calls it sharping? If any of those men had
become angry, we could have found ourselves in a
very ugly situation."

"That's why you choose respectable middle-aged
men for your marks." Fisk shuffled the cards and
fanned them. "Pick a card."

I pointed to the nine of horns.

"You also wager only a small sum, so no one really
minds losing." Fisk shuffled deftly. "And it helps if
dinner, or some other pleasant distraction, is coming
up soon."

"I see," I said, smiling at my squire's forethought,

which impressed me more than the flimflam with the cards. "As long as you don't actually cheat anyone, I don't mind. But you might warn me next time."

"You'd have argued," said Fisk simply. "And Sir Michael . . ."

"Yes?"

Fisk pulled the nine of horns out of the well-shuffled deck. "This is sharping." He grinned, wickedly, at my astonishment.

Next morning before we set out, I purchased another bedroll, and enough trail food to replenish our supply. I don't know why I bothered, for Fisk persuaded me to spend the next night at an inn, where he repeated his previous success.

The third night of the journey, the old weaver Fisk challenged had seen the trick before; Fisk laughed and bought the man an ale. Even with several small setbacks, we had replaced the gear I gave the Savant by the time we reached our destination.

Uddersfield was a town on the verge of becoming a city. In over a century of peace, buildings had sprouted outside the old siege wall. The chimes of its tower clocks rang over the countryside—one of them a few seconds slower than the rest.

We followed the river road in, past rope makers,

coopers, smithies, and a rawly stinking dye yard. As we approached the great gate, I paused to admire the sweeping arc of the wall over the river. Once it had been part of the city defenses, but now small boats slipped between its supports and fishing lines descended to the water. The shade beneath a bridge is always a good place to fish.

Hooves and cart wheels clattered on the cobblestones that paved the road in front of the gate. As soon as we passed through it we encountered a mob of street sellers offering fruit, hot meat pies, pins and ribbons to take home to the wife, a guide to your dock, sir, or your inn, or wherever you need to go, just ask Mart.

Two brightly painted players stood on opposite sides of the street extolling the virtues of their troupe's entertainment and shouting out the name of the inn where they worked. A couple of women, almost as heavily painted as the players, lounged on the steps—they didn't have to shout to announce the service they were selling.

One looked me over, and I smiled without fearing I might raise her hopes. Fisk had washed and mended my clothes, but I looked far too rough to afford her time. Fisk might seem a possibility.

I turned to make sure he was passing temptation by,

and found that Fisk and Tipple were no longer at my heels. I reined Chant to a stop, ignoring the curses that rose as traffic slowed around me, and stood in the stirrups looking about. There, in a shadowy alley, Fisk sat on Tipple's back, talking to a man whose gaudy rags and missing hand proclaimed his profession as surely as the players' painted faces.

I maneuvered Chant through the crowd toward them. The press of bodies thinned, but 'twas still too noisy to hear what Fisk was saying.

The beggar shrugged and shook his head.

Fisk took a few coins out of my purse, which I hadn't lent him, and dropped them into the beggar's cup. "Pass it on, if you see him."

The beggar shrugged again and settled back at his post, rattling his cup with a practiced air. Fisk turned Tipple back toward the street, almost colliding with me.

"Sir, ah . . ." He held out my purse. "I saw that fellow in the alley and I thought we should start asking about Long Tom."

I tied the purse back on my belt—although I wasn't sure why I bothered. "Next time, ask for my purse instead of . . . Oh, never mind. Did you learn anything?"

"Doesn't know Long Tom, never met him, never

heard of him." Fisk sounded irritatingly cheerful for someone reporting total failure.

"That's odd," I commented as we rode down the street. "I'd think a beggar would know his competitors, even in a town this size. Was he a local?"

"It doesn't matter. Jack Bannister used to say that the beggars know more of what goes on in a town than the sheriffs. I'm sure he knows Long Tom perfectly well."

I gazed at Fisk's smug expression in bafflement. "But he *didn't* know him."

"He *said* he didn't. No guild member will turn one of his brothers over to a stranger. But he'll pass the word, and sooner or later Long Tom will find us."

"Beggars have a *guild?*"

"Of course," said Fisk. "A tight one too. They pay a tithe, like anyone else, and in return the guild redeems them if they get in trouble with the law, supports them if they can't work, the usual things. And a few unusual—beggars are more vulnerable than most."

"Supports them if they can't *work?* I thought they turned beggar *because* they couldn't work."

"Begging is work," said Fisk curtly. "Cursed hard work. That's another thing the guild does—it keeps amateurs and riffraff out of the trade."

"Like you?" I hazarded a guess. For a moment I thought he wasn't going to answer, but . . .

"I was younger then," said Fisk. "A lot younger. Now what kind of room do you want, Noble Sir? Cheap, but clean and respectable; cheaper and clean, but not respectable; even cheaper, but neither clean nor . . ."

'Tis annoying to have a squire who knows the contents of one's purse.

We settled for clean but not respectable, and Fisk found such a place with remarkable ease for someone who had never been in Uddersfield before.

The rest of the day we wandered about the city, paying beggar after beggar to tell us that they'd never heard of Long Tom. I was beginning to think the stable lad had been mistaken, but Fisk seemed confident that "the message will get out." As we worked from the docks through the fruit and fish markets, through the craftsman's yards and into the shops and homes of the merchants, I realized that Fisk was orienting himself in the city—that while I could tell east from west by the sun and the sea breeze, but hadn't the least idea where our inn was, Fisk was building a street map in his mind.

The acrid, fatty stink of the soap makers' yard blended with the scent of fresh bread at the bakeshop where we purchased mid-meal, and I spent twenty minutes wandering around the horse market pens.

There was a sorrel stud with a deep chest and strong withers that I'd have recommended to Father if there was any way he could get the message in time. If he would have accepted my advice. Since there wasn't, and he probably wouldn't, I left the horse to whatever lucky fellow could afford him.

Looking around, I discovered that I'd lost my squire again. He wasn't in the square that opened off the horse yard, so I ran my eyes over the shop signs. Not the brass workers', surely, or the chandler's, or the saddler's. An herbalist, a spicery, a . . . yes!

I made my way to the bookseller's and found Fisk, nose deep in a book whose title proclaimed it to be a retelling of the Miros ballad cycle. Looking over his shoulder, I discovered that Fisk was reading not the ballads, but the introduction.

"You read introductions? No one reads those things!"

"Jacobin usually translates ancient plays," Fisk murmured absently. "I'm curious to see why he'd do a ballad cycle. He once wrote that ballads were nothing but 'the wretched meanderings of modern minds, and only the ancients—'"

"It's only five gold roundels, sir," said the bookseller.

Fisk came back to the real world with a start and returned the book to its table. He left the shop briskly, but the look he cast back over his shoulder reminded me of the last look I'd given the chestnut stud.

It hasn't escaped me that my squire is far better educated than he likes to admit, mayhap better educated than myself. It did escape me why he didn't admit it, but 'twas no use to pry with a creature as untrusting as Fisk.

That evening I decided to go to one of the plays I'd heard extolled at the gate, for I don't often get a chance to see one.

Fisk hesitated when I proposed this, and I asked if there was danger in roaming the streets at night. The inn where the play was to be held was in a respectable part of town, but our inn was not. Yet Fisk said 'twas safe enough, and by the time we reached the inn yard I had forgotten all about it.

Intermittent clouds veiled the moons, which don't seem to shed as much light in the city as they do in open lands. The inn yard was lit by dozens of torches, flickering in the breeze that whispered between the buildings.

A good-sized crowd had gathered—merchants, craftsmen, shopkeepers, and their wives. But I still followed Fisk's advice when he suggested I tuck my purse inside my doublet. It may be cowardly to shrink from trouble, but 'tis foolish to invite it.

Plays are best after dark—the torchlight conceals the tawdriness of the actors' costumes, and glass jewels glow bright as the real thing. The flickering light works its magic on the players' faces, too, transforming the exaggerated paint to make these ordinary folk seem more than human.

The story was highly unlikely: The Gifted and lovely heroine, who was being pressured to wed a local baron, discovered that one of their village headsmen was in league with pirates who planned to capture a shipment of gold ore as it passed through the humble hamlet. 'Twas exciting, despite its silliness, and I applauded with enthusiasm when they'd finished.

For all that, I was troubled as Fisk led me through the darkened streets toward our inn. The wealthy baron had been almost as villainous as the headsman, and when the damsel and her heroic lover had defeated the pirates' scheme, they fled to a town, seeking protection from the baron's wrath. A play like that could get the players whipped off a noble's estate. Of course, if they offered it in the countryside, the villainous suitor would become a wealthy merchant or a tax collector—a creature who is never popular.

I had turned to say as much to Fisk, wishing to hear his opinion, when a hand grasped my collar and a knife blade appeared across my throat, cutting off speech, movement, and breath. I swallowed and felt the sharp edge slit my skin, so tightly was the blade pressed. I resolved not to do that again.

A twitch at my belt revealed the loss of my dagger. For one mad second I wished I'd worn the sword that was currently back in our room—not that they wouldn't have taken it just as easily.

"Nobody move," a soft voice muttered in my ear. I had no intention of moving, or even speaking enough to tell him where my purse was until that knife blade backed off.

Shifting only my eyes, I saw the silhouette of a second man, holding Fisk in the same position. My heart hammered with the need to move, to fight, to do something. . . . I could all but hear Fisk's comments on such an idiotic impulse.

Then the man behind me shifted, but the knife never wavered, and rough-skinned hands tugged my wrists behind my back and bound them with scratchy twine. I found being bound strangely heartening, for if they intended to slit our throats, they'd not trouble to tie us up.

"My purse is in my doublet," I murmured, trying to ignore the blade. "Left side."

A soft snort reached my ears. "This isn't a robbery, Baron. Don't piss yourself over it."

Then what under two moons was it? I swallowed again, and wished I hadn't as something warm trickled down my neck. I thought of several moves I could make, but most of them entailed kicking and running, which would gain me nothing but a slit throat.

Then the knife lifted away, and a rough sack that smelled of oats was pulled over my head. In the darkness I probably couldn't have seen through the coarse weave anyway, but they took no chances—a strip of cloth bound my eyes closed and secured the sack in place.

A sharp prick in the ribs told me where the knife was now, but even without that silent message I wouldn't have tried to fight. Between the cloth that blinded me and my bound wrists, I was helpless. But I didn't have to like it.

"You took your time finding us. I was beginning to think I'd have to send a town crier." Fisk, sarcastic enough to cut cloth. I might have found that reassuring, except I've come to realize that Fisk is particularly sarcastic when he's scared right down to the soles of his boots.

Soft chuckles emerged from the darkness, and my wits suddenly caught up with what Fisk had said: The beggars' guild had found us.

The two men guided us, stumbling, for quite a long time, over cobbles that felt rougher than they had before. Walking blind in the hands of our captors was horridly unnerving, and they stopped several times to spin me around, so I couldn't tell the direction of the turns we made. They had pulled up my hood. Anyone we met would see nothing out of place unless they looked closely, and the knife that hovered near my ribs would have kept me from crying out—but we encountered no one.

Several dogs barked as we passed the yards they guarded, and once I smelled the distinctive, sour odor of a pigpen, but I couldn't have retraced our path. Then the hands that gripped my elbows held me still, and the soft voice murmured, "Eight steps down, Baron."

They helped me down the wooden stair, and I heard Fisk's steps coming down the planks behind me. At the bottom they pulled me forward, and I tripped over a doorsill and onto a wooden floor.

The men who'd brought us left without a word—I heard the door close behind them. I was about to speak to Fisk, to find some way to untie each other, when a new set of footsteps came from the other side of the room.

I stiffened, for if this was some new threat there was nothing I could do about it. The cloth that bound my eyes jerked, then loosened, and the sack was lifted away.

I blinked, wishing I could rub my eyes. Only two candles lit the cellar, and though the ceiling almost brushed my head, the walls stretched away till they lost themselves in darkness. From the size of the room, I thought we must be beneath a warehouse—"borrowed," no doubt, for the occasion, since the man who stood before me, in gaudy beggar's rags, couldn't possibly have owned such a building.

There was gray in his thinning hair, but the lines around his eyes were only visible when he smiled, a little wryly, as he went to unbind Fisk's eyes. "I apologize, sirs, for the inconvenience, but you'll understand that a humble man like me gets nervous when he hears that strangers are asking for him."

I eyed his stocky, ordinary body—he was shorter than Fisk. "*Long* Tom?"

A spark of mischief lit his eyes. "It refers to . . . another part of my anatomy."

Fisk emerged, blinking, from another oat sack. "You could have asked us to meet with you."

I was relieved to hear that the cutting edge in his voice had vanished, despite the fact that we were still bound. Since Fisk seemed to understand these strange events better than I (at least I hoped he did!), I relaxed a bit myself.

Long Tom strolled over to the sturdy table that held

the candles and Fisk's and my daggers—the only piece of furniture in the room. He leaned against one corner and eyed us shrewdly. "Well, you're here. I hope it's something worth my while—you do realize that I'm not going to be able to work for the rest of the time you're in town? Longer, if you go to the sheriff. You could cost me a lot of money, young sirs."

"We won't go to the sheriff," I said. "As long as we're unharmed. All we wanted was to talk to you!" It came out sounding more aggrieved than I'd intended, and Long Tom smiled.

"I'll still miss work."

"If you tell us what we need to know, we'll leave town tomorrow morning," Fisk told him. "And his purse is in his doublet. Left side. We'll pay you well for any work you miss."

"All right," said Long Tom. "How much?"

I opened my mouth to offer him eight gold roundels, which was all the gold I had, but Fisk spoke first.

"Five silver roundels. That's plenty for a few minutes' talk, now isn't it?"

They eventually agreed on nine silver roundels. As the beggar plucked my purse from my doublet, I realized there was nothing to stop him from taking it all—and slitting our throats, too. But he extracted nine silver discs, set my purse on the table, and eyed us expectantly.

"What do you want to know?"

I tried not to hope too much. "Did you meet a man named Hackle, somewhere near Willowere, who bought your clothes?"

Long Tom's brows lifted. "Yes, though he didn't give me his name. Gray haired, but strong still, with a peg leg?"

"That's him. What we want to know is, did he say anything, give you any clue at all, as to where he might be going next?"

The sympathy in Long Tom's eyes answered my question before he spoke. "I'm sorry. He never said a word about where he was going. Seeing he was truly lame we talked about that—one 'cripple' to another, so to speak—but aside from that he was strictly business. He took my clothes and I took his, and three silver roundels into the bargain."

I stared at Long Tom's perfectly hardy legs and then at the leg brace leaning against the table. There was something subtly askew about it, and I realized that it would make a straight leg look crooked.

Long Tom followed my gaze and laughed. "I use a crutch, too, when I'm working. It's not a bad rig."

"But if you're not crippled, why beg? Surely you could do something else. Something easier."

"Not a lot." Long Tom held out his hands, flexing

them stiffly, and I saw that his fingers twisted like gnarled roots. "I was a weaver, before my hands went," he said calmly. "There's some things not even magica can cure. I could run errands, but that pays less than begging—and having spent the first part of my life sitting in front of a loom, I find the road has some appeal. I spend my summers traveling, and the winters snug in town with a warm mug to ease my aching fingers. Not a bad life. That's something most don't understand—that you can lose the use of your hands, or half a leg, and go right on living. That's what the old man and I talked about, mostly. He used to be a huntsman."

"How did he lose his leg?" asked Fisk.

"Sacrifice to the Furred God. The involuntary kind. One winter the wolves were so bad, the bounty on wolf pelts rose to three gold roundels. He got greedy and set out steel traps."

A chill went down my spine. "That's a mistake. You can never tell what a steel trap will seize."

"True enough, young sir. He trapped himself a magica wolf—and not being Gifted, he had no way of knowing, so he didn't seek out a Savant. Several days later, he stepped into one of his own traps, buried under the snow in a place he swears he never put one." Long Tom shrugged. "He lost the leg. The Savant buried it with the wolf and promised he'd have no more trouble. It put an end to his days as a huntsman, but he said a lady rescued him and he had a better job now."

A lady rescued him. And he had returned the favor. Fisk and I exchanged grim glances. How far would Hackle go to protect his lady? You could do the sacrifice in advance, if you really had to kill a magica creature. A huntsman would know how to trap and kill a magica boar, too. Though after his last experience with killing magica . . . I shivered. Old Hackle had courage.

'Twas Fisk who came back to the point. "He didn't say *anything* to hint at his future plans?"

"Not a word."

"What about his clothes? Maybe they'd give us some clue."

"I'd show them to you if I had them," said Long Tom. "But there weren't any clues there—a tight-weave linen shirt, dark blue doublet, and britches. You could buy them in any town on this coast . . . probably any town in the realm."

"Where are his clothes, then?" Fisk asked stubbornly.

I knew how he felt, for my own heart was a leaden lump at the thought of traveling so far for nothing.

"I sold them in the next town and bought these." He gestured to his warm, sturdy rags. "All I know is where the old man came from—where he was going, I haven't a clue."

"He told you where he came from?" That didn't sound like closemouthed Hackle.

"He didn't *tell* me," said Long Tom. "He didn't have to. I recognized his accent."

I heard Hackle's voice in my memory, the softening of the last syllable of some of his words.

"There's a fishing village about two days' ride north," the beggar continued. "It was originally settled by Lealanders when their city was sacked. They've been there for hundreds of years now, but they've still got a touch of the accent. That's where Hackle came from. But I've no idea where he is now."

Long Tom had stuck my dagger into the tabletop, so I had no difficulty cutting myself loose while he made his "escape."

I had to rub the feeling back into my hands before releasing Fisk, and while I waited I retrieved my purse—nearly full.

"He didn't rob us," I commented.

"Beggars aren't thieves," said Fisk. "I told you that the guild keeps riffraff out. If they didn't, there's not a town or village in the realm that'd have them."

"So they govern themselves?"

"Just like any other guild." Fisk turned his back and held out his wrists. "They don't admit unredeemed men, thieves, or simple ones—it takes sharp wits to be a beggar."

I was beginning to realize that.

We left Uddersfield the next morning, traveling north, because we had no idea where else to go. 'Twas *possible* that Hackle's friends and family knew his whereabouts.

The fair weather broke during our second day on the road. A lashing wind rolled out a carpet of thick, dark clouds, and it rained until the water soaked through my cloak, doublet, and shirt and trickled coldly down my back. We stopped early that evening, for the fishing village Hackle came from was too small to offer lodging. The inn was near empty, since few venture out in such weather, and steam from the cloaks set before the fire fogged all the windows. Fisk cast his eyes over the small, surly crowd and decided to refrain from plying his craft that night.

The next morning was overcast and dripping, but the rain had stopped. We reached Hackle's village by midmorning, a collection of weathered timber cottages that might have looked welcoming on a brighter day. Folk stared as we rode down the street, for we had turned off the main road to reach this place and I doubted they saw many strangers. I tossed a brass roundel to a curious urchin, and he told me that

"Master Hackle" was down at the beach.

There might well be more than one Hackle in this village—few men had no family at all. But who more likely to know his whereabouts than family? My heart beat quicker as we rode down the slope to the strand.

Wind beat the waves to a churning froth, and several fishermen had chosen not to put out in it. Most of them were mending—sails, nets, rope. But Master Hackle, to whom one of them directed me, had taken the opportunity to beach his boat and scrape the hull.

He had almost cleared one side, though several barnacles remained. As we rode nearer I saw that they'd been marked with red dye, and realized that those particular pests must be magica. Fishermen, who often net magica fish, must have close relationships with their Savants. Too many things can go wrong at sea, and the consequences are often fatal.

When we hailed him Master Hackle turned and laid down his tools. Under the drab knit cap, his face was round, and, for all the creases wind and sun had etched there, he looked younger than his brother.

"Master Hackle?" I asked politely.

"That's me. What can I do for you, young sir?" His accent struck a chord of memory, and my hopes flared.

"I'm looking for your brother. His lady is charged with murdering her husband, and I fear your brother has taken her into hiding. I need to find her and return her to justice."

Fisk choked and started to cough. But remembering the last time I hadn't told the truth, I wasn't about to repeat that mistake.

The good cheer vanished from Master Hackle's face, but he answered readily enough. "Sorry, young sir, but I don't know where Nate is. We don't see much of each other since he went to Cory Port to work for Lady Ceciel. In fact, I haven't seen him for . . . over a year now, it would be."

I opened my mouth to question him further, but, as usual, Fisk beat me to it.

"To work for Lady Ceciel? Not for Sir Herbert?"

"That's what I said. He went north looking for some sort of post after he lost the leg—there was nothing for him here. The baron said he'd no use for a maimed man and would have tossed him a few coins and sent him on his way, but Lady Ceciel hired him as her steward."

"It seems . . . strange that Lady Ceciel would be so kind to a stranger, and then kill her husband so foully."

I was thinking aloud, but Master Hackle answered. "I don't know how Sir Herbert died, so I can't speak to that, but I do know Lady Ceciel for a right kind woman."

"Mayhap the judicars will consider that," I said. "But you must know your brother's habits, the places he knows. Where would he go if he wanted to hide?"

Master Hackle snorted. "He used to hide out in the tavern cellar, but I doubt he'd take Lady Ceciel there. I told you, I haven't seen much of him for the last ten years. As to where he might hide the lady . . . sorry, sirs, I just don't know."

"At least he didn't try to beat me up," I said gloomily. The damp sea wind bit at our backs as we rode from the village. "That's an improvement."

"That depends on how you look at it." Fisk smirked. "He didn't try to beat you up, but he sure lied a lot."

I turned to stare at him and my hood blew over my eyes. I thrust it down impatiently. "Why do you think he was lying? He answered all our questions in a very straightforward manner."

"That's what makes me think he was lying," said Fisk. "Look. You told him you were trying to track down his brother, whom he seems fond of, and Lady Ceciel, whom he obviously respects, to bring them to justice—yet he willingly answered all our questions in a very straightforward manner. Doesn't that strike you as suspicious?"

It did, now that he mentioned it. But . . . "But there's no way to force him to tell us the truth—and what truth, anyway? Do you think he knows where his brother is?"

"Maybe. He knows something he's not saying. Hackle's not likely to have stashed his lady in some other part of the countryside and then run home to tell his brother about it. But I'm not sure it matters. There are ways of forcing him to speak, but I'm not up to using them, and I *know* you're not."

I was glad to hear that Fisk wasn't either—not that I'd ever considered him capable of such things. Besides . . .

"There must be people who know both Hackle and his mistress more recently. One of them might be willing to talk. Especially if they're hiding out somewhere near their home."

"Cory Port?" said Fisk thoughtfully. "It'd be risky, going to ground where people might recognize her."

"But they'd know the territory," I argued. "And they'd be in Lord Gerald's fiefdom—he might try to force her into marriage, but she can be certain he won't hang her. And they might have friends in the area who'd help them."

"Or enemies. Who'd betray them."

"Exactly. We're going to Cory Port."

Cory Port was a three-day ride in dry weather—Fisk and I rode in at sunset on the fifth day, damp, weary, and almost as muddy as the horses. The smallish town rolled over half a dozen hills before sloping down to a surprisingly large harbor.

We had agreed (or rather Fisk had persuaded me) to be cautious about advertising our purpose here. He told the innkeeper I was looking for a port with cheaper shipping rates than Uddersfield. I quietly resolved to see the harbormaster before I left, so it wouldn't be a lie—my father would be delighted to pass such information on to Lord Dorian.

A roaring fire and a good meal raised my dampened spirits, and I finally asked the question that had been haunting me for the entire ride. "Fisk, do you think she's guilty?"

He had been talking about how to find Lady Ceciel's hypothetical enemies without alerting her friends. Now he set down his mug, adapting easily to the change of subject. "He was poisoned, and I don't know of anyone else who had a motive. As you've said, several times, that's for the judicars to decide. All we have to do is bring her back."

And I would be redeemed. Honor satisfied. Father satisfied. Rupert's steward for the rest of my life. I sighed and realized that Fisk was looking over my shoulder.

One of the stableboys stood behind me, dripping on the scuffed planks of the taproom floor.

"I hope you'll forgive us, sir, but we seem to have

lost one of your horses." He had the oddest expression on his face—guilt and alarm struggling with . . . a desire to laugh?

"What do you mean 'lost'?"

"Oh, we found her again. The little spotted mare. She'd slipped her tether and, ah, followed a cart." His cheeks turned red and he had to stop and bite his lip before going on. "A brewer's cart. One of the bungs was loose and the ale ran into the cart bed. Big kegs, sir. The driver didn't know she was back there until he stopped. She's at a tavern, about eight blocks away. I'm afraid she's . . . she's . . ."

"Drunk," I finished for him.

Fisk was shaking with silent laughter, so hard I could feel the table vibrate.

"Go ahead and laugh," I told him. "She'll be too hungover to ride tomorrow."

He began to whoop, which shattered the boy's composure as well.

My own lips twitched as I went on. "Which means we'll have to double up on Chant. Or hire a horse, or *you'll* have to walk. 'Tis really"—the laughter rose—"not funny." I gave up on dignity and joined their merriment.

Fisk was the first to recover.

"We'll hire a horse," he announced, wiping his eyes.

Fisk had come a long way in the last few weeks, from the sullen, frightened, "Yes, Noble Sir" criminal I had redeemed. He'd been acting, lately, like the companion and comrade a squire should be. I smiled at him. "We'll hire a horse."

We went together to fetch Tipple. The stableboy gave us clear directions to the tavern, near the harbor district. The cobbles were still slick with rain and mud, and the moons played peeking games through the fast-flowing clouds.

Tipple was tethered in the tavern yard, head down, swaying. Her eyes were closed.

"We're going to have a time of it getting you up those hills, you sot," I told her severely, and Fisk snickered again.

She blinked foolishly and snuffled my neck.

"Wait till tomorrow," I said. "You'll see."

'Tis a great advantage to have four feet when you're drunk. I put Fisk on one side of her and I took the other, hoping we could put her upright if she started to fall. But aside from a tendency to lean on us and the occasional stumble over objects that weren't there, Tipple managed fairly well.

"Will she really be hungover tomorrow?" Fisk asked. Tipple swayed toward him and he shoved her shoulder, hard, before she could overbalance.

"She'll be as miserable as you'd be, and grumpy with it, too. We really will have to hire a horse."

Tipple stumbled and came to a stop, looking carefully for the invisible thing that kept tripping her.

"The inn ought to lend us a horse," said Fisk. "They're the ones that let her get away."

"We should have told them of her trouble," I said ruefully.

Tipple raised her head and peered blearily into the alley to our left, ears pricked—'twas all the warning we had.

Four men in dark clothes burst from the shadows, cudgels in their fists. They split neatly around Tipple— two headed for me and two for Fisk. My heart began to gallop, while time seemed to slow. I could see every detail, from the pattern of stitches in their knit caps to the rough stubble on the bigger one's chin. One of them rushed me, cudgel lifted, and I surprised him by stepping forward to catch his arm and punching him in the stomach with my free hand.

He doubled over, dropped the cudgel, and grabbed my right wrist with both hands. The other man made a grab for my other arm, but missed. I pivoted, swinging his comrade between us as I tried to twist free.

When that failed, I drew my dagger and slashed at

my opponent's throat, kicking his groin at the same time. This was a mistake, for neither of the blows connected firmly enough. He yelped and leapt back, but he kept his hold and his comrade dodged around him and grabbed my other arm.

I heard a cry of pain and saw one of Fisk's opponents stagger into a wall, his arm pressed against his side. Fisk had drawn his dagger, holding it low and weaving in the manner of a skilled knife fighter. He *could* fight, curse the bastard.

Thrashing in their grasp, I tried to stamp on the toes of the man who gripped my knife arm, but he danced aside, yelling for help. The man Fisk had injured stumbled toward us, cudgel in hand. I couldn't defeat three of them.

I aimed a kick at my opponent's knee—it struck a glancing blow, but it threw him off balance. I twisted my arm again and his grip loosened.

Tipple's hooves clattered on the rough stones. In the tiny corner of my mind that wasn't screaming *Fight! Fight!* I hoped that she could manage on her own. After that, there was nothing—not even darkness.

CHAPTER 9
Fisk

My head hurt. For a long time that was all I could think of, but then a memory stirred: Jack, a long time ago, telling me that when you woke up in a strange place after being hit on the head, you should lie still and listen.

Like a lot of Jack's advice, this was probably sound, but easier said than done—I'd already moaned a couple of times. *Had* I been hit on the head?

I vaguely remembered waking several times before, but I'd felt too rotten to notice my surroundings. I now realized I was lying on a wool-stuffed tick spread over what felt like a web of ropes—it was awfully uncomfortable. There was a blanket over me, and the air on my face was fresh despite a strong smell of vomit. Someone was sick. Besides me. Sir Michael?

I opened my eyes and wished I hadn't, although the

sunlight arrowing through half a dozen fist-sized air-holes, high in the opposite wall, wasn't very bright.

The wooden room held nothing but ten rope beds, one of which I occupied, and an unlit candle lantern suspended from the low ceiling. But the lantern, the whole room, was swaying like . . . like a ship. I was on a ship. *Cudgel-crewed.* Curse it.

I lifted my aching head and looked for Sir Michael. He lay in another bed, three down from mine. One of the men between us had been sick. The other lay with that absolute stillness that can't be mistaken for sleep, whatever the ballads say.

Some people would have tried to stand up at that point. Not being an idiot, I rolled carefully out of bed and crawled down the tilting floor, and, as I did, memory leaked back. Cory Port, and the stableboy laughing about Tipple. The men who'd rushed us from the alley. I'd had time to draw my knife and I thought I'd cut one of them, though I wasn't sure. If I had, I hoped he was a local thug and not one of the crew who'd want blood for blood. On a ship, there's no place to run.

I gave wide berth to the half-dried pool of vomit, and the whimpering man in the bed above it, but I stopped to check on the still one, just in case. What I could do if he was alive I didn't know. The question didn't arise.

Sir Michael wasn't dead. Drawing nearer, I saw that his brows were crimped with pain, and relief turned my already wobbly limbs to mush. He lifted a shaky hand to his head.

"Owww."

"Me too," I said.

"Fisk?" His eyes opened, blinking in the dimness. After a moment they focused on me. "I don't know what I drank, but the room is moving. I never drink that much."

"You're not hungover," I told him. If he never drank that much, how did he know the symptoms so well? "The room *is* moving. We're on a ship. We've been cudgel-crewed, I think."

"Oh." There was a long, pained pause. "Curse it."

I laughed, which made my head throb, and leaned against the wall—which they probably called something different on ships. I wouldn't know. I was a landsman, and happy to stay that way.

Sir Michael said nothing. Eventually he opened his eyes and looked around the room. His expression changed when he saw the dead man, but I spoke before he could move.

"There's nothing to be done there."

He closed his eyes again. "Do you think *she* arranged this?"

"It'd be a pretty big coincidence for us to get

cudgel-crewed accidentally."

"But how did she know? We didn't tell anyone why we were there."

"Except Hackle's brother," I said dryly. "Noble Sir, we've got to be more subtle about this."

Sir Michael sighed. "Well, 'tis cursed shabby of her to use poor Tipple's weakness—Tipple! Chant! What's going to happen to them?"

He was so agitated he started to sit up. I could have warned him that was a mistake. Sweat broke out on his pale face, but I was pleased to see he didn't get sick. And I was *very* pleased that the constant roll of the floor (the deck?) wasn't making me sick, either.

"Don't worry about the horses," I told him as color seeped back into his face. "The innkeeper will keep them for a week, then sell them. They're probably better off than we are."

"But Chant's lame! What if—"

"He's also big, well trained, and gentle. Someone will take him. And there's nothing you can do about it, anyway."

Sir Michael closed his eyes and fell silent. Then his eyes opened again, and turned to me. Blazing. "You can fight."

It sounded like an accusation, and my aching brain took a moment to remember why. "Ah . . ."

"You *can* fight. You lied to me."

"I didn't see that getting beaten up with you would do any good. Noble Sir."

"That's not the point! The point is that you *lied*." Splashes of red appeared on his pale cheeks. I'd never seen Sir Michael angry before. I knew that he didn't lie, but he wasn't crazy enough to expect someone else to follow his example. Was he?

"So what? I fought when it was necessary. Not that it helped."

"That's *not* the point," he said again. "The point is . . . ah, forget it."

He lay back again, pressing a hand to his head.

"What?" If I was to be blamed for something, I wanted to know what it was. "I don't see why—"

The door at the end of the room swung open and two men entered, one carrying a tray holding ten steaming mugs. The men wore the rough wool britches and shirts of sailors and their feet were bare. One was long, lean, and young, while the other was short, round, and old. They both looked grim.

They started passing out mugs on the other side of the room. The first man accepted his in grateful silence, but the small man in the second bed grabbed the older man's arm, demanding to know where he was and what had happened.

"You've been cudgel-crewed, mate," the older man

told him, with a kind of rough gentleness. "You're on a cargo ship, the *Golden Albatross*, and you're going to be here for a while, so you may's well stop fretting about it. I'm called Cracker; I'm the cook and the closest thing we've got to an herbalist. This tea'll help your head and your stomach, so drink up. The captain'll be here in a few minutes, and he'll be answering your questions."

The small man burst into tears, but Cracker ignored him and went on to serve the rest of us. He sighed when he saw the dead man, but the look on his face told me he wasn't surprised.

The tea was bitter and minty and I'd no idea what might be in it, but Sir Michael drank his without hesitation, and since he knew something about medicines I drank too. It had a good effect on my headache, which had gone from nearly intolerable to merely painful by the time the captain came in.

For some reason, Cracker's words made me expect a big, beefy fellow, but the captain was small and slight, with neat, tiny hands. His bald spot was reaching for his forehead, and his boots, which added two inches to his height, still didn't make him tall. And none of it mattered. I've never seen a man so obviously in command—shrimpy and bald or not.

His eyes swept over the room, gathering ours, before

he spoke. "By now you'll have figured out that you've been cudgel-crewed aboard my ship. That means you'll be crewing for me for the rest of the voyage, like it or not. This isn't something I usually have to resort to. I'd a bit of trouble a few days back, but I've seen a Savant and made sacrifice, so you've nothing to fear. This is a fine ship, and you'll be as safe aboard her as any sailor can be."

Ten of his crew evidently hadn't believed that, and I hoped, passionately, that he was right and they were wrong.

"You'll have the rest of today to recover from your injuries. Tomorrow will see you up on deck learning a bit about the ship, and the next day you'll start training as seamen. By the end of the trip you'll *be* seamen." He paused a moment and studied us, swaying expertly with the roll of the ship.

"I'm sure some of you are thinking of escape. Don't. Any time we're within reach of shore, you'll be locked in this room. Any attempt to escape will be punished with the lash. Work well, and when we reach our final port I'll pay you a salary, same's the rest of the crew. Work very well, and if you like I'll sign you on to come back, and turn you loose one fiefdom short of Cory Port."

He must have been desperate for crewmen—kidnapping us made it impossible for him to return to Cory

Port, since Lord Gerald's sheriffs would be waiting to arrest him. I hoped again that he was right about this ship being safe from the Furred God's vengeance—I'd already dealt with the slaying of magica once, and that was once too often. But the captain was continuing.

"The rules on this ship are simple. The penalty for slacking is the lash. The penalty for brawling is the lash. The penalty for theft is the lash. The penalty for disobedience, or disrespect to an officer, is the lash. Mutiny, and I'll throw you over the side. Kill someone, I'll throw you over the side. Don't try anything stupid and you'll do fine. Any questions?"

Then he turned away, for at that point only an idiot would have asked a question. So I wasn't surprised when Sir Michael said, "Captain? Where are we going?"

The captain looked surprised, but I was relieved to see that a reasonable question didn't offend him.

"We're headed for our home berth, Tallow Port." A rustle of dismay swept the room. Tallow Port was halfway around the realm. "We should get there in about three months, wind and weather permitting. If you're smart, you can be back here in six months—your sweethearts won't have time to miss you, and your kiddies won't have grown an inch. If you're not smart . . ." He shrugged and departed, and Sir Michael and I stared at each other in consternation. In six months Lady Ceciel could hide herself anywhere. And the trail would be cold.

The next day, we crept up on deck, blinking in the fitful sunlight, for the autumn weather had shifted again. It *was* called a deck, I learned. And though the interior floors were called floors, the interior walls were called bulkheads, the beds were called bunks, and there were many other bits of useless wordplay.

That first day, most of the new "crewmen" sat in a wretched huddle, but Sir Michael wandered around asking questions about this or that, and I did a bit of learning myself.

We ate with our fellows in misery, and the meals added to that misery. Breakfast consisted of a bowl of boiled wheat with dried meat in it, and hard biscuits. Mid-meal was a bowl of boiled, dried meat, with wheat in it, and hard biscuits. Dinner was a bowl of dried meat, with a wedge of cabbage, or a few carrots, or a potato, and hard biscuits. My only consolation was that the captain and his officers fared no better.

As we ate, we learned something of the men who'd been kidnapped with us. One was a carpenter, one an apprentice tanner, and so on. Several were sailors, and they were fairly resigned to their lot, though they'd not have chosen this ship. We also heard, that first day, the story of the seagull that had soared through an open cabin window and snatched a broiled fish right off the captain's plate like . . . well, like magic. The captain beat it to death with a chart weight, for he was sensitive about receiving proper respect, even from seagulls. The response when Sir Michael introduced himself as a knight errant, and me as his squire, was tiresome, but it soon passed. The only one of us who really stood out was Willard.

Willard was the man who'd cried when Cracker told him he'd been cudgel-crewed. He was a merchant's clerk by trade, and physically not unlike the captain—small and slight with thinning hair, though he was only in his early twenties. But far from possessing the captain's hard competence, Willard couldn't seem to do anything right. He tried his best, but he dropped so many things that after three days' trial Cracker banned him from the galley. Perhaps fear made him clumsy, or perhaps that was simply the way Willard was.

The captain finally gave up and assigned Willard to act as ship's clerk, recording all matters of cargo. There wasn't much clerking to do while we were at sea, so for most of his work shift the first mate set Willard to scrubbing the deck and cleaning and polishing the metalwork. He still dropped things, but if he screwed up these simple tasks he wouldn't sink us.

A few questions determined that the crew was loyal, and the officers were the only ones armed, so I resigned myself to my fate. Perhaps when we were released in Tallow Port I could persuade Sir Michael to declare my debt repaid and let me go. Jack once told me that any connie who couldn't make a fortune in Tallow Port ought to give up and get an honest job.

As the first few weeks of our training passed, I became a reasonably competent apprentice seaman. My hands were deft enough at knots, and the rest of the job consisted of hauling on, or releasing, whatever rope they told you to. Each rope had a specific name and function, and I got them all memorized at about the same time my hands and bare feet grew callused. I learned to ride the pitching deck better than I could ride a horse. I should also mention that all our feet were bare, not through cruelty or stinginess on the captain's part, but to give us better purchase on the deck—especially when it grew slick with rain or high waves, or when Willard tipped over his wash bucket.

But if I became reasonably competent, Sir Michael took to the sea as if he'd been born to it. Of all the "new crewmen," he was the only one allowed to climb into the nets of rope that spiderwebbed up from the deck. He seemed to take a special pleasure in this cramped, noisy, tilting world, surrounded by the endless expanse of wind, wave, and open sky.

I wouldn't have left the safety of the deck for a hundred gold roundels, but I had noticed before that a year of supporting himself with odd jobs had given my noble employer an unusual expertise at manual labor.

Then came the afternoon when Sir Michael summoned me to the railing with a direct look, and a jerk of his head so slight it was almost devious.

I sauntered over to him. It was a good afternoon for sauntering, not a cloud in the sky and the sun so warm our feet stuck to the pitch that sealed the deck planks.

"Look, Fisk." He was leaning against the rail like a man with nothing on his mind. "No, not that way—out to sea."

At first I saw nothing but water. Then a wave tossed us up and I glimpsed a line of low humps on the horizon. "Land?"

"Land! I've been up in the rigging and I think 'tis no more than a mile off. Can you make it?"

"Make it what? Wait a minute, you don't mean . . ."

Sir Michael nodded, his eyes still resting casually on the busy deck. "Over the side, right now, before they lock us up."

"You're mad," I told him. "You'll freeze. You'll get eaten by sharks or something." But my heart began to pound. If Sir Michael was forced to leave me behind—through no fault of mine—he'd never declare me un-redeemed. Not Michael.

"The sun's been on the water all day, Fisk. It won't be that cold. They'll order us below soon. *Can you make it?*"

My freedom. Free, and in Tallow Port—half a realm away from past misdeeds and crazy knights errant. Still . . . A foolish qualm of conscience seized me.

"Are you sure *you* can make it?" I asked.

That caught Sir Michael's attention and he stared at me—about time, too. He was being so casual, he was about to look suspicious. "Almost sure. I can't guarantee our safety, but if I thought 'twas truly dangerous I wouldn't propose it. What—"

"Then you should go," I told him, trying to sound courageously resigned, which was tough the way my heart was singing. "You'll have to leave me here, Sir Michael. I can't swim. But I'll be all right, and it's more important to bring Lady Ceciel to justice. Go. Now."

"You can't *swim?*" I glared, and he went on more softly, "Fisk . . . is that the truth?"

I realized he was thinking of the time I'd told him I didn't know how to fight. Heat flooded my cheeks.

"Of course it's true," I snarled. (As it happens, it was.) "Where would I have learned to swim? The city sewer? Get out of here, Michael, while you've got a chance!"

His eyes widened. Then he drew himself up and took a deep breath. "No. I won't leave you. We'll find another way."

"What other way? You'll never get a better opportunity!" He was looking noble and stubborn, curse him. "I'll be fine! What about your redemption? Your honor? What if Lady Ceciel kills again?"

Sir Michael shook his head. "I don't think so. If she was going to kill anyone, it would be *us*. And she hasn't, Fisk. Doesn't that strike you as odd?"

When I thought about it, it did, but . . . "Not really. Lots of people hate their spouses more than they could ever hate a stranger. Maybe she had a good reason to kill Herbert."

"Mayhap she did. I wish I knew what it was."

"Then go find out!"

"No, Squire." He took my arm and pulled me away from the rail. "I won't desert you. We'll find another way."

"Thanks a lot, Noble Sir."

The son of a bitch laughed.

Shortly after that, they ordered us down to the room where we bunked and locked us in. We might have tried to cry out or throw a message out an airhole. But as the captain pointed out, he'd committed no crime in this fiefdom, so even if we did attract attention, no one would do anything about it. And as I pointed out to Sir Michael, even if the law interceded for the rest, they'd let the captain keep us since indebted men have no legal rights.

Sir Michael said that shouldn't weigh with us if we could help the others, and the ensuing argument kept us from boredom as the evening dragged on.

Another week passed. Since the weather stayed fair, the captain ordered us to paint all the ship's trim—at sea, you have to keep wood painted or oiled, or it rots.

Sir Michael, Willard, and I were applying scarlet paint to the aft deck rail. It was a bright, clear day with just enough wind to keep the ship moving, and we were all dipping our brushes in the same bucket. Then Willard moved his foot and knocked it over. Sir Michael grabbed for the bucket—we'd both been saving the paint from Willard all morning—but this time he missed, and the paint spilled down to the main deck.

Willard winced. "Sorry. I'll clean it up."

I was about to make some reply when I noticed that Sir Michael, who'd leaned over the rail in his attempt to catch the bucket, had evidently frozen there. Then he moved back, stiffly, his expression so grim that my jaw dropped.

I was going to ask what was wrong when I heard footsteps coming up the stair to the aft deck. Bootsteps.

The whole left half of the captain's face was scarlet, and paint splattered his clothes. He looked like a player who's been hit with a fruit pie, but no one laughed; this was the man who had beaten the seagull to death. This was the man who regarded an offense against his dignity as the ultimate crime.

We'd been painting the underside of the rail, so all three of us were on our knees, anyway.

"C-c-c-captain." Willard's body crumpled under the weight of the captain's rage. He cowered, twitching with fear, and I thought that his own terror, combined with the shock and pain of flogging, might actually kill him.

"I did it."

We all turned to Sir Michael. The captain looked startled, but Willard's face revealed a shamed, desperate hope. I opened my mouth to protest, but Sir Michael grabbed my wrist, squeezing hard, commanding silence. He stood and faced the captain, and I realized the whole ship had fallen silent, watching.

"My apologies, sir," Sir Michael said, in a clear,

carrying voice. "'Twas an accident."

The sailors in the rigging might have seen what happened. I looked up at them—all but two were watching Sir Michael and the captain, and those two were looking at Willard.

Willard crouched on the deck. He tried to speak but produced nothing but little choking sounds. His white face twisted like a man about to retch. I put my hands on his shoulders, squeezing him into silence. The two sailors above said nothing. I said nothing.

The officers herded the crew off to one side and drew their swords, but we all knew no one would try anything. Sir Michael was pale, but except for a couple of lines between his brows, his face showed no expression. He pulled off his shirt when they told him to, and they tied his wrists to the main mast so we couldn't see his face.

Cracker and his assistants were summoned from the galley—everyone had to be present. Cracker's shrewd eyes took in the whole scene, and he went to stand beside Willard. Willard clutched him and began to babble.

The captain, who had gone to his cabin, returned wearing an old shirt and old, dark britches. He carried a whip—a long, leather one, like ox cart drivers use. That kind of whip takes some skill, and for a moment I hoped he wouldn't know how to handle it, but of course he did. It could have been worse—I've heard of sea captains using whips tipped with metal barbs. He flipped out the coil, then flicked it expertly, so the slack rolled down the length of the leather and the end snapped against Sir Michael's bare back. Sir Michael flinched but didn't make a sound. A red stripe appeared, and a drop of blood rolled down his skin.

In my opinion, heroism is vastly overrated.

The whip whispered and cracked again. I was about to start cursing my employer for every kind of fool, when I realized this might well be the fate Sir Michael had spared me in Deepbend.

Sir Michael stayed silent at first—though Willard flinched and whimpered at every cut. But that couldn't last. After a few minutes (I refused to count blows, for that only makes it worse) blood began to splatter on the deck and Sir Michael began moaning, softly.

An odd, sick smile lit the captain's face. He'd been waiting for Michael to scream and wouldn't stop until he did. Something Michael would fight to the last.

Vastly overrated.

But those soft moans marked the beginning of the end of Michael's self-control—a dozen more blows set him screaming. The captain stopped soon after that and went to change his clothes again.

Willard clung to Cracker, crying.

I wanted to go below and help tend Sir Michael, but they told me that was Cracker's job and sent me back to work.

Sir Michael was young and strong. He'd be fine in a week or two, no doubt. Absolutely no doubt. There was no reason for my hands to shake for the rest of the afternoon . . . but they did.

CHAPTER 10

Michael

"Shh, lad, shh, just hold on a bit. Shh." Cracker's voice was the second thing I became aware of. The first was my back, which felt as if thorns were being raked across it every time I drew a breath.

The air was thick with the burnt-bitter scent of mallow salve. Cracker's clothes rustled and I gasped at the sting as he rubbed salve over the whip cuts, but the sting was followed by blessed numbness. For superficial scrapes like these, it would give several hours of ease—more if 'twas magica, but that wasn't likely on a ship like this one.

I gritted my teeth, and Cracker worked quickly. In only ten minutes the mallow had taken full hold and I was able to sit up, carefully, and drink a mug of clear broth, thick with the taste of various herbs.

"I've got to get back to the galley now," said Cracker. "But your mate can tend you through the night."

I thought of trying to explain that Fisk was my squire, not my mate, but the pain of lying down again stole my breath, and by the time I recovered it Cracker had gone.

I suspect that some of those herbs were soporific, for within minutes I found my eyelids drooping. The light coming through the airholes was pink with sunset, and I realized, sleepily, that this was going to leave me with some rather explicit scars. Not respectable at all. But remembering poor Willard's twitching face, I found I had no regrets—rescuing the weak is what a knight errant is supposed to do. And all I had to do, to keep Father from finding out, was to never take off my shirt. 'Twas simple. I was still thinking how simple it was when I drifted off to sleep.

I woke again sometime in the night. My back throbbed and burned, and my throat was tight with thirst. Light hands smoothed salve over the aching welts, and I hissed at the sting.

"Cracker?" I asked. When you're lying on your stomach, turning your head requires more back muscles than you'd think.

"No, it's me. Fisk." 'Twas a good thing he added his

name—his voice was so gentle I barely recognized it. Moving very slowly, I turned to look at him.

"You don't have to sound so kindly. 'Tis not that bad."

"Thank goodness. Being that kindly was a terrible strain."

I didn't dare laugh, but I was glad he sounded more like himself. He leaned down, his eyes searching my face. The rocking candle lantern cast shifting shadows over his. He evidently found what he was looking for— he relaxed and straightened. "You'll be all right."

"That's what I told you."

I waited for him to tell me that *this* had not been a smart thing to do either, but he said nothing more. His fingers on my back were feather soft—a pickpocket's touch. How had I ever managed without a squire?

I said as much when he helped me sit up so I could drain a mug of rum-spiked water.

"Don't get too content with it," he replied. "I'm hoping that someday you'll declare my debt repaid."

"Someday," I agreed, yawning despite the pain.

"I don't suppose you'd put a time limit on that?" He tried to sound tough and indifferent, but the softness had crept back into his voice.

"Not yet." I fought the impulse to yawn again as he laid me down. My back was numb once more, and between that and the rum, I was almost comfortable. "I'll let you know."

"You do that," Fisk said. I wondered if he realized he was smiling.

The next time I awakened I found Fisk sitting, sound asleep, against the wall beside my bed. Ships are never silent, but there's a deep stillness that prevails over the darkest part of night, and I sensed it now.

The mallow's numbness was wearing off, and I realized that Fisk must have reapplied it several times without waking me—and had sat up all night to do it. I hated to wake him, but there was a bodily necessity I had to take care of, and I couldn't sit or stand without help.

"Fisk?"

He woke with a start, stiff and disoriented, and for a moment I forgot my growing discomfort. Fisk is a complex person. I would have to remember this kindness the next time he infuriated me—though the last time, he hadn't even understood that it was his lack of trust that angered me even more than his lie about being able to fight.

"You're a very good man," I said. His face crimsoned from collar to hairline, as if I'd accused him of something shameful.

"I just don't like pain." He rubbed his face briskly, regaining control. "Especially if it's mine. What can I do for you, Noble Sir?"

I'd always known 'twas going to take time.

By morning I could sit up by myself, although I tired quickly when Willard came to speak with me. Or mayhap 'twas simply that 'tis exhausting to be thanked, not to mention wept over. I was relieved when Fisk arrived and kicked Willard out, with a briskness that was not unkind.

The next morning, I felt weak and hot, and there was a place over my lower left ribs that throbbed dully.

I couldn't see Fisk's face when he salved my back, but I felt his hands hesitate when he reached the throbbing place. Shortly after that, Cracker came in to examine me, and I realized that one of the cuts had become infected—a thing that magica duckroot will cure easily . . . but this ship had none.

Cracker soaked the infected weals with warm water to soften them and then rubbed plain duckroot powder over them and replaced the warm damp rags, hoping that heat would take the herbs deeper into the wounds.

My fever rose that night, and my head throbbed in rhythm with my back. I felt vaguely nauseated and was rather cross with Fisk, who sat up with me again, wiping what he could of my face and arms with cool water.

Fisk was allowed to abandon his duties to sit with me. He hadn't had much sleep the last two nights. Dark circles shadowed his eyes, and he hadn't shaved this morning. I saw that he was frightened for me and thought that I ought to be frightened, too, but I felt too ill to bother. Fisk would take care of it.

Once when I drifted out of sleep, Willard was there, not apologizing, but talking sensibly of the cargo to be off-loaded at Granbor.

"He means to put in on the early tide," the little clerk said, "off-load as soon as he gets permission, and depart six hours later. Master Fisk, are you sure about this?"

"No," said Fisk curtly. "But I don't have a better idea. Help me get him up."

My blankets were peeled away, and I shivered as cool air swept over my skin. I could see the point in laying three or four clean blankets over my mattress, then putting another tick over them and making the bed again on top, for the extra padding would be more comfortable. But even in my indifferent haze, I wondered why Fisk was cramming four ballast stones into the corners of my bed.

He and Willard talked as they worked. Fisk was

strangely concerned about the cargo manifest "looking" right, and Willard kept reassuring him. Willard was nervous, too, and I wanted to reassure him, but I was too tired. Fisk would take care of it.

Time passed. I woke, slept, and woke again in a daze where nothing seemed quite real.

The pain of Fisk's grip on my shoulder roused me. His face, lined with exhaustion, held an expression of such firm command that it cut through my stupor, and I realized he wanted me to be silent. I nodded understanding and he pulled me out of bed, leaning me against the wall where he had sat for so many nights. 'Twas night now, I saw, and our fellow crewmen slept soundly. They missed a remarkable performance.

In near miraculous silence, Fisk pulled the extra bedding off my bunk and, with the aid of a ball of twine and a knife he must have stolen from the kitchen, he shaped the extra tick into a rough likeness of a sitting man.

He weighted it with the ballast rocks so the roll of the deck wouldn't tip it awry, and it looked extraordinarily real. I started to tell him so, but his hand clamped over my mouth. I was quite aggrieved, until I remembered I was supposed to be silent. I nodded, and he went back to work.

The dummy in the bed was easier to construct, and only moments later Fisk helped me stumble into the passageway.

The cold, fresh air that poured from the open hatch roused me, and my dazed brain recognized that we were escaping.

"What a good idea," I told Fisk.

"Shh!"

I was walking toward the ladder that led to the deck, but Fisk steered me around it and on down the corridor.

"Aren't we going up on deck? I thought—"

"Shh!"

This was not a squirely response, especially the second time. I was going to tell Fisk that, but he clamped a hand over my mouth and glared. Silence. Right. We were escaping.

Fisk snarled under his breath and rushed me through the corridor and down the three steps to the hold so fast I didn't have time to lose my balance. Then he propped me against the wall and turned to shut the hold door behind us. I gazed at the shadows the lamp cast through the crates and wondered why the door had been unlocked. But when Willard emerged from the shadows, I understood, for the ship's clerk had access to the keys.

"Have you got the manifests rigged?" Fisk asked.

"All I have to do is fill in the blanks," Willard told him. "Once the ink dries, there'll be no way to tell they weren't written at the start of the voyage."

"What if the captain recognizes your handwriting?"

"He won't." Willard smiled nervously. "I tried to imitate the previous clerk's writing."

Willard a forger? There was something different about him tonight—his voice was crisp, and though his movements were as clumsy as ever, his face held a new confidence. Willard had found his courage. But even so . . .

"Real courage is that you shouldn't become a forger," I told him, and then frowned, for that wasn't quite what I meant to say.

He and Fisk looked at me.

"This can't work," Willard told Fisk quietly. "Sooner or later the guards will notice you're not moving and raise the alarm. You'll be no use to him if they flog you, too."

"A good herbalist is the only thing that can help him now." Fisk wore a fierce expression I had never seen before. "What have you picked out for us?"

"This one for Sir Michael." Willard gestured to a long narrow box. "The manifest says it's full of tapestries. I thought it would be best for him to lie down."

"That's fine." Fisk had somehow acquired an iron crowbar and now he started prying up the box's lid. He worked carefully, but the nails screamed softly as they withdrew from the wood, and Willard flinched.

"Don't worry. There's too much wind for them to hear us on deck, and everyone else is asleep."

"I'm . . . I'm not sure I can close that up again. I'm not much good with a hammer," said Willard.

"I'll do it. All you have to do is fasten me in. What did you choose for me, by the way?"

Willard gestured to an old wine barrel, more than five feet tall. "It's got a big, carved chair in it. They're part of a shipment that no one will miss till we get to Tallow Port. All you have to do is tell me who to send you to."

"Who to *send* us to?" Fisk stopped prying at the nails and stared at Willard.

"An address that your . . . containers should be shipped to. The harbormaster won't accept them without an address."

"Send us wherever the rest . . . no. They might give us back to the captain. Send us to Master Greenman. There's a dozen Greenmans in every town, right?"

"Maybe, but the harbormaster will want to know which one—he's not going to take a crate he can't deliver. You've got to have a name, Master Fisk."

"But I don't know any merchants in Granbor!" Fisk hissed, wrenching up the lid of the tapestry box. "Help me get these out—we'll drop them in the bilge. Come on, Willard, you live on this coast—you must have heard of someone—the richest merchant, the local baron, the town brothel keeper . . ."

"I haven't." Willard grunted as they hefted a big roll of fabric out of the box.

"Well, I've never even heard of Gran . . . Wait a minute, I have. Granbor and tapestries, by the two moons! Lady Kathryn, I *will* teach you to sew! Paid or not! Send us to Mistress Kara the weaver."

"That will be wonderful," I told them. "With a needle, Kathy needs all the help she can get."

"He's talkative tonight," Willard observed, as they laid me down on a folded tapestry in the bottom of the long crate. "How are you going to keep him quiet?"

"Can't—he might suffocate if I gagged him. And, Willard, if we do get caught, don't get stupid and heroic and confess. There's no sense in you going down with us."

"Don't worry." Willard smiled. "I'm not such a fool. Though it's rather flattering that you think I might be."

Fisk snorted. "It might be flattering to your courage, but it's a cursed insult to your intelligence. You're a brave man, Willard, and a smart one. We owe you for this. I'll tell the judicars what happened, both here and in Cory Port, but that won't do much good. Is there anything else I can do for you?"

"You owe me nothing," said Willard. "At least, he doesn't. But if you could tell my wife—"

At this point they lowered the lid on the crate and the rest of the conversation was lost as Fisk nailed me in, which was a pity.

The tapping stopped and I heard nothing afterward but a few muffled thumps—presumably the carved chair being removed from the barrel and thrown into the bilge. I was sorry that they were destroying another's property, but 'twas dark in the crate, and peaceful, and Fisk would take care of any problems. . . . I went to sleep.

CHAPTER 11

Fisk

The only light in the barrel was a small circle that shone through the bunghole. Then Willard turned down the lamp and left, and it was completely dark. A yawn took me by surprise—I hadn't slept much lately. I sat with my back against one side of the barrel and my toes pressed against the other, contemplating all that could go wrong with this lunatic plan. Every scenario I imagined ended with me flogged and Michael dead. But then, not escaping ended in Michael's death too.

I was considering whether it would actually kill me, or just break most of my bones, if the crane rope broke and dropped my barrel onto the cobbles when I fell asleep.

I roused a little when the barrel lifted off the floor, but it was the smack as it swung into the edge of the cargo hatch that woke me. If I yelped, no one heard it.

The barrel swayed and spun. I rubbed my bruised forehead, and then tried to rub some of the stiffness out of my neck. I hoped Sir Michael, in his long, narrow box, fared better than this. Was he ahead of me, or still on the ship?

I tried to look through the bunghole, but all I saw was a dizzying swirl of masts and sky, and my neck muscles cramped so painfully I had to sit up.

The barrel descended in a rush, bounced on its tether so suddenly that my teeth cracked together, and settled with a bump. I commanded my stomach, firmly, to stay where it was.

A little shaking told of the removal of the sling ropes. I was off the ship! Sir Michael? I bent and peered though the bunghole and saw nothing but legs. Something thumped down beside me, but it was out of sight. I sat up, rubbed my neck, then bent and peered again. I heard the clop of hooves and a horse's legs passed, followed by turning cart wheels. More men's legs. Another thump as something else lit near my barrel.

I didn't dare try to remove the lid—for all I knew I was in full view of the ship's deck, with the captain looking on.

I leaned back, trying to get comfortable and failing. With any luck someone would leave me alone in a warehouse and I'd pop the lid—Willard couldn't have fastened it too tight, could he?

It was outside the barrel that my problems would really begin. I could free Michael—desperate as I felt right now, I could demolish that crate with my bare hands. But then what? I needed money for an herbalist, and more money for magica.

The old thought was so familiar that sweat broke out on my forehead. That was a long time ago—*this is now*, I told myself firmly. I was grown up. I could get the money. But how?

My first thought was to run a con, for con games are safest, but any game that would produce a big enough score would take too long to set up. And I needed a big score—not only for magica herbs and a healer, but enough to pay room and board throughout Sir Michael's recovery. And he *was* going to recover. I wouldn't let lack of money defeat me again. Ever.

It was at this point that my barrel tipped sideways, shot into the air, and bumped upright. I suppressed a startled yip, and realized I had been lifted onto a cart.

I crouched and peered through the bunghole. From this height I could see along the dock, a row of ships and buildings, curving away. But the sight that made my heart leap was the corner of a long, low box, right at the edge of my field of vision. It was perfectly still—

but what did I expect it to do? Get up and dance? Michael was probably asleep. And when he woke up, he was going to need a healer.

I sat back and wrapped my arms around myself, warding off the chill of fear, and thought of all the ways I knew to get money fast.

The fastest way is picking pockets, but it's *not* safe and the chances of a big take are low.

My barrel lurched and I felt the cart moving. I abandoned planning and watched fences, shops, and anonymous walls pass by until my neck complained again.

A simple burglary was the best bet—you could score big and fast. Unfortunately burglary isn't that simple, and the faster you rush into it, and the less you know about your target, the higher your risk of getting caught.

If we ended up in jail, would the judicars pay for a healer? Now *there* was a thought. A cursed stupid thought, but the fact that I contemplated it as long as I did said a lot about my state of mind.

The cart jerked to a stop. Warehouse? No such luck. The view through my peephole showed a stone house with windows of old glass. I heard voices, but I couldn't understand the words. Then a man's doublet appeared in my view—close up. I barely had time to brace myself

as the barrel was lifted off the cart and laid on its side—
then it began to roll. I wedged my arms and legs so I
rolled with it instead of tumbling around inside. Up,
down, up, down. The sweeping loops made my stomach
flutter, even after all those weeks at sea. I heard a
grunted curse about the load balance.

They lifted the barrel up the short flight of stairs,
and the hall must have been too narrow to roll me
down for they continued to carry me—which would
have been welcome except when they picked up the
barrel I ended up head down, lying on my shoulders
with my neck twisted like a hanged man's. I didn't
dare try to right myself for they might detect the
movement.

The barrel slammed into the floor, crimping my
neck even further, and the voices receded. A woman's
voice had joined them. No matter, they were gone and
I could move! The contortions I went through to turn
myself right side up set the cursed tub rocking, but by
the time the voices returned I was sitting up, trying to
catch my breath.

The bunghole was now near the top. I rose to my
knees and put my eye to it. I saw a huge, half-filled
loom and the corner of a rack that held twists of yarn
sorted by color. Mistress Kara must have had every
color there was, for the small section I could see held

nothing but various shades of blue fading to black. I cursed under my breath and put my ear to the hole. A woman was saying . . .

". . . for the delivery. I know I wasn't expecting anything. You're sure my name was on the manifest?"

"Quite sure, Mistress."

"Well, I suppose the long box is someone returning a tapestry, for I do tell people to send them back if they change their minds. But I can't imagine what's in the barrel. Isn't it odd there wasn't a sender's name on the papers? I'll have no way to know if it was meant for someone else, unless the contents provide some—"

"Ah, Mistress?"

"—clue, and even if it's something that might go to anyone, like dishes, if I put the word about, someone's bound to claim it. Oh, you need my signature?"

The voices receded again and my heart began to pound. I was alone—this was my chance.

I reached up and thumped the heel of my hand against the barrel lid. Nothing. I struck it harder and hurt my hand. Cursing under my breath, I tried hitting the lid with both hands—all around the rim and then in the center. Maneuvering awkwardly, I tried the floor with the same results. Thanks a lot, Willard—tamping down this lid was the first physical thing he'd done right in all the time I'd known him.

I had to go through more contortions to get my shoulders braced against the lid. When I finally managed it, I pushed with all my might and got nothing for my effort but muscle cramps. The barrel was too small for me to get any leverage.

I had dropped back to a sitting position when Mistress Kara returned. Her voice was the only one I heard, and I couldn't make out words, but I was left in no doubt of her intentions. The crack of a wooden mallet on the lid of my barrel made me flinch. I ran my hands over my hair and tried to think what I was going to say. Play it by ear. Jack always said I was good at that, but in this case—

The mallet hit the lid again, and it tipped and lifted away. Light flooded in, but I wasn't so blinded as to miss the horror that dawned in Mistress Kara's widened eyes.

I summoned up my most reassuring smile. "Hello."

Her shriek all but split my eardrums. Her face vanished, and I heard running footsteps and the creak of an opening door. It was so quiet I could hear her draw in breath to scream again, and I waited resignedly. But she didn't scream. Except for her rapid breathing, the house was still. She must be alone here. No wonder she was alarmed.

Then I heard footsteps, very tentative, coming

toward me. A rush of steps. Stillness. Then a series of quick footfalls as she marched right up to the barrel and looked in.

This time she held an iron crowbar, raised to strike, and her mouth was set in a determined line.

"Don't!" I showed her my empty hands. "I'm not going to hurt you. I don't want to hurt anyone—honest!"

Some of the fear left her face, but the crowbar didn't waver. "Who are you, and what are you doing in my house?"

"My name is Fisk, and I'm escaping." I pumped all the I'm-a-harmless-good-fellow energy I could summon into my next suggestion. "Look, would you let me get out of here? I really don't mean any harm."

She took a cautious step back, but curiosity began to replace the fear in her expression, and I knew I'd won.

"All right. But move slowly."

As if I had a choice in the matter. After all those hours in the barrel, my legs refused to straighten. When I finally stood, they buckled and the barrel tipped over. I had to crawl out of the cursed thing, which had the good effect of calming Mistress Kara. She lowered the crowbar and gazed at me in assessing silence.

She was somewhere in her early twenties, with dark hair tucked into a neat starched cap, and clear dark eyes held the beginning of a sympathy I intended to make full use of. Thank goodness for softhearted marks. She was small, and her figure was full without being overly plump, which is not a bad thing at all.

"Ah, would you mind lending me that?" I gestured to the crowbar in her hand.

"No!" She stepped back, her grip tightening. "I mean, yes, I do mind. Do you think I'm an idiot?"

Her eyes were wary again. The long box was very still, but snarling at her would only harm my cause. I tried another reassuring smile, but I'm not sure I brought it off.

"Don't worry, it's just that my employer's in there and—"

"There's another man in *that* box?" She lifted the crowbar.

I couldn't blame her. "Well, yes, but he won't hurt anyone either. In fact, he's sick, and I'm worried about him. You can keep the mallet and stand behind me. I really need to get him out, because he was flogged, and the wounds got infected, and . . . and curse it, woman, either hand me that thing or open it yourself!"

I wasn't smiling anymore, but Mistress Kara didn't look frightened. She glanced at the mallet that lay on the table and then went to the fireplace that dominated one wall and picked up a poker. It was about the same length as the crowbar, and, while not as heavy, the sharp hook on the end made up for it. She came back and handed me the crowbar.

I scuttled over to the box and began working on it. My hands were unsteady, but I had the nails out quite shortly. I tossed the crowbar across the floor to relieve Mistress Kara's fears, took a deep breath, and lifted the lid.

The damp, stuffy scent of illness welled out, but Michael's back moved—he was breathing. Then I saw red streaks reaching out from the angry, swollen patch on his left side. I could feel the heat of his body from where I knelt.

I heard the startled catch of Mistress Kara's breath. She stared at Sir Michael with horror and pity in her eyes. She looked at me, she looked at him, she looked at me again, and she laid the poker on the table.

"Let's get him to bed," she said.

Mistress Kara was strong for a small woman, but she was a small woman, and my legs showed a tendency to collapse. Between us, however, we finally managed to get Sir Michael up the stairs and into bed in a small, snug room overlooking the kitchen garden.

Mistress Kara was indeed alone in the house; her maid had the day off, and the cook was at the market.

She left me sponging Sir Michael's face and arms with fresh water, while she ran for the herbalist. She came back with two men—the other was the sheriff. Softhearted, but not entirely a fool.

Trying to hear what the herbalist was muttering over Sir Michael, I answered the sheriff's questions briefly but honestly. Almost honestly. I saw no point in revealing that Sir Michael and I were both indebted men. And when I told him we had been in Cory Port on business, I didn't mention what that business was. Why complicate matters? So what came out was a simple, straightforward story of a mishap that was relatively common in seaports. Except for Sir Michael's bravery in saving Willard—I milked that tale for all it was worth, keeping an eye on Mistress Kara as I did so. She looked a lot calmer with the sheriff in the house, but could I soothe her enough to let us stay?

The sheriff, a middle-aged man with a kindly face, a comfortable potbelly, and the shrewdest eyes I've ever seen, heard me out. Then he checked Sir Michael's and my wrists for tattoos that mark a permanently un-redeemed man. Finally he looked at the calluses on our hands and feet.

"As far as I can see, he's likely telling the truth. There's no writs out for either of them, and one of my deputies reported that the captain of the *Albatross* is looking for a couple of crewmen who 'deserted' him, so—"

"So it's the most wretched business I ever heard of!" Mistress Kara's voice snapped with indignation. "This poor man . . . Can't you *do* something about that captain? Arrest him for loitering, or—"

"Not in Granbor." The sheriff interrupted with the firmness of someone who knew Mistress Kara well. "He's committed no crime against any of Lord Lester's folk. We'll keep an eye on him to be sure he doesn't try to cudgel-crew more men, and if he does we'll arrest him. Aside from that . . ." He shrugged. "What you need to do is figure out what you're going to do with these men."

"What *I'm* going to do? Why me? I'm not—"

"They were delivered to you." The sheriff's eyes sparkled mischievously, and I fought down an impulse to swear at him. "So it's your decision. You can send for their captain—"

"As if I'd do anything of the kind! I'd like to do something *to* the sadistic son of a—"

"Or you can throw them out—"

"Into the street? Without a fract between them, and one of them half dead of infection, and—"

"Or you can keep them here," said the sheriff, "with no one in the house but you and old Maudie. I don't recommend it, Kara."

"I'll make my own decision, thank you very much. I mean to—"

"Or you could lodge them with the herbalist until this one recovers. It mightn't cost that much. . . . I'll pay a bit of it myself, and if there's any good in him Master Barton will cut his rates. How about it, Barton? Is there any good in you?"

"Why do people always expect healers to offer their services for free?" Master Barton turned from Sir Michael's bed, wiping his hands. "Do you expect free bread from the baker? Or free carpentry? No, indeed. So why should I do it?"

I couldn't fault his logic, but my guts knotted. I didn't have any money. Mistress Kara noticed my expression.

"Stop it, you stingy man, you're scaring Master Fisk. He doesn't mean it," she assured me.

Master Barton sighed. "I'll offer my time for free, but this man needs magica to heal and I can't give that away—it costs too high. I can't board them, either. There are two boys with mumps in my sickroom."

"Then they'll stay here," said Mistress Kara firmly. "I'll hire Milly's brother to help with the heavy nursing, and he can keep Master Fisk from murdering us in our beds and making off with the silver."

"I wouldn't count on it," said the sheriff.

"But what about magica herbs?" Master Barton

asked. "They're going to cost—"

"Wait, they do have money!" Mistress Kara's eyes snapped with excitement. "That was a very fine tapestry Sir Michael was lying on—at least, I'm sure it *will* be fine, when I have a chance to look at it. I'll buy it from them, and probably make a profit on the resale! Besides, there's a . . . Master Fisk, are you all right?"

"I am now." I drew a shuddering breath and blinked hard. "Mistress Kara, I thank you. If you hadn't—"

"Nonsense, anyone would do the same. Well, anyone as curious as I am. But you're worried about your friend, and tired out too, so—"

"He's not my friend." I was wondering if there'd be any money left after we paid Master Barton and spoke without thinking. "He's my . . . ah . . ."

They all stared at me. Mistress Kara's face was bright with interest, and Sir Michael would tell them anyway as soon as he recovered. And he *would* recover, thanks to Mistress Kara.

"He's a knight errant," I said. "And I'm his squire."

The sheriff frowned, the herbalist smiled, and Mistress Kara's eyes lit with delight. "I knew it! This is a story I've got to hear."

It all came together as Mistress Kara had decreed. Milly-the-maid's brother—a groom by trade—was perfectly

willing to nurse "a two-footer." Especially at the fee
Mistress Kara offered. Master Barton left, returned
with his magica herbs, and chased old Maudie out of
the kitchen to brew them. Then he chased me out of
Sir Michael's bedroom while he applied them, prefer-
ring Milly's brother's assistance.

I was so stupid with fatigue that I was standing in
the hall staring at the bedroom door when Mistress
Kara came by.

"Master Barton's treating your friend? Don't look so
nervous. He's a very good healer, and he never lets
anyone in. I have a commission to finish—not that it
looks like I'll get much work done with all this fuss
going on—but I have a hunch your story will make up
for it. And the moment I finish, I'll start looking for a
buyer for your tapestry."

"I hope you find a generous one," I said, inserting
the words into one of her brief pauses for breath.
"You've been spending pretty freely, considering you
haven't examined the tapestry yet."

"Then let's have a look at it, for I must admit I'm
curious. If it belongs to one of the big houses, I might
be able to sell it back to them. A lot of family tapestries were seized as loot in the warring times. Sometimes you can . . ."

We went downstairs to Mistress Kara's weaving

room and unrolled the tapestry on the floor. It was big, roughly ten by fourteen feet, and unlike the spiral story I had seen on Mistress Kara's tapestry at Seven Oaks, this was designed in the usual way. The big scene in the center showed a bloodstained knight lying with his head in the lap of a slender maiden. The knight's blood covered her skirt and hands, and they both looked quite unhappy. It wasn't something I'd want on my walls, though the weaving was good.

Mistress Kara saw my expression and grinned. "It was probably commissioned to portray an old family story. It gives the owner an excuse to tell everyone about his heroic ancestor who did thus and such. Besides, look how the crest on the knight's shield is displayed."

The shield lay at the knight's feet; the painted ship sailing into an outstretched hand was clearly visible.

"And the same device is woven into the corners. See, the ship sails around the border, encountering storms and monsters, but at each corner it sails into the hand. Family tapestry. But it may be hard to find out who originally owned it, since it's not a liege's crest."

The older and more important a family, the simpler their crest—across the length of a dusty battlefield, it's much harder to tell the difference between a ship sailing into a hand and a bull charging a tower than between a shield that's half red, half black, and one that's blue with a yellow circle in the middle.

Mistress Kara looked the tapestry over. "Yes, this was made for some petty baron who wanted to brag about his ancestors. I'll give you thirty gold roundels for it."

"Forty-five," I answered before I could stop myself; after all, she could still kick us out.

She showed no sign of kicking us out, but her eyes began to glitter. "Thirty-three. And considering that I might not be able to track down the family, who might not want it back if I do, that's a very good offer."

"Forty."

We settled on thirty-five, for Mistress Kara was a shrewd bargainer and she had the advantage.

Master Barton joined us for mid-meal. He said Sir Michael's fever would break sometime tonight and, seeing my resolve to sit up with him, Mistress Kara persuaded me to take an afternoon nap.

It was late when I awakened, for full dark had fallen, and I swore as I poured water into a basin. The face that stared back at me from the mirror was still hollow-eyed with weariness, rough with stubble, and looked so disreputable that I was astonished Mistress Kara had agreed to let us stay.

I was even more surprised, when I went down the hall to Sir Michael's room, to find Kara sitting with him.

I thanked her, implying as politely as I could that she could leave if she wished. In her shoes, I'd have been worried about being alone in the same room with me.

But she settled firmly into her chair and declared that she'd like to hear my story now. "For I consider that story your rent, Master Fisk. I collect good stories, you know. I use them as inspiration for my tapestries."

The lamp was turned too low to read, so as not to disturb Michael, and I needed to do something to keep myself awake. Besides, "stories" are part of a con artist's repertoire.

I began with breaking Lady Ceciel out of Sorrowston Tower, and I made a good tale of it, for I glossed over a few of the less glamorous aspects, like the mud, and went for a saga of true heroism . . . after a fashion.

Mistress Kara was an attentive listener. When she interrupted, her questions and comments were the kind that led the story on and on. After a time, my recitation became less heroic and more true. When I reached the point where she opened the barrel, and finally fell silent, I realized that I had revealed not only that Sir Michael and I were both indebted, but my own criminal past. Mind, it would have been hard to explain how I became Sir Michael's squire without revealing both those things, but I could have lied. Either I must have been more tired than I thought or Mistress Kara was a *very* good listener. Getting people to talk is part of a con artist's trade. She might have been a good one, if she wasn't so talkative herself.

My revelations didn't seem to disturb her. She was gazing at Michael's flushed, stubbled face. "He's quite heroic."

I looked at the scabbed-over cuts that crisscrossed my employer's back. "Vastly overrated," I muttered.

"But do you think he's entirely competent at it? I mean, most of his efforts don't come off, do they?"

"He's not incompetent!"

Her brows lifted at my vehemence, and heat rose in my face.

"I know how it sounds, but he isn't. It's just . . ." I stopped. A dog barked somewhere in the distance. Mistress Kara waited, her bright, curious eyes fixed on mine.

"It's that . . . his reach exceeds his grasp. He tries to do things no one else would even dream of attempting—and he usually brings about three quarters of it off. The last quarter sometimes trips him up, but the parts he does manage are remarkable. And no one else would have tried."

A thoughtful, distant look crept over Mistress Kara's face. Was I looking at an artist being inspired? *I hoped not.*

"I see," she said. "Thank you, Fisk. Good night."

She left without another word.

I watched Michael sleep for the rest of the night, and Master Barton was right: His fever diminished. When Milly's brother took my place at dawn, I felt no more than normal warmth when I laid my hand on Sir Michael's face. Even the red streaks were fading. I went to my own bed and fell asleep without worry for the first time in days.

I woke in the early afternoon and checked on Sir Michael. He was still sleeping, so I took the time to shave and wash before going in search of food.

I found Mistress Kara in her weaving room, up to her elbows in paper and charcoal. I was surprised to find her sketching instead of weaving, but it was no concern of mine. As politely as possible, I asked to be paid for my tapestry.

She first subtracted the money she'd paid out to Master Barton and Milly's brother. The amount left was smaller than I'd hoped, but if she'd charged us more rent than a story, there would have been nothing left at all.

I spent the rest of that afternoon in town, buying some inexpensive but decent clothes for my employer and myself. Returning with my purchases, I took the time to change before going to Sir Michael's room and was pleased to find him awake. Quite ridiculously pleased.

He took in my restored appearance and his first words were "Where did you get the money?"

I could have indignantly denied that I'd stolen it. Or told him I'd robbed half a dozen widows and orphans. But his eyes were laughing, and since the owners of the tapestry would no doubt consider that I *had* stolen it, I sat down beside the bed and told the truth.

To my surprise, Sir Michael made no protest. "When we get back to Cory Port, we'll repay them" was all he said.

"With what? And how are we going to get back to Cory Port?" I laid the old purse Mistress Kara had given me on the bed. "This is all that's left."

Sir Michael rolled onto his side, wincing, to lift the limp purse. He shook it, sighed, and handed it back to me.

"Keep it. You're better at handling money than I. And if you've got it, at least I'll know where it is."

I felt myself blush, and he grinned. "Don't worry so much, Fisk. As long we pay for the tapestry, the owners won't care—'twas on its way to be sold, after all. We simply have to find them."

"Well, I can describe the tapestry," I said absently, wondering why Sir Michael was changing the subject. Where was *he* planning to get the money to carry us home? He clearly had some idea—and he didn't want to tell me about it. "And it had a crest on it, too, a ship sailing into a hand. Sir Michael, how, exactly, are you—"

"A what?" he interrupted sharply. "Fisk, say that again."

"I want to know how you plan to—"

"No, forget that. About the ship and the hand."

"It was on the tapestry," I replied blankly. "The device on the knight's shield, and in the border, was a ship sailing into an outstretched hand. Why, do you know it?"

"That's the coat of arms of Craggan Keep. 'Twas embossed on Lady Ceciel's belt—you didn't notice?"

I hadn't, but I also hadn't tied the lady into a rope sling, or helped her on and off several horses.

"But that doesn't make sense," I protested. "With Sir Herbert dead, and no other heir until this mess with Lady Ceciel is settled, no one would have the authority to sell off the keep's valuables except . . ."

Lady Ceciel herself. I saw my realization echoed in Sir Michael's face.

"No," he said.

"She went home. We've been scouring the country-side, from Crown City to the leeward shores, and she *just went home.*"

"No."

"It explains how they were able to find us in Cory Port so quickly," I went on. "Hackle's brother probably sent word the instant we left him."

"No!"

"And it explains how she was able to find a ship captain willing to kidnap for her—he was already selling her valuables. She just offered him extra to take us, too."

I thought Sir Michael was going to protest again—instead he began to laugh, low, but quite hard.

I glared at him. "It's not funny."

"Yes, it is." His voice shook with mirth. "And the joke's on us. She went home. You're right, Fisk. We're amateurs."

"But we thought about that! Why isn't she afraid Lord Gerald will marry her off to some henchman, and then hand her over to justice? Why hasn't he done that, if she's been sitting in Craggan Keep all this time?"

"I don't know. Mayhap someone is protecting her. Mayhap she has some hold over Lord Gerald or some way to prevent him from knowing where she is. But only the heir could sell family valuables. She is the heir. Therefore, she went home." He began to laugh again.

"That's a cheerful sound," said Mistress Kara, poking her head through the door. Her face lit with pleasure, and I suddenly wondered if she had some interest in my employer that went beyond charity or artistic inspiration.

"Lunatics do this all the time," I told her. "Ignore it. We've figured out who owned your tapestry."

She listened with her usual bright-eyed interest while I explained our deductions.

"Well, how wretched of her," said Mistress Kara. "She could have had the decency to run from you!" Her lips were twitching, and Sir Michael chuckled again. He seemed none the worse for all that laughter, but his face was paler—time for him to rest. But Mistress Kara continued. . . .

"So I'll probably have a harder time selling that tapestry than I'd hoped. Oh well, the story was worth it. I've been asking questions about your Lady Ceciel. She sounds . . . interesting." She stopped talking and smoothed her skirt nervously—a gesture I'd never seen her make. "They say she hires simple ones from all over the area to be her servants. That sounds charitable, don't you think?"

Her eyes were lowered. I had no idea what the problem was, but Sir Michael noticed her reluctance.

"It sounds as if you've heard something else," he said gently. "If you feel uncomfortable repeating it, then don't. We understand that you don't wish to gossip unkindly."

He'd obviously hit the mark with Mistress Kara, for relief lit her face—but he was wrong about me understanding. If there was something scandalous about Lady Ceciel I wanted to know it. And I never met anyone who could resist spreading gossip.

"They were saying she poisoned her husband, of course," said Mistress Kara slowly. "But that wasn't the worst of it. I'm really not sure."

"Then you needn't say more." Sir Michael smiled.

I wanted to howl with frustration, but Mistress Kara was gazing at Sir Michael. "You're going after her, aren't you?" It wasn't a question.

"We must," said Sir Michael. "'Tis a matter of honor. And justice."

Evidently perceiving my employer for the naive twit he was, Mistress Kara sighed. "Then I'd better tell you. If you're going to confront her, you should know."

But at this interesting point, she hesitated again. I could no longer contain myself. "Know what? Please, you've heard our story—we need all the help we can get! What's being said about the wench?"

Sir Michael opened his mouth to object, but I sent him a glare that silenced him on the spot.

"Well . . ." Mistress Kara leaned forward, the anticipation of really good gossip relieving some of the distress in her eyes. "They say . . ."

CHAPTER 12

Michael

"She's probably a witch," Fisk told me. "Which means we should be careful how we approach her."

The sea wind ruffled my hair, cool and brisk, for Appleon had turned to Oaken during our stay at Mistress Kara's, and winter was creeping up on us. We sat in the prow mending sails—a task at which Fisk, the seamstress's son, was far better than I.

Fisk's outrage, when I proposed that we work our passage home on a sailing vessel, had been so intense 'twas comical. But it was the only practical way to get back—especially when you considered our lack of funds. I challenged him to think of another way for us to reach Cory Port before winter . . . and he couldn't. I think he was reluctant to leave Mistress Kara's home. In the weeks it had taken me to recover, he'd become inordinately attached to her library.

But I finally succeeded in prying him away from her books, and we found an ore freighter willing to take on a couple of hands. The *Floating Shoe* was older, dirtier, and slower than the *Albatross*, but the captain was an honest man, and his crew laughed at the thought of him ever flogging anyone.

I wondered if some of Fisk's reluctance to leave Mistress Kara's was fear of Lady Ceciel.

"What makes you think she's a witch? That's the only thing they *didn't* say about her."

"Think about it. She's studied herb lore, she's evil, and she's borne no children."

"'Tis a myth that you can gain a Savant's power by sacrificing your fertility to the Furred God," I told Fisk. No one really knows where the Savants get their ability to placate the gods—to intervene between nature's magic and man. "In fact, I'm not sure that witches aren't a myth. Have you ever seen one? Or known anyone who's seen one?"

As logic went, 'twas pretty poor, but the thought that someone might gain a Savant's power over nature and magic, and then use it against humanity, horrified me. The other horrifying accusations against Lady Ceciel ranged from infidelity (most often with the simple ones she'd taken on) to human sacrifice. (Also with the simple ones.)

Listening to the ugly gossip, I understood Mistress Kara's reluctance to repeat it. Especially since, as she pointed out, it couldn't all be true, "For there isn't enough time in the day for all she's supposed to be doing!" Some of the rumors had even contradicted each other, but still . . .

"I don't think she's a witch," I told Fisk firmly. "Witches are supposed to live wild, as the Savants do. And even if she was, how could anyone know it?"

"I know one way," said Fisk, with an exaggerated leer. The sacrifice of their fertility was supposed to leave certain parts of a witch's body cold to the touch. To my considerable annoyance, I felt myself blush.

Fisk's lips twitched, but when he spoke his voice was serious.

"Sir Michael, we've *got* to get smarter about dealing with this woman. Even if she's not willing to kill us— and I'm not as sure of that as you are—her little delaying tactics are dangerous! If you won't tell Lord Dorian where she is—"

"You know I can't. The terms of repayment require that *I* bring her back."

"They might make an exception when they find out she's holed up in a keep, surrounded by armed guards."

"We don't know whether she's surrounded by guards or not."

"If she isn't, she's a fool. And she's not a fool."

For a moment the ugly gossip faded, and I remembered the composed, sharp-tongued woman we'd taken from Sorrowston Tower. She wasn't a fool. But there was something in Fisk's face . . .

"You have an idea, don't you?" I demanded. "You know how we can seize her."

My squire's neat stitching never wavered as he spoke. "My only thought is that I'd rather grab her when she's outside the keep instead of in the midst of her servants, surrounded by armed guards. And she may ride out surrounded by guards, in which case it doesn't make much difference."

"We don't know if—"

"That's my point. We don't know enough. Lady Ceciel saw us once, on a dark night. If we change our appearance, we might be able to get work in the keep, as servants or grooms. If we find out enough about her habits, maybe we can come up with a workable plan for a kidnapping."

I stared at my practical, craven squire in astonishment. "Are you out of your mind? She'd recognize us in a heartbeat and—"

"Not necessarily," said Fisk. "Haven't you ever met someone you know in a different setting and not known them?"

I had, of course. Last year when I was working in

the mines, one of Lord Dorian's stewards came to buy ore; I didn't identify him until he announced his name and business.

"But—"

"No one really looks at servants, and besides, I know a lot of ways to change a person's appearance," Fisk said shamelessly. "Voice is the hardest part."

"But—"

"But the most important thing is that she doesn't expect to see us. She thinks we're on a ship, bound for Tallow Port. She won't see us, because she won't be looking for us. That's the real trick of disguise."

"But what about Hackle? He met us twice, once in a good light, and as steward, he's probably the one who *hires* servants."

Fisk's hands stilled. "I think we can fool Hackle, too. He'll be tougher than the lady, but he won't expect to see us either. This is . . . part of my craft. I know what I'm doing."

I'd known Fisk was a good man when I redeemed him, but I never dreamt he'd be so useful. Still . . .

" 'Twould be a lie, Fisk. And even if I was willing, I don't think I could carry it off. We must find an honorable way."

Fisk started sewing again. I couldn't read his face, but his voice was mild as he said, "I've heard you lie before. And you were very convincing."

"When? What do you mean?"

"To the captain of the *Albatross*. When you told him you'd dumped that paint." Fisk's voice was still neutral, but my face grew hot.

"That was necessary! If I hadn't lied, he'd have taken Willard, and—"

"So lying is justified if it serves some greater good?"

The philosophical trap yawned at my feet. The trouble was, I didn't know how to avoid it.

"There has to be another way. An honorable one."

"Well, when you think of it, Noble Sir, let me know."

Fisk continued to stitch. The silence stretched. Hard as I thought, I couldn't come up with any other plan. And Fisk had a point. If Lady Ceciel had murdered her husband, a lie was small cost for bringing her to justice. My father wouldn't approve, but I'd stopped trying to win Father's approval a long time ago.

"All right, Fisk, how do we start? Changing our appearance I mean."

The expression flickered over Fisk's face so quickly I couldn't identify it—astonishment and . . . gratitude? Whatever it was, 'twas rapidly swallowed by a sparkle of pure mischief.

"There's a lot I'll need to coach you on," Fisk told me demurely. "Changing your walk, doing something about your accent. But first we have to cut your hair."

◇ ◇ ◇

In truth, I only objected because Fisk seemed to expect it, for I have no problem with being regarded as a peasant. But it still felt odd to hear the shears snick so close to my scalp.

"Why don't we pretend to be armsmen instead of servants?" I asked as clumps of hair fell to the deck. "That way we'd be carrying weapons if something went wrong."

I was a little nervous that he was doing this by lantern light. I wasn't worried about getting a bad haircut, for hair grows out, but I liked my ears the way they were.

"Men-at-arms sleep in the barracks, ride out with the lady, and never get into the house at all," said Fisk, combing my forelock straight with his fingers. "Servants sweep, mop, and empty the privies. They get into every room, and you'd be amazed how much they know. Not to mention that men-at-arms generally own their own weapons, armor, and a horse, and even when we get paid we can't afford any of those things."

All of this was painfully true, but 'twas the thought of Chant and Tipple that made me sigh as cut hair began to fall over my nose. I hoped they'd found good homes, for Chant was well trained, despite his weak leg, and Tipple a sound little mare, despite her weakness for beer. Wherever they were, there was nothing I could do for them.

"There," said Fisk abruptly. He pulled off the gunny-sack that shielded my shoulders and shook it out, then toweled my head with it and stood back, considering his work.

I ran my fingers through what little was left of my hair. My head felt oddly light, as if 'twas floating on my shoulders.

"Not bad," Fisk pronounced. "Not bad at all. In a week it'll grow out enough to look natural."

The wicked glint in his eyes made me nervous. I ran my fingers through the stubble again. "I wish I could see it."

There were no mirrors on the *Floating Shoe*. Fisk frowned thoughtfully. "Come with me."

He took me to the galley and spent some time searching among the pots. "Ah, here it is!" He buffed the shiny copper kettle lid on his sleeve before holding it out to me.

My reflection bent around its dents and curves, but I could see enough. Stripped of my hair's softening presence my bones stood out sharply, making my face look thinner and more angular—mayhap my recent illness added to the effect. Even my hair color was different, a darker brown, for the sun had never reached the hidden roots that were now revealed.

"Gods' mercy. I don't think *Kathy* would recognize

me! This is excellent, Fisk. I look like a peasant."

"No one would take you for 'Sir' Michael," Fisk agreed. "I think I'll start calling you Mike. Just to get in practice."

I winced, for while I've wished that Fisk would call me Michael (as he did on the deck of the *Albatross*, when he tried to convince me to save myself and leave him behind), "Mike" is a name I've never cared for—perhaps because my brother Justin used to tease me with it.

In the days that followed, I learned much of the art of disguise. Fisk altered my walk by placing cloth pads under my heels, but after several attempts we concluded that I couldn't utter a sentence without giving away my origins—well, that's what Fisk concluded. He taught me to fake a stammer, and told me to speak no more than a few words—he'd do the talking.

Even if I never spoke an untrue word, 'twould still be a lie.

I wondered what Fisk intended to do with his own appearance—he'd made such changes in mine that I was certain he could do the same for himself when the time came.

The *Floating Shoe* didn't stop at Cory Port, but for a small fee (actually, a reduction in our wages) the captain agreed to land us near a village to the north. The crew rowed us to shore before dawn—just half a day's walk from our destination, so there was no way that the tale of our strange doings could travel back to Hackle or Lady Ceciel. I didn't believe that Hackle could possibly know what we were doing now, but I'd thought the same just before I walked into his last two ambushes. I vowed to take more care this time.

Fisk went into the village alone, and returned with some travel food and a small bottle of walnut stain, which he used to darken his hair when we stopped for breakfast. My confidence suffered a blow, for he looked like Fisk with dark hair—quite easily recognizable. But he laughed at my qualms.

'Twas a fine day for travel, the wind blowing off the sea brisk enough for cool walking and the sun bright enough for warmth in a sheltered place. In a few hours we came around a bend and saw Craggan Keep looming on a hilltop.

Fisk slowed, gazing up at it. "We've got two choices. We can go into town, tell people that we're a couple of servants looking for work, and let them refer us to the keep, or we can walk up now, bang on the gate, and ask. The first way establishes our identity if anyone thinks to check, but asking now would be in character."

"Let's get it over with," I said. "We can go into

town and establish things later."

Fisk cast me an odd look, and I sensed his reluctance now that the time was upon us. But he made no protest, simply pulling me off the road to change into our better clothes.

"They'll know we haven't been walking all day in these," I objected. "Not dusty enough." I put the cloth pads under my heels and minced back and forth.

"But we would change clothes if we'd seen the keep and decided to ask for work," said Fisk. "Just remember to stammer and we'll be all right."

I wished he wouldn't look so worried when he said that. Since we had no alternative, we needed to succeed.

We set off up the road to the keep, me mincing, and Fisk's walk suddenly acquiring a slight roll, although he still looked like Fisk with dark hair.

Craggan Keep was a square stone fortress, its gray walls unsoftened by the feathery clasp of ivy or climbing roses. As I drew closer I saw why—the bushes near the walls had recently been cleared to create a killing ground, a thing I'd never seen in my lifetime, for the realm has been at peace for many generations. Two armsmen patrolled the parapet—something else I'd never seen. Lady Ceciel was not a fool.

"I'm glad I don't have to assault this place," I murmured.

"That's the idea," said Fisk.

Under ordinary conditions climbing the hill to the keep would have been easy, but with my heels unnaturally elevated, I arrived at the top with aching shins. How would my legs feel if I had to walk like this for days?

We stopped before the great iron-hinged doors. In Fisk's eyes, I read a plea that we didn't have to go through with this. *Yes we do,* I thought at him. Evidently it got through, for he sighed, stepped forward, and banged on the doors.

"Hello! Hello the keep! Anyone in there?" I felt my jaw drop, for the voice wasn't Fisk's—'twas higher, timorous, and his face . . . I swear 'twas fatter. His expression was petulant. His lips looked fuller. How did he do that?

A narrow portal in the door slid aside, so suddenly that both of us jumped. A man peered out—probably one of the guards, but we could see nothing but his eyes and nose.

"State your business." He sounded bored.

"We're looking for employment." Fisk managed to sound both nervous and firm. "In the house, mind. We're not stable hands, nor scullions. We'd like to see the steward, if you please."

"We're not hiring." The portal started to close.

"Wait! Wait, wait, wait, my good man. All we seek is

an interview. Surely that can be . . . arranged?" 'Twas
the jingle of our purse, not the plea in Fisk's voice, that
opened the portal again. The guard surveyed us and
saw no threat. The portal slid closed and the great
door opened, for 'tis hard to palm a bribe through a
peephole. A silver roundel changed hands.

"I can't do much for you." The guard was a sturdy fellow, with freckled skin and thick arms. "I told you, she's
not hiring. Leastways not normal folk, and you look too
smart to meet her other standards. Although . . . what's
his name?"

I knew a moment of panic, for I'd not thought to
provide myself with one. But I had to say something.
Fortunately, I remembered to stammer. "S-s-s-s—"

"Sammel," Fisk cut in. "He can't talk much, but he's
a good worker. If there aren't any posts in the house,
we might consider lowering ourselves to—"

"Sorry, mate, no posts anywhere. Try the port."

"My good fellow, if we could just see the stew—"

"Sorry. Can't help you."

The door was closing.

"Wait!"

The door closed.

"Curse it." Fisk kicked the door. "I hope your nose
rots off!" he yelled.

I heard a chuckle on the other side of the thick

planks, but there was no other response.

Fisk swore under his breath all the way down the hill. "At least we can go to Lord Dorian now," he finished.

"No."

"What do you mean, *no*? She's locked up in that place like a payroll in a vault! She's got guards patrolling the walls! She probably never goes out without *dozens* of them. Noble Sir, we're licked. Beaten. Finished. We. Can't. Do. This. Am I being too subtle for you?"

The darkness of Fisk's hair emphasized his familiar glower.

"I admit this is a setback," I told him. "But we haven't even started yet. We should go into town and establish our identities. If we had references, the steward might agree to talk to us." And given a few more days, mayhap I could think of a better scheme than this dishonorable charade.

We rounded a bend and the keep vanished from sight—which also meant they couldn't see us. I took Fisk's arm and led him off the road.

"I want to scout the area." Sitting on the first convenient log, I pulled off my boots, removed those accursed cloth pads, and rubbed my aching shins.

"There's not much point in scouting a mark you

don't intend to rob." Fisk's expression was a weird mixture of determination and pleading. "Haven't you got it through your head? This woman is dangerous!"

"Look, all I want to do is circle around the keep." I tried to sound more confident than I felt. "There's only two guards and they're watching the killing ground, not looking into the trees. I want to see the terrain—"

"In case we have to make a run for it?" Fisk asked dryly.

I couldn't deny it. "I also want to see who comes and goes. Mayhap we can get a job delivering their supplies. Or we might think of something else, if we observe them a bit."

Fisk's gaze was steady. "Sir Michael . . . you're crazy."

I laughed. "You've only just realized that? Really, Fisk, most people figure it out the moment I introduce myself. "

His lips twitched, and I knew I had him. Smiling, I pulled my squire into the woods behind me.

Moving in a wide circle through densely wooded hills is harder than you'd think. By the time we stopped for mid-meal our boots were muddy, and we were leafy, scratched, and itchy with sweat. I hoped Fisk was enjoying himself as much as I was.

"Never more than two guards," I noted. "If those

clouds come in, a man in a dark cloak could probably make it across the open ground without being seen."

"And then camp outside the walls, waiting for the guards to come out and skewer him when the sun comes up." But Fisk looked thoughtful, despite his words. "Besides, if those clouds come in it will probably rain. Maybe even snow, if it gets any colder. That'd be wonderful, for a man wearing a dark cloak in a killing ground."

There was more conversation in the same vein. By late afternoon we'd circled two thirds of the keep, and we still hadn't any idea for getting in—much less getting the lady out.

"What's wrong with going to Lord Dorian?" Fisk grumbled behind me. "He's supposed to be the upholder of justice, so let him uphold it. That's his job."

"So it is, but . . . Lord Dorian wants to claim Cory Port," I said. "I greatly fear he may care more about that than he does about justice."

"Of course he cares about justice. His sheriffs arrested me, didn't they? I think that's a fine indica—"

Fisk was so involved in his speech that he walked into me before he realized I'd stopped moving.

"What is it?" He peered around me.

I didn't answer. The meadow stretched before us,

nearly covered with evenly spaced blood oak saplings.

"The keep's burying grove." Fisk's voice was hushed. "They had to have one . . . didn't they? Sir, what is it?"

"Look at the trees, Fisk. They're all young. All these graves have been dug within the last . . . ten years, I'd guess."

We both knew how long Lady Ceciel had lived in the keep.

Fisk took a deep breath. "She's been busy, hasn't she? Come on, she couldn't have killed that many people. There are, what, forty graves here? Someone would have complained when all their neighbors went missing. And if she killed them, wouldn't she conceal the graves?"

"Then how do you explain it? Only plague results in groves like this, with all the trees so close in size. And there's been no plague on this coast in the last ten years."

"So maybe . . ." Excitement lit Fisk's face. "Maybe she's trying to hide something else—like treasure!"

"Of all the . . . and you called me crazy! Why under two moons would she bury treasure?"

"Because she's afraid it might be taken away," said Fisk promptly. "Because it was gotten illegally."

"By being in league with pirates, like in that stupid play? That's absurd. And even if something like that *was* true, you'd hide your money where you could reach it quickly, in case you had to flee."

"It might be hard to hide treasure," said Fisk stubbornly, "in a house full of servants."

That was ridiculous. But so was assuming she could kill this many people without anyone stopping her.

"I know one way to find out," I said. "Come on. If we cut straight west we'll hit the road, and be in town by sunset." I turned toward the woods, walking off so abruptly that Fisk had to scramble to keep up.

"Why are we going to town?" he asked.

"To buy a shovel."

We had to buy a lantern as well. By late evening a blanket of clouds had indeed rolled in, bringing with them a scent of rain that foretold a storm later in the night.

Away from the torches that lit the streets 'twas very dark. The Creature Moon was almost half full, but the huge Green Moon showed only a sliver of itself, and the light that leaked through the clouds was barely enough to keep us on the road.

The woods were worse, for the thrashing branches distorted what little light there was, slowing our pace to a groping crawl. But even Fisk didn't propose we light the lantern. The guards' attention was directed to the ground around the keep, but a moving light will draw anyone's eye.

We had no fear they'd hear us; the wind whistled in the treetops, sent fallen leaves skittering over our feet like panicked mice, and altogether made enough noise that we had to stand close to hear each other, since we didn't dare to shout.

Actually we didn't have much to say. The closer we came to the burying grove, the quieter Fisk became, and I knew neither of us really expected treasure. He made no protest when, on arriving, I took up the shovel and handed him the lantern.

There were several hills between the grove and the keep, so we could light it without risk. It took several minutes to find the newest grave—so freshly dug that when I loosened the earth around the sapling and lifted it away, the soil around its roots held the shape of the bucket it had been potted in. No expensive magica to mark this grave. If what I suspected was true, 'twas strange she'd marked the grave at all.

Fisk held the light and I dug—carefully after the first few feet, for the thought of my shovel piercing . . . anything . . . sent a chill creeping up from my belly.

Not that I didn't feel chills already, for there's no spookier task than digging up a grave on a dark, windy night. Had I been alone, I don't think I could have done it.

When my shovel blade struck the yielding mass, my stomach turned over. Fisk set down the lantern to help me clear the earth from the canvas-shrouded body and heave it up beside the grave. The stench of decay reached through the wrapping, and I swallowed, bracing myself, before drawing my knife and slitting the stitches that held the shroud together.

I looked up and met Fisk's somber gaze. The lantern shone steadily, which meant his hands weren't shaking. He was doing better than I. He nodded readiness and I flipped the edges of the shroud aside. But neither of us was ready for the sight that met our eyes.

Fisk stepped back, choking. The light flashed away, but not soon enough—the image of the mutilated body was imprinted on my mind. I swallowed hard, trying to quell my nausea, listening to Fisk's harsh breathing.

"Sorry," he said. But he didn't bring the light back to the corpse for several minutes, for which I was grateful. I found I was standing several feet away from the grave, with no memory of having moved.

When Fisk turned the light back, we were both prepared. And indeed, someone had restored the body to a semblance of dignity.

'Twas a boy in his early teens, with the flatish face of a simple one. His torso, which had been slit from throat to groin, had been stitched back together, though little effort had been made to conceal the fact that his internal organs had been terribly disturbed—removed and thrown back haphazardly, from the lumpy look of his abdomen. His head had also been opened, and roughly stitched.

I was still trying not to be sick when Fisk said, "Dissected. We aren't the only ones to be curious about this boy's death."

"If that's true, then he was dead when it happened."

The fact that my squire was able to make deductions and I wasn't shamed me into looking at the corpse more dispassionately. Fisk was right—this was a healer's investigation, not a sadist's sickness. The thought calmed me somewhat.

"We'll never be able to figure out what he died of, that's for certain," I said. Even if the body hadn't been so badly mistreated, I don't think I could have touched it.

"It can't have been anything obvious." Fisk knelt and pulled the canvas back over the boy's corpse. "Or they wouldn't have needed to dissect him. Poison perhaps?"

"Or disease." My eyes wandered over the grove. Some of the graves were quite small. I shuddered. "Or even natural death. The simple ones frequently die young."

"*This* many of them?" Black fury grated in Fisk's voice, and I knew how he felt. I'd only said it because I didn't want the horror to be true. If she had killed all the poor children she'd so "charitably employed," I had to bring her in. A wave of desolation told me, for the first time, how much hope I'd clung to. That somehow she'd prove innocent, and I'd find some way to escape spending the rest of my life as Rupert's steward. Day after day of safety and sameness, as season followed season in an endless cycle until I died.

'Twas only now, as I truly faced its loss, that I realized how much I loved the life I'd led this last year. For all its discomfort and uncertainty, every morning had promised new adventure, every curve of the road new beauty, and every stranger the possibility of interest, or friendship, or even enmity. I didn't want to give it up—I *couldn't*.

"We should have thought of the simple ones." Fisk's quiet voice held a deep, hot anger I had never heard in him before. "They were the only people she could kill without anyone protesting."

Outrage burned away despair. I could never ignore this, never condone it. Even if it meant life as Rupert's steward. "We need help, Fisk. Lord Gerald. He's her liege lord. He has to act on this when we tell him."

"Are you certain? Cory Port still brings him . . ."

Fisk's gaze fixed behind me. Turning, I saw fire in the woods, four wind-whipped torches . . . coming straight toward us.

"They'll have men behind us too," I said. "That's how I'd do it."

Fisk dived for the lantern and turned it out, but the glow faded too slowly. He threw it into the grave, plunging us into darkness, and I heard the glass shatter.

"How under two moons does she always know where we are?" he howled in a whisper. "Come on!" He grabbed my arm and started for the woods, stumbling when I didn't move.

"You go. I'll hold them as long as I can."

"Are you out of your mind?"

"No. Think, Fisk! If she catches us both, she'll kill us. She has to—we've learned too much. But if you get to the authorities, she won't dare kill me. Run. Now!"

'Tis very useful to have a practical squire. A nobler man might have stayed to argue and gotten us both killed. Fisk cast one more look at the approaching torches and took off like a deer . . . well, almost. He tripped over something once, but he rolled to his feet and ran on without a second's pause.

I hoped he remembered what I'd said about men behind us, for those too-obvious torches had to be beaters, driving us into ambush. If I saw that so clearly, surely Fisk would . . . or would it be as obvious to a townsman? I wished I'd said more. I wished . . .

Four men stepped out of the woods. They looked surprised to find me waiting, but not disappointed. Their torches were set in spiked holders, and they thrust them into the ground as they advanced, drawing short clubs that reminded me of the last fight Lady Ceciel had arranged for us. Why not swords? I had no idea, but at the sight of those clubs hope flared in my heart—not of winning, not against four, but of holding them long enough to give Fisk a chance.

The flickering light concealed their faces, but I didn't have to see their faces. I was fighting for my squire, myself, and for all the poor souls whose graves lay around me, whose murder these men had willingly ignored.

I was quite ready to bash someone. I waited until they were almost upon me, raised my shovel, and charged.

CHAPTER 13

Fisk

Running like a madman through the cursed, tripping darkness, I heard Sir Michael's war cry. I tried to close my ears to the thuds, grunts, and shouts that followed, for he was right—the best way I could help him was to escape, and come back with a sheriff and a big gang of thugs.

Something, a fallen branch, a tree root, wrapped around my ankle and brought me down. This time I crashed into a tree when I fell. Lying there, stunned, with the dead leaves rattling past my face, I realized that if I continued to run around like a wounded moose, they'd be able to find me by sound alone once they'd finished with Michael. And hadn't he said something about other men? Yes. Other men behind us. That was how he'd do it.

It was possible Lady Ceciel wasn't that smart, but I wasn't prepared to bet my life on it.

Two lives, really.

I shivered and crawled into the shadow of the great tree on which I'd almost brained myself. At this point, I wouldn't bet a brass fract against Lady Ceciel. How, how, *how* did she always know where we were? The first few times I could understand it, but tonight?

I could no longer hear the fight, so either it was finished, or I'd passed out of hearing range. No matter. The only thing I could do for my stubborn employer now was to get out of here. I waited for several minutes but saw and heard nothing. Not that I could have heard anything short of a shout. With all these dry leaves, on a quiet night I wouldn't have stood a chance.

Picking out another large tree, I waited for the next patch of clouds. In the ensuing darkness I hurried forward, tripped, fell flat, and crawled the rest of the way.

I hate woods.

I spent a lot of the next ten minutes on my hands and knees. The damp forest mold was soft, but there were scores of stones and branches buried in it, and I swear I crawled over every one of them. I was crouched by a thick clump of bushes, catching my breath and rubbing a bruised palm, when a shout came from behind me.

"Ho, the woods! We got one—did you get the other?"

"What other? We haven't seen anyone."

The answering shout came from a rock a hundred yards ahead of me, and my heart leapt into my throat. I'd planned to use that rock for cover.

"What do you mean, you haven't seen him? He ran this way."

The voice was coming nearer. With fervent thanks for the rushing wind, I burrowed into the bushes. My cloak was a sober brown. Surely on a dark night, in the midst of a clump of bushes, half buried in fallen leaves, I would be invisible. . . . Of course, the branches were bare. It would depend on whether or not my pursuers looked.

The man behind the rock emerged. "What do you mean, he went this way? I told you, we haven't seen anyone."

"Curse it, you must have missed him. How could you? She said it's our jobs on the line if we let them get away!"

They were close enough now that they didn't have to shout, and I could still hear them clearly. I kept my eyes shut, not for any sensible reason, but hoping like a child that if I couldn't see them, they wouldn't see me.

"I tell you, no one passed this perimeter." I heard the footsteps of other men approaching and a rumble of agreement. "He must have circled back while you were fighting with the other one."

"Could he have been that smart?"

I wished I had been. I'd have been on the road by now, instead of cowering in a pile of leaves. I also wished that someone would say something to indicate that Michael was all right.

"If he circled around he's likely long gone, but we'd better try. Have everybody fan out and sweep toward the road."

A long pause was followed by a sigh. "I guess. But we'd better make it fast—we've got a lot of digging to do tonight. Spread out, lads. Head for the road, and keep your eyes open."

Luck is something I never trust, but I've never despised it either. The fact that they started their search on the other side of my bush was pure luck. I lay there for five minutes, listening to the search pass beyond me, breathing the scent of decaying leaves, before it hit me.

Digging. Lots of digging, and they must have twenty men. She was going to dig up the graves, remove the bodies. Remove the only evidence that would confirm my story. I had to get to a sheriff—fast.

It wasn't possible to run all the way to Cory Port, though I tried. It was probably a good thing I couldn't—my brain only seemed to function when the stitch in my side forced me to walk. It was during one of those lucid periods that I realized that in a small town like Cory Port the sheriff would be appointed by the local baron. Which might mean that the Cory Port sheriff had belonged to Sir Herbert, and hated Ceciel. Or he might not care who paid him, in which case he now belonged to the lady.

As I stumbled down the rutted track, alert for the sound of pounding hooves behind me, it also occurred to me that he might care more about justice than getting paid, but I wouldn't bet on it. A few months ago the thought would never have crossed my mind. Association with Michael was rotting my brain. I had to get away from him—as soon as I saved him. Thunder rumbled over the sea, and I rubbed my side and started running again.

I guessed it was about the sixth hour of the night when I stumbled into Cory Port, which left four hours till dawn. Most of the torches had blown out in the wind, but I found the largest inn without difficulty. The stable lad on gate duty roused after only a few shouted threats.

A sleepy groom was persuaded that he had the authority to rent me a horse, since we both knew his employer wouldn't want to be awakened *or* miss the profit if I went down the street. Quite a large profit, since I couldn't provide references or say how long I'd need it. Thank goodness I was the one who'd been carrying our purse.

The groom claimed the fidgety roan was the best horse for rent in the town. Looking at the beast, I had my doubts. But then, what did I know about horses?

As the groom saddled him for me, I brought the conversation around to the sheriff. And I did it casually enough to keep him from becoming suspicious, which isn't easy when you're trying to rent the fastest horse in town in the middle of the night. But I'm pretty good at that kind of thing. The groom was yawning when he told me that the old sheriff had been replaced, only a few weeks ago, by a new man.

Between thunderclaps, he mentioned other changes the new "lady baron" had made, such as decreasing the town's taxes if they'd agree to drop their shipping fees. I tried not to shiver, although my blood was running cold in my veins. I would get no help from the law in this town.

Uddersfield was the nearest town big enough for the sheriff to answer to both Lord Gerald and a town council. Lord Gerald might want to keep Cory Port in his hands, but Uddersfield's town council would resent another port's competition. They'd probably be delighted to order the sheriff to arrest a baron who

might lower the shipping rates . . . and they'd doubtless be outraged by the murders, too.

I would have set out for Uddersfield then, but as I
led the roan toward the stable door a peal of thunder
shook the building. Rain began to fall—a spatter of
drops that soon became a sheet, a blanket, a mattress
of rain. To set out in the dark, in a downpour, was suicide. Riding off a cliff wouldn't help Michael—not to
mention what it would do to me.

A chill that had nothing to do with the damp air settled into my guts, but there was no help for it. I bribed
the groom to let me sleep in the loft, and wake me as
soon as it was light enough to ride.

The roan had the roughest walk I've ever encountered,
but he was a steady goer so I forgave him every jarring
step. It's a four-day ride from Cory Port to Uddersfield.
I made it in three and a half, despite rain, mud, and
being forced to stop when darkness fell.

Remembering my experience with Mistress Kara, I
took the time to shave when I rose on the third
morning. Little could be done for my travel-stained
clothes, or the marks of strain and weariness on my
face, but they lent credence to my story. Besides, I
was telling the truth.

I handed the tired roan over to the sheriff's man

and climbed stiffly up the steps to the town hall. I was reporting a serious crime. I was on the same side as law and justice, no matter how strange that seemed, so of course they would help me.

Clearly, I was out of my mind—but at the time I felt nothing but exhausted relief as I approached the clerk and demanded to speak to the sheriff.

"You want us to assault Craggan Keep? Are you out of your mind?"

The sheriff was about my own height, but with an air of hard competence I'd never possess . . . though I might be able to fake it. Unfortunately his competent manner and craggy face concealed the mind of a guard dog. Lots of teeth; no imagination.

"I don't want you to assault it," I explained as patiently as I could. The impulse to pace back and forth on his carpet and rant at him was almost irresistible. "I want you to go in and demand Sir Michael's release."

"And suppose she says she hasn't got him? Then what?"

"Then arrest her!" I waved my arms wildly. "Threaten her! Search the keep! How do I know— *you're* the sheriff."

"And you want me to do all that on nothing but

your word? You've been very forthcoming, Master
Fisk, about how you and your employer have been
pursuing Lady Ceciel, but you haven't told me why."

He thought he was being subtle. Curse country gossip. I had no choice but to brazen it out.

"What do you mean, why? I told you, Sir Herbert's
brother found that Sir Herbert had been poisoned.
She—"

"I don't mean that, I mean why you? Why send a
couple of"—he searched for a sufficiently offensive
word and failed to find it—"outsiders to bring the lady
back instead of appealing to Lord Gerald through the
High Liege?" He paused again, to watch me squirm. "I
know that Sir Michael is indebted, Master Fisk. And so
are you, unless he's pronounced on you in the last—"

"He did," I lied without hesitation. "When I rescued
him from the *Albatross.*" And so he should have, the
ungrateful bastard.

Then a hideous thought crossed my mind: If Sir
Michael died without pronouncing my debt repaid,
I'd be permanently unredeemed. They'd tattoo broken circles on my wrists, and even the beggars
wouldn't have me . . . unless Sir Michael's heirs set
other terms. Sir Michael's heir was his father. I tried
to keep any trace of my reflections off my face.

I must have succeeded, for the sheriff pursed his

lips and said, "All right. Since there's no contrary evidence I'll accept your word for that, but it does your cause no good. Sir Michael Sevenson is unredeemed. If you abuse the law, then you're outside its protection until you've made restitution."

"He's in trouble *because* he's trying to make restitution," I snarled.

"Sorry." The sheriff shook his craggy head. "I have no official interest in helping Sir Michael Sevenson. On the other hand . . ."

For once, I had the sense to hold my tongue.

"This talk of graves disturbs me. Even simple ones are entitled to justice."

Another pause. My fingers began to cramp, and I unclenched my fists. Pounding his head into the desk wouldn't speed his ponderous thought process, no matter how much I wanted to do it.

"Tell you what, Master Fisk. I'll go to Lord Gerald and ask if I can take some men to look at that burying grove. Yes, I remember you said she planned to move the bodies, but I'd like to check it out. You can come with us. This may not result in a chance to free your Sir Michael—if she has him—but who knows what we'll find once we start *digging*?"

He chuckled at the awful pun and I smiled. I felt so grateful I'd have kissed his feet—smiling at bad jokes was the least I could do. But Lord Gerald wanted to keep Cory Port.

"Sir, shouldn't you bring this matter before the town council? If it concerns a rival port, surely it concerns them, too." I'd told him about the shipping fees and taxes, and this was his town. So why was he shaking his head?

"I'll certainly take it to them, but the council doesn't meet for eight days. If Lord Gerald agrees, I can notify my deputies, and we'll leave from the back courtyard at dawn tomorrow. Meet us there."

"I will, but . . . dawn, sir? It's been four days already, and you're right about the need for haste. Couldn't we—"

"Master Fisk, it's late afternoon, and I still have to meet with Lord Gerald. There's no point in riding through the night when you'd just have to rest your horses and sleep during the day. If Lord Gerald agrees, we'll be in the courtyard tomorrow at dawn. And if he doesn't, I advise you to tell Lord Dorian to go through the proper process next time!"

"But—"

"Good day, Master Fisk."

I spent the rest of the day seeking out an inn that had a stable to care for the weary roan, and was cheap enough that I could afford it. Old rough-gait had been expensive, and our purse was almost empty. *Again.* When we got out of this, I was going to have a word with my employer about our finances. When we got out of this . . .

I was almost as tired as the roan, but I woke several hours before dawn, dressed, and stole softly down the inn's creaking stair. A sleepy stableboy helped me saddle up, and I was waiting in the back courtyard of the town hall when the eastern stars first began to dim.

The black sky faded to charcoal. Steam puffed from the roan's nostrils, and I clutched my cloak around me. It was very quiet; not even the birds were awake. The only sound was a distant chiming from some tower clock.

Sir Michael had been in Lady Ceciel's hands for four days now, but, knowing I'd escaped, she would wait to see if I brought help. And she'd know it would take time. If I were in her shoes, I'd give it a month before I did anything . . . rash.

I shivered and pulled my cloak tighter. The sky paled. A rooster crowed, not too far off. Colors appeared in the hall's stained-glass windows. The sun slipped over the horizon.

It was still early. The roan fidgeted and I soothed it. The sheriff said dawn, but that could be loosely interpreted. Especially in towns. I'd spent too much time in the countryside lately; only farmers thought that dawn meant dawn, right?

I waited for another half hour before I faced the truth. Lord Gerald wanted Cory Port. He'd told his sheriff not to go. But Lord Dorian wanted Cory Port, too—he'd be happy to go to the High Liege with my tale . . . and by the time anyone did anything, Michael would probably be dead.

There was nothing I could do about it. The rising sun didn't warm me.

Nothing I could do. It was over a week's ride back to Lord Dorian's fiefdom, and he wouldn't send troops over another lord's land without the High Liege's permission. Not for an unredeemed man. And Lady Ceciel might not have played it safe. He might be dead already.

I needn't even tell Lord Dorian; why should I go to so much trouble to avenge someone who by that time would be long dead? If Lord Gerald and his sheriff didn't care about the simple ones she'd killed, why should I?

I was free. I could tell the world Sir Michael had pronounced my debt repaid. He wouldn't be around to deny it. I could ride off, and never again have to sleep in haylofts or mend chicken coops—not to mention camping out, skinning game, brawling, and *quests*. No more lunatic knights for me. What was it he'd said about debts of honor? More binding than a chain. But if he was so crazy, why did I feel invisible shackles closing around my throat?

I had to save him. It was impossible, and insane, and would probably get me killed, but I *owed* the lunatic son of a bitch. I had to save him. Somehow.

Heroism is *vastly* overrated.

CHAPTER 14

Michael

I wasn't unconscious when they took me into the keep, but I was badly bruised and stunned, so I had only vague impressions of being dragged up flights of stairs and down long hallways.

Midway down one hall, they thrust me into a small, dark room and shoved me toward a bed. A true knight errant would have sprung back into the fray the moment they released his arms. I toppled onto the bed with a whimper of relief and didn't even stir when the cold metal shackle closed around my ankle.

I don't know what woke me—I didn't hear a thing. When my memory returned, I muttered a curse and opened one eye—the other was swollen shut. Someone had lit a lamp, and I could see the stone wall that the bed rested against. No paneling. No window. Rolling over, carefully, I learned that the room was about ten feet square and, besides the bed I lay on, held a chamber pot, a small table with a lamp on it . . . and Lady Ceciel, who leaned against the wall by the door, watching me.

I sat up hastily, and a sickening throb all but tore my skull apart. I moaned and sank back to the bed, eyes closed.

If she came near to tend my hurts I could use her as a hostage—assuming I could sit up and grab her. But she stayed where she was. I rolled slowly onto my side, the chain attached to my ankle rattling, opened my good eye, and gazed at her.

It was still night, for she wore a bed robe and slippers, and her hair was braided down her back. She should have looked childlike and innocent, but no child ever wore such a complex expression—amusement mixed with cold fascination. Thunder rumbled in the distance.

A smile that held no warmth touched her lips. "Well, Sir Michael. Are you going to arrest me?"

If I'd had any hope she didn't know what Fisk and I were doing, it would have died right there. But I'd never entertained much hope on that score.

"Consider yourself arrested," I said wearily. "You *will* be, you know, by Lord Gerald or Lord Dorian or someone. You can't get away with murder."

"I didn't kill Herbert." She said it absently, gazing at me with dispassionate interest. "You have the magic-sensing Gift, don't you?"

"What does that matter? Your own sister found the poison—how can you deny it?"

She smiled. "Poor Agnes. She had quite a crisis of conscience. I heard about your fight with Peter, too. You've had a rough time of it, you and your . . . squire."

I don't usually mind being laughed at, but this time I did.

"My squire has gone to the authorities," I told her. "You'll answer for your crimes as soon as . . . ah, Fisk did escape, didn't he?"

The change of tone must have been ludicrous, but this time she didn't laugh. There was a moment of silence while we both sought a reason for her to lie to me, and couldn't find one.

"Yes," she said finally. "The dolts haven't laid hands on him yet, so I think he's gotten clean away."

"Then 'tis over. As soon as Fisk tells the authorities what we found, they'll come for you. You might as well give up now." And not hurt me. I hoped she under-stood that implication. Thunder rolled again.

"Ah, but that depends on which authority he goes to." Her lips were twitching, curse her. If she con-trolled the local sheriff . . . No, Fisk would think of that. Fisk was so cynical, it would never cross his mind that the local sheriff might be honest.

So he'd have to go farther for help, which would take him longer . . . which might give them time to capture him. Could I convince them he'd walk right into the local sheriff's hands? *Try*.

"You mean the local sheriff is your man?" 'Twas far too easy to sound frightened. I bit my lip and sat up.

"Yes, but I'm not counting entirely on him. Your Fisk doesn't strike me as a fool. And he didn't strike Hackle as one, either. We'll wait and see what he does."

So much for deceiving Lady Ceciel. Her voice sent a shudder down my spine.

"You don't dare kill me as long as Fisk is free." Now I struggled to keep the fear *out* of my voice. "They'll know you have me. If I die, they'll know you did it."

"So? If I killed my husband, I'm dead anyway. They can only hang me once."

I found myself with nothing to say.

Lady Ceciel's expression changed. "You mean it, don't you? You really intend to see me hang."

"I'm not your judicar." I folded my arms to keep myself from shaking. "If there were extenuating circumstances . . . I don't know. There would be none for killing me."

"Not even the fact that you're trying to get me

hanged? Oh don't look so frightened. I'm not going to kill you—not for a long time. I have something else in mind."

Something else? I had no chance to ask, for she turned and went out, closing the door behind her. I wrapped a blanket around myself, but I was still shivering long after she'd gone.

Eventually my fear wore off, and I began to feel foolish, so I unfolded myself and investigated the room. It wasn't promising. In addition to having no windows, the floor and walls were of stone, and the heavy beams and planks of the ceiling looked every bit as impregnable as the floor.

Standing up, I examined the furniture. The table was crude and heavy—too heavy to pick up and swing, too solid to break apart. The lamp was a cheap one, of tin and thick glass, too flimsy to do more than irritate anyone you threw it at. The chamber pot was lightweight tin as well.

I'd been trying to ignore the shackle, but now I sat and looked at it. 'Twas iron, of depressingly good workmanship; the only way out was to pick the lock, a skill I'd never learned. I bet Fisk knew how. If . . . *when* I got out of this, I'd have him teach me.

The chain could have stopped a charging bull, much

less me, and the other end was attached to an iron ring that circled one of the bed frame's horizontal bars. The bed frame was even sturdier than the table, its joints pinned together with tight-set wooden pegs. I might have pounded the pegs out, if I'd had any tools.

The mattress was canvas, stuffed with wool, and the slats beneath it were the best weapon I found, thin enough that I could break them out of their frame, but still heavy enough to stun someone. Only it didn't matter how many people I stunned, because I was chained to the bed frame, and even if I could maneuver it out the door . . .

A sudden vision of me running through the keep with the bed frame dragging behind me made me smile. It felt good, despite my bruised face, and 'twas still lingering when the bolt clicked and the door swung open.

I spun, my heart thumping—which was silly, since Lady Ceciel had said she didn't intend to kill me for a long time.

A girl stood in the doorway. She looked to be about fifteen, big for her age, with a round face and curly, reddish hair. Her jaw dropped slightly at the sight of the room, and the tray in her hands sagged. This made me nervous, for the water, cloths, and especially the pot of salve, were something I'd prefer to see used on me rather than the floor.

"Oh." Her voice was breathless and childlike. "You've messed up the bed."

I saw no reason to apologize.

Her eyes wandered from the bed to me and she frowned. "You're messed up too."

She was one of the simple ones. "That's all right," I told her gently. "You're here to help me, aren't you?"

"Aye, and like to take all day at it. Get in, girl, do."

Hackle pushed the girl through the door. He glowered at the ravaged bed, but made no comment. I glared at him, despite the fact that he carried a water jug and a basket that almost certainly held food. The girl might have been persuaded to bring me the shackle key, but there was no way to corrupt Hackle.

He lingered by the door, as Lady Ceciel had. The chain wasn't long enough to reach him unless I dragged the bed across the room.

He wasn't inclined to chat, so I focused on the girl instead. Her name was Janny, she'd been with the lady three years now, and she was willing to let me tend my own hurts while she fixed the bed. She'd probably be willing to do anything anyone suggested, including bringing me a saw. That would be why Hackle was there.

I mopped the blood off my face, with Janny telling me when I missed a spot.

The humming energy of magic that touched my

senses when I picked up the salve gave me further hope—you don't waste magica on someone you plan to kill. 'Twas easy to rub the salve into the right places, for my tender nerves told me where I needed it. The pain was already fading as I smoothed a second coat over my swollen eye.

Janny picked up the tray to depart. "You'll be better soon. The lady's potions work fine. She's so smart. She—" An enthusiastic gesture slopped water onto the floor. "Oops."

She frowned at the damp patch, unsure how to clean it with the tray in her hands. I was about to take the tray, but she solved the dilemma herself.

She stared at the spill and once more I felt the buzz of magic along my nerves, in the exposed skin of my face and hands—but this was different from anything I'd felt before—strong, focused. Not existing passively, as it did in plants, or exercised instinctively, as animals will, but magic being generated . . . deliberately.

The small puddle evaporated, shrinking in on itself until the floor was dry. *Human* magic. It seemed so unnatural that I took an involuntary step backward, sitting abruptly when my knees hit the bed.

Janny gave me a sunny smile and departed—her job well done. Hackle's smile was tinged with malice. To my disgust, I found that I was shaking again.

〈〉 〈〉 〈〉

Three days dragged past. My captors weren't unkind—with the next meal they brought me a selection of books: a ballad cycle, an account of some explorer's adventures in the southern deserts, and a treatise on astronomy.

I chose the explorer's story, though my suspicion that it would prove as fantastical as the ballads proved correct. I might have believed in the strange animals he described—I hadn't been there, after all. Even the bizarre customs of the savages weren't beyond the realm of possibility. But no one was as courageous and resourceful as the explorer made himself out to be.

In a real adventure, things went wrong. In a real adventure, you couldn't escape from a simple stone room and a shackle in a civilized keep full of servants, and had to sit there tamely waiting for your *squire* to rescue you. In a real adventure fear rapidly gave way to boredom, and you found boredom could wear away your resolve faster than fear. Father would be horribly embarrassed to have a son who couldn't get out of an ordinary cell.

Hackle always accompanied Janny, who brought my food and emptied the chamber pot. At mid-meal on the third day I asked, politely, to speak with Lady Ceciel.

She arrived about an hour later. She'd obviously been working in an herbarium, for her big apron was marked with soil and sap, and her hands were stained green. Smudges on her face showed that she'd pushed trailing wisps of hair out of her eyes, and the scent of bruised plants encircled her like perfume.

"What do you want, Sir Michael? I'm very busy."

"I want to put a stop to this nonsense," I told her. "You can't keep me prisoner forever—Fisk knows where I am. 'Tis . . . 'tis ridiculous! You have nothing to gain by it and a great deal to lose. Let me go."

She leaned against the doorsill and folded her arms.

"Oh, I don't know. While you're here, I don't have to worry that you're plotting to ambush me and haul me off to a hanging. I've been investigating, Sir Michael; I know the terms of your repayment. No wonder you've been such a pest."

Hot blood rose to my face, but a question surfaced as well.

"How did you always know where we were? Not the time you had us cudgel-crewed—Hackle's brother must have warned you. But at first, when you set the boar after us outside Willowere. There wasn't time for Mistress Agnes to contact you."

"Oh, that was Hackle's doing. I'd sent him to tell Aggie I was safely home, and he got there shortly after you and Fisk left. He hoped it would discourage you, but it didn't work."

"If you know the terms of my repayment, you should understand that." I began to pace, ignoring the jingle of the chain. "But what about this last time, in the burying grove? How did you know we were there?"

She laughed. "You won't like it."

"Tell me anyway," I said gloomily.

"It was sheer luck. One of my maids sneaked out to meet a lover. She passed by the grove, saw your light, and reported it. So I sent out the guards."

Sheer luck. Outrage welled through me, and I sought for some witty, cutting comment. I didn't find one. "Fisk will hate that." I sank onto the bed, kicking the chain out of my way.

She laughed again. "We've also learned a lot about Master Fisk. You seem very sure he's going to return with the authorities."

"Of course. Unless . . . You haven't caught him, have you?"

She paused a moment, drawing out my suspense, but she answered honestly, "No. He bypassed my sheriff entirely and set out toward the south. I've sent men after him, but they haven't returned."

"They wouldn't have, if he's . . ." I broke off, aghast at my uncontrolled tongue. 'Twas probably the result of having no one but Janny and Hackle to talk to.

"If he's headed for Uddersfield," she finished calmly. "But what makes you certain he'll go to the authorities at all? A criminal, a con artist. And indebted. What's to stop him from running off now that he's free of you?"

"Fisk wouldn't do that." As I spoke the words, I realized that I believed it. "He's a better man than you think. He'll come back with the authorities, and then . . . Lady Ceciel, this is absurd. Let me go now, before the law enforces it."

"Ah, but the law won't protect you, Sir Michael. Have you forgotten? I can do anything I like with an indebted man." She waited for me to reply. When I said nothing, she smiled and went out.

I was so accustomed to the idea that the High Liege's law protected all his subjects that I had forgotten I was now outside it. How stupid of me. And how stupid of Father to have done this to me. Thank goodness Fisk wasn't stupid. He would appeal to the authorities on behalf of the simple ones, and Sir Herbert. When they arrested Lady Ceciel for those crimes, I'd be set free.

I have no doubt of him, I reminded myself. The man who'd helped an old drunk up the steps at his own sentencing would never abandon me. Being indebted made him uncomfortable, but I had sensed the beginnings of friendship between us. Fisk might be a con artist, but he wasn't that clever a liar. Still . . .

I found myself gazing at the joint at the bottom of the bed frame that held the shackle hoop. As solid as it was, 'twas made of wood. Wood can be ground or sanded away. And at the joint two pieces were pegged together . . . with a *wooden* peg.

After some thought I lay down on the floor, braced my hands against the head post, and kicked the bottom of the foot post twenty times. It didn't seem to have any effect. Then I lay on the bed and kicked the top of the post, twenty times. I rolled back onto the floor, the chain jingling.

'Twas better than reading.

More days dragged past. I worked at breaking the bed frame apart but made little progress, and Janny was replaced by a simple boy, several years younger than she, who said very little.

On the sixth day of my captivity they brought me water for bathing, clean clothes, and a razor to shave my growing beard. Hackle drew his sword and watched me intently every minute I held it. A three-inch razor against a three-foot sword. I didn't try anything.

The eighth day of my captivity was the first day it would have been possible for Fisk to return. Barely possible, if he'd had perfect traveling weather and a fast horse, and if the sheriff of Uddersfield had agreed to set out instantly. I told myself not to be foolish, and worked harder on the bed frame.

On the ninth day the bed post was beginning to shift in its socket, so I propped the other three legs on books, lay on the edge of the mattress, and tried wiggling the post with both feet. It did seem to shift, but the position was so uncomfortable I couldn't keep it up for long.

Every time the door opened my heart leapt. In a real adventure things go wrong. I told myself I couldn't expect Fisk for at least twelve days. Four days to reach Uddersfield, two to get the authorities in motion, four days back, and another two to allow for the unforeseen.

So I was taken by surprise, on the evening of the tenth day, when Hackle told me, "Our men came back."

"What? The men you sent after Fisk? When?"

The serving boy stared at me, unaccustomed to such vehemence. Hackle's expression was dour, but something under it looked uncomfortably like compassion.

"Are you going to tell me?" I asked.

"It took 'em a few days to find him. Your man, Fisk, went to the sheriff at Uddersfield, and the sheriff went to Lord Gerald. The lady's had some dealings with him, you know."

"We'd guessed she might." I spoke calmly, but my stomach was beginning to twist.

"Anyway, they knew you were indebted so they refused him. Then Master Fisk sent his horse back to the stable he rented it from—by renting it to someone else, the thrifty rogue—and set off walking east. They didn't wait to learn more."

My heart was pounding. I wrapped my arms around my stomach to quell the rising sickness. It didn't mean he'd given up, I told myself firmly. He'd gone to Lord Gerald's sheriff and been refused, so he'd decided to try elsewhere. He'd . . . He'd rented his horse. It would have taken several days to find a rider going to Cory Port. He must have felt he had all the time in the world. *He'd given up.*

I swallowed hard. He'd tried. He'd gone to Lord Gerald's sheriff. He'd try another! Lord Leopold's fiefdom was to the east, and he had no stake in who owned Cory Port, so Fisk had decided to go there . . . on foot? He'd given up!

The boy was staring at me, eyes wide in wonder. I didn't want to be stared at.

"What happened to Janny?" The roughness of my voice surprised me.

"Ah, she died, poor girl," Hackle said absently. "Pick up the tray, lad. I don't think he wants dinner tonight."

He was right. I lay on the bed, gazing at the ceiling. The lamp was low, but I never turned it out completely since I had no way to relight it.

Janny was dead. The fact that Fisk had abandoned me suddenly seemed less important. She'd been simple, but she'd also been kind, sweet-natured, and alive. She had a right to all the life she could get, short as it was bound to be. I had to do something. I was deluding myself trying to break the bedpost—even if I freed the chain, there was a bolted door and a keep full of guards between me and freedom. But Lady Ceciel was deluding herself, too. If she was going to kill me she'd have done it immediately, or when she learned Fisk had failed. She couldn't keep me here forever. I had to get out, go to Lord Dorian, go to the High Liege if necessary, and get some protection for those children. Janny was dead.

Next morning when they brought my breakfast, I told them I had a proposal to offer Lady Ceciel.

She came almost immediately, and she was excited about something; there was color in her cheeks, and she fidgeted from foot to foot in the safety of the doorway. I hated her, but I had to conceal it. I had to get out of there. 'Twas too late for Janny, but the others might still be saved.

I took a deep breath, trying to keep the anger out of my voice. "You've heard that Fisk failed with Lord Gerald's sheriff."

"Frankly I was amazed that he tried—I mean, a man with his past."

I ignored the pain of betrayal. "He does seem to have given up, which . . . well, it leaves me in an awkward position."

Her lips twitched. "Yes, I can see you might find it . . . awkward."

I hated her. I lowered my eyes to keep her from seeing it. "I can't arrest you. Fisk isn't going to bring the authorities. So . . . so I give up. I'm not going to try to take you back, Lady Ceciel."

I thought I was lying rather well, but when I raised my eyes her smile was sardonic.

"So I'm supposed to let you go?"

"What else can you do? You can't keep me here forever. And I don't believe you'd kill me." That was true—although I didn't know why.

An expression that was almost shame crossed her face, but then the excitement returned.

"You're right, Sir Michael, I'm not going to kill you. I'm going to give you an opportunity beyond any man's dreams." She stepped forward and leaned over the table, bathed in the lamplight, her eyes intent, like a peddler making a sale. "How would you like to be the first intelligent human to work magic?""

"Not in the least," I said. "Not that it matters. No humans except . . ."

The monstrous concept swarmed into my mind and stretched, leering evilly. She waited, watching, while I figured it out.

"That's what you're doing." My voice emerged in a whisper. "You're *experimenting* on them. You're trying to make it possible for humans—normal humans—to work . . ."

"Magic." She smiled. "The power the gods gave us, and then took back. But I don't think it's a god power. I think it's something alchemical, and genetic, like the sensing Gift."

"That's how you killed them, dosing them with your potions. That's how you killed Sir Herbert. You needed a normal person to . . . to . . ."

Her face changed again. "How I *killed* them? You think I'd hurt those children?" She stamped her foot. I hadn't thought anyone did that, outside of ballads.

"How dare you think I'd harm those poor creatures? I *help* them. I take them in, mostly starving, some of them beaten, all unwanted, all abandoned. I feed and clothe them, and teach them to work at what they can. They're *willing* to help me. And yes, I dose them. And I've increased their powers!"

She leaned forward, selling again. "Hackle thinks it's only because I encourage them to work their small magics—growing plants, removing stains, kindling fires—instead of punishing them. But he's wrong. I've made their magic stronger, and it will work on an intelligent person, too. I'm *sure* it will. I may not have the sensing Gift, but I trained with my sister. I know everything she does about medicine and anatomy, and I haven't killed *one* of those children. In fact, I've kept some of them alive longer, although I can't save them forever.

"And if I can give the world magic . . . think of it! Think what a healer like Aggie could do with magic, healing broken bones and wounded flesh directly instead of through herbs. Think of a judicar who would know if a witness spoke the truth! Of what farmers and craftsmen could do to improve their work, their lives!"

Or what a criminal like Fisk might do.

"I might believe you," I said, "if you hadn't killed your husband."

Her back straightened. Her mouth set, bitterly. "Think what you will, Sir Righteous. It doesn't matter. You're unredeemed. I can do anything I want with you."

"I won't take your potions."

"Yes you will." There was no doubt in her voice—

only a flicker of pity, more terrifying than any diatribe. She turned and went out, leaving the door open. I wasted several seconds staring at it before my mind woke up. She'd be back in a moment! I spun and kicked the bedpost as hard as I could.

'Twas solid as a rock, and I almost broke my heel. That's what it felt like, anyway. I was sitting on the bed, clutching my foot and swearing, when Lady Ceciel returned.

The object she laid on the table was a funnel carved from cherrywood, hard and smooth grained, the narrow end oddly curved. 'Twas designed to be pushed into someone's throat, and my own knotted so tightly I couldn't speak. The thought of having that thing forced down my gullet was so revolting, I almost decided to take her cursed potions rather than submit to it.

There were teeth marks in the wood.

I had to swallow several times before I could speak. "It seems not all your victims are willing."

Her face went scarlet from collar to hairline. "The potion sometimes makes them sick. Cramps, nausea. It's a small price to pay for magic, but they don't understand. I know what I'm doing. It's safe. I swear it."

"If you know 'tis safe, why don't *you* take the potion?"

"Because one of the ingredients is argot." The color in her face was fading. "No woman who might be pregnant should take it, and in magica form, no woman who might still bear children should ever take it. I'm looking for a substitute, but argot has—"

"And if I die, you'll just dissect me to find out what went wrong and try again?"

"It might be hard to find another subject. Normal folk don't line up to volunteer for this." A smile touched her lips. "And I don't often capture indebted men who are trying to kill me. But I won't kill *you*, Sir Michael. In a few days I'll be ready. I'll give you a Gift beyond imagining. And then you'll understand."

She left, bolting the door and taking the funnel with her. Her workroom must be nearby for her to have fetched it so quickly. I wished she'd left the sickening thing so I could smash it. If I got out of this, I'd have to apologize to Father. He was right—there were worse things than being Rupert's steward.

I lay down on the edge of the bed, braced both feet against the post, and worked it back and forth, trying to ignore the way my stomach quivered. The thought that she might succeed horrified me—but it wasn't likely. Even her loyal Hackle didn't believe she'd increased the simple ones' magic. How could he condone what she was doing? Be a part of it? And Sir

Herbert must have condoned it, too; it had obviously been going on for years before his death. Had he agreed to take the potions? Was that why she claimed she hadn't killed him?

But how could she be so sure it wouldn't kill me? Truth be told, I was more afraid that she'd succeed than I was of dying.

She wouldn't succeed. Magic and intelligence couldn't exist together. I was sure of it. But then, I'd been sure of Fisk, too.

'Twas not easy to work the post while crying with fear, but I managed.

CHAPTER 15

Fisk

It took me nine cursed days to get back to Cory Port—almost a day just to get out of Uddersfield. I had to get rid of the roan. I could imagine nothing more conspicuous than riding into town, in a new identity, on a horse that half the town probably knew, and which might have been reported stolen. I found a mark going north, and charged him almost as much as I'd paid for the beast.

I also took the time to write four letters. The first two, almost identical, went to Sir Michael's father and Lord Dorian, describing what we'd found, what had happened to Sir Michael, and my plan to get him out. I sent them east with a traveling bookseller, who was known to be a reliable mail carrier. By the time they reached their destination it would all be over, but if I failed, I wanted someone to know where *I* was, in case they felt like mixing a little rescue with their vengeance.

The third letter went to the town council of Uddersfield, and it focused less on Sir Michael and myself (though I certainly mentioned us) than Lady Ceciel's plan to lower Cory Port's harbor fees. Would they allow a multiple murderess to plot with the local lord to steal funds that should rightly go to their fine town? Knowing town councils, it would take them several weeks to decide what to do—but they might get moving before Lord Dorian, who would have to go to the High Liege.

The fourth letter went to Willard's wife, telling her what had happened, and that he intended to make his way home to her—after all, I had promised.

I finally set out from Uddersfield on foot. I know of no better way to discover whether someone is following you than to move so slowly they overrun you. Not to mention the fact that I'd need every roundel in my purse.

I slept in a barn without the farmer's knowledge, which saved half an hour's haggling and a few coins— and curse what Sir Michael would think of it.

Arriving in Kempton, I sought out an herbalist. A decent woman, she flatly refused to fill my order until I told her the whole story of why I wanted it . . . and she still had qualms.

She soothed them by charging me the most outrageous sum you ever heard of. (She was a decent woman, not a stupid one.) I spent the next few days hanging around her workroom, learning how to sound like an herbalist—the patter, the catchphrases, and just enough knowledge to fool a layman. I might have to fool an expert, but that's actually easier. With a layman, you have to know more than they do—with an expert all you have to do is ask knowledgeable-sounding questions, show interest in their answer, and then make comments like "So you have no reservations about any part of this process?" Experts are easy.

I spent the evenings working my deck-cutting scam, with less restraint than usual. I drew some sullen looks from the losers, but no one beat me up. Fortunately I was leaving town soon.

The last thing I bought before leaving Kempton was a bottle of bleach. That night the walnut stain washed out, and over the next few days my hair became lighter and lighter. I didn't think the guard I'd bribed would recall the dark-haired servant he'd turned away, but the dark-haired man who'd rented the roan in the middle of the night was more memorable.

I worked my way north on the back roads—not quite as fast as the main one, but they let me pick up some new clothes that were both shabby and flamboyant, a small cart with a donkey to pull it, a handful of ribbons, a few jugs of lilac water brewed by an old countrywoman, and finally a sign proclaiming my new name and profession:

MASTER MARION GELANTRY, RESTORER OF YOUTH, BEAUTY, AND ROMANCE TO WOMEN WHOSE FACES NO LONGER REFLECT THE EXQUISITE SPIRIT WITHIN.

In short, I was selling wrinkle cream.

I rolled into Cory Port and set up for business in front of an inn of the better sort. They sent a couple of muscular grooms to suggest I leave, which I did. I drifted down the social scale, ending on a corner between a high-class brothel and a wheelwright's shop. The wheelwrights were amused by the show, and some of the girls bought cream—or I traded it to them, increasing my stock of fripperies. Then the lady of the house came out and shooed the girls away—much to the disappointment of the wheelwrights. She was about to shoo me away too, so I made my first real play—I sold her a vial of the real cream, the special cream, the one that worked, the one that was . . . magica.

Mistress Lucille knew the worth of magica skin cream—high-class prostitutes are the only kind who both need it and can pay for it. Magica skin cream really will take ten years off a woman's apparent age . . . as long as she continues to use it. The effect wears off after about four days and the sudden return of all those wrinkles has a horrible effect on a woman's self-esteem. But many women—and men—can't resist looking so much younger, if only for a few days, weeks, as much as they can afford, and often more.

Mistress Lucille wasn't sufficiently high class to buy much. She'd heard of magica skin cream, but she'd never expected to see it in this backwater port. I sold her a very small vial at cost, for the privilege of leaving my cart where it was and sleeping in her garden shed.

I was afraid she'd try to save it for a special occasion, but she didn't. Over the next few days she looked younger and younger, and the news spread like wildfire.

I sold small pots to the richer townswomen, sorrow-fully displaying my rapidly depleting stock. My prices started at outrageous and went up. Husbands began to eye me askance. The new sheriff's wife was one of my customers.

Generally this was the point at which I'd have abandoned my donkey and cart and sneaked out of town with a nice fat purse—but this time, I had other plans. I began to mention, with great outward regret and some inward trepidation, that I couldn't possibly sell the formula, not for any price. The next day, a couple of guards arrived to escort me to Craggan Keep.

The guards had been told to bring "my wares" with them, and since they weren't sure what Lady Ceciel wanted, we took the donkey cart and the donkey, too. They let me drive up to the keep, but they watched closely to be sure I didn't make a break for it.

Under ordinary circumstances (had I been fool enough to let matters reach this stage), I'd have been looking for a chance to escape. As it was, I congratulated myself—my plan was working. So why did I feel like I was climbing the platform steps to be sentenced? Michael had saved me from that and I was going to return the favor . . . if he lived.

I turned a bright smile on the guardsman to my left and commented on the beauty of the day. He sneered at me.

As we rode through the killing ground, I wondered again why she'd bothered to clear it. No keep could hold against a determined assault. . . . But she could hold out until help came from Lord Gerald, whose troops were quartered outside Uddersfield. I quelled a shiver. If Lord Gerald was that deep in her confidence, I'd been lucky to get out of Uddersfield alive.

This time the great doors opened, and we clattered onto the cobbles of the courtyard. The keep was square, with round towers at each corner, and glass gleamed in what used to be shuttered arrow slits. The guard's shout for the stableboys echoed off the stone. Could Michael hear it? Was he even here? He had been in her hands for thirteen days.

She wouldn't do anything rash, I assured myself. Not until she knew it was safe, and she couldn't be sure of that yet. Surely.

The patrol leader gathered up one vial of each product, a handful of ribbons, and all the tawdry jewelry. Then he and two of his cohorts marched me up the steps and into the keep.

It was the same vintage as Sir Bertram's—Sir Herbert must have felt right at home. The bright, late-afternoon light did little to alleviate the gloom of the local gray granite and age-darkened wood. The banners that hung from the rafters were faded. We were climbing the steps to the gallery when I noticed large dark patches on the walls. Of course! She'd sold the tapestries. I had a fanciful notion that the keep missed them.

We traveled almost a hundred feet down the main hall to reach the stairs to the third floor—good architecture for defense. I was glad I planned to burgle the place rather than assault it. On the third floor they led me toward one of the corner towers. The burnt green smell of brewing herbs grew quite strong.

When the guard announced us the lady waited a moment before looking up, her attention fixed on a kettle sitting over a small firepot. She wrapped her apron around her hand and whisked the kettle off the flame and onto a trivet to cool. She looked tired, older than I remembered, but somewhere in the preoccupied face was a deep flame of . . . excitement? Passion? I had no time to pin it down—the need to act, to be the person I claimed I was, swept the thought to the back of my mind, where it wouldn't trouble my performance.

I stepped forward and bowed, with a flourish. "Gentle lady, what a finely appointed workplace! We shall pass pleasant hours discussing our common craft, for I am Marion Gelantry, wholly at your service."

Her lips twitched. My fake noble accent has that effect on those who are familiar with real nobles. Mind you, I can do a good noble accent too—these past weeks in Michael's company had helped me perfect it. For now, I put on a disdainful face but let my nervousness show through.

"An herbalist are you, Master Gelantry?"

"Of a sort, fair lady. I specialize in the preparation of beauty enhancements for women less lovely than yourself."

She snorted and motioned for the guard to lay his booty on her worktable, where she cleared a space for it. Every flat surface in the room was covered with herbal concoctions in some stage of preparation. The work looked orderly, but the room showed small, telltale signs of being overused: soot stains on the walls above the bracketed lamps, a pile of broken crockery in a corner bin, the number of empty and near-empty jars in the wall racks—all told of many hours working on . . . what? No way to know, unless she could be induced to tell me.

"Lady, may I inquire what aspect of the craft you are currently embracing?"

"No." She uncapped a jar of wrinkle cream and rubbed it between her fingers. "Magica?" I remembered that she had no sensing Gift.

"Tragically, lady, 'tis not. I have sold all my magica cream, and you know how difficult and time-consuming it is to create. Why, 'tis a wonder I sell it at *any* price!"

She smiled. "I do know, and it's actually quite easy. The reason . . . This is good!" She had just sniffed the old countrywoman's lilac water.

"Made with the freshest of dew-wet lilacs, to adorn the fairest of the fair. I will gladly offer you that bottle as a tribute to your beauty."

I smiled winningly, but she wasn't buying. She capped the bottle.

"As I was about to say, the reason most herbalists don't make it isn't because it's hard, but because it wastes magica that could be used in medicines. All it produces is an illusion that does nothing but harm in the long run. And we also don't make it because it's too much temptation in the hands of clever con men, Master Gelantry."

"My lady, you wound me! I protest! I—"

"That being the case, give me one good reason I shouldn't turn you over to the sheriff."

If she wanted the sheriff to handle it, she wouldn't have bothered to interview me. *I hoped.* "Mayhap 'cause I haven't broken any law." I let my accent start to fracture, as if my composure was dissolving. "There's nothing says, to say, that you can't sell magica beauty cream. I'm not a con artist, long as I don't lie about the effects, and I didn't. You won't find one woman in town sayin' I didn't warn 'er it'd wear off after three or four days. 'Cause I did. I know the law."

My accent was pure city gutterling now, and her lips twitched again.

"But you're also talking about selling the formula for your magica beauty cream. I'd like to see this formula, Master Gelantry, to be sure it's as real as your product."

I licked my lips nervously and glared at her. In the back of my mind I was still me, but in my heart I was a third-rate connie, defending himself against a wealthy lady with nothing but wit and guts. "I never said any such thing! I told 'em I *couldn't* sell 'em the formula for any price! You can't arrest me for that, and you know it, lady."

Her eyes narrowed. The silence lengthened.

"You're right," she said finally. "You've broken no law."

I'd been careful not to.

"But I'm not just the lady of this keep, I'm the baron."

I tried to look appropriately surprised and alarmed. It was hard, because my heart was pounding with hope—my plan seemed to be working, for a change. Surely any baron would banish a troublemaker like me.

"It's my duty to protect my people. I have duties to Lord Gerald and my neighbors."

So my men will escort you to the border tomorrow. Come on, lady, say it.

"So I order you to leave Lord Gerald's fiefdom as soon as may be. If you aren't off his lands in two full days, well, I'm sure we can find something to arrest you for. Loitering, trespass, disrespect to authority . . . Benno, throw him out."

"What? I mean, lady, have mercy!"

"I am being merciful." She frowned. She *was* being merciful; that was the problem. If she threw me out now, instead of ordering her guards to escort me off Lord Gerald's land in the morning . . .

"But . . . but it's almost dark! S'pose I meet up with bandits? That cart's all I got!"

"That cart, and the money you made over the last few days," she said dryly.

"But the money's in my cart!"

"Don't worry, there are no bandits in the area. You and your cart will be quite safe." She laid her wrist on a clay pot to judge its temperature and frowned thoughtfully. The guard grabbed my arm. I was losing her.

"Lady, wait, I . . . I haven't told you everything."

That got her attention. The guard stopped pulling at me.

"I . . . I made some enemies the last few days. I've been honest, but the price . . . some of the women . . . ah, curse it!" The nervous sweat on my face arose from a different fear, but she had no way of knowing that. I fed that fear into my voice as I went on, "Lady, let me stay here till morning. I could sleep in the kitchen. I'll give you five bottles of that lilac water you liked, if you just let me stay the night. Please, lady . . . ten bottles?"

"All right." Her eyes fell to the vial of lilac water. "If nothing else, it will get you out of here. You can sleep in the stable with your cart. Benno, put a guard on the stable door. We don't want Master Gelantry's 'enemies' to sneak in."

The guard chuckled. I tried to look insulted, but the

relief broke through. "Thanks, lady. Though you got a bargain. That's the best lilac water this side of Crown City, and—"

She snorted, and gestured for the guard to lead me out. I went to the stables peacefully, my hands shaking with the narrowness of my escape. I'd been prepared to be locked in a dungeon cell, waiting for morning to be thrown off Lord Gerald's land. I'd even thought they might take me to the sheriff . . . *in the morning.* Who'd have thought the murderous bitch would be merciful? It didn't matter. I'd be inside the wall tonight, and that was all I needed. That, and a way to find Sir Michael, get him out, and delay pursuit until we were safely away.

But I was inside. My plan had worked.

In the stables I encountered Chanticleer and Tipple, comfortably housed in two big stalls. I didn't stop to chat with them, for fear they'd give me away. I had a bad moment when Chanticleer poked his big head over the stall door and huffed at me, but he didn't neigh, and no one heeded it.

The grooms pointed to a corner by the tack room, where they'd put my donkey cart, and told me to stay out of the way. But after a while I got up and wandered down the long row of stalls, stroking horses' noses, and apologizing for not having any treats. I wanted the horses to become accustomed to me, so they wouldn't get nervous when I roamed about tonight.

Chanticleer and Tipple came to me eagerly, but they acted more bored than abused. Their coats gleamed, and they'd put on a few pounds—actually, they looked better than they had when we were caring for them. I accused them of getting fat and soft while their masters worked, and they snorted.

When we left it would be on these horses, for I knew Sir Michael would refuse to leave them. And it would be all but impossible to get two horses out of the keep. I didn't know how to get Michael out—or me, for that matter. I decided not to tell Michael I'd found them . . . assuming I could find him. Assuming he was alive.

The grooms took me into the kitchen to eat dinner with the staff. It was one of those cavernous rooms with a fireplace you could roast a whole cow in, but I was more interested in the door. It opened with a simple lever and latch, but there was a thick bolt in the center. I could slide a sharp probe past the door and work the bolt back, but that would take time, and the kitchen door was clearly visible from the outer wall where the guards patrolled. As was the front door, which was probably even more secure. I doubted there would be other doors in a keep this old—every door was a place they'd have to defend if the wall was breached.

The staff was large for a keep this size, maybe thirty servants. The guards ate elsewhere. I noticed that about a quarter of the servants were simple ones, and the memory of the corpse in the burying grove promptly cost me my appetite. Lady Ceciel was dangerous. I mustn't forget that. Ever.

I flirted with several maids and sold three bottles of beauty cream. I thought about trying to bribe someone to leave the kitchen door open, but I didn't dare.

Back in the stables, I pulled the donkey cart into a stall and prepared for the job, which mostly consisted of removing everything that could either jingle or catch the light. I was already carrying all my lock picks, and a few other useful items. The only thing that presented any difficulty was money. I pulled my purse from beneath the seat of the donkey cart—the closest thing to a hiding place I had—and shook it. It was fat as a pregnant sow, and undoubtedly jingled. I'd done rather well these last few days. I sighed, extracted a handful of gold roundels and tucked them into every pocket, compartment, and fold of my clothing, one in each space so they couldn't rattle. With a little ingenuity I stowed away nine of them, and put the rest back under the cart seat. If I found a way to take the horses, maybe I could take the money, too. Taking the horses began to look more appealing, though I still didn't see how I could manage it. Never mind. Worry about getting out after you've gotten in.

I rolled myself into a pile of blankets and listened to the grooms finishing their chores. They exchanged good nights with the guard at the stable door as they left, but I wasn't worried about him . . . much.

I found a knothole in one of the wall planks, and watched the grooms enter the keep through the kitchen door. They probably slept in the kitchen—lower servants often did. The question was whether they used the privy on the other side of the stable midden or something indoors. And if they used the outside privy, did they leave the kitchen door unlocked?

The sunset faded and moonlight took its place. The setting Green Moon was just a sliver, but the Creature Moon rose in full, golden glory, and the sky was clear. Why is it never overcast when you need it?

Through my knothole, I watched the windows go dark until only the light in Lady Ceciel's herbarium remained.

I tucked my boots under my belt and slipped down

the corridor to the loft ladder. Several of the horses roused as I passed, but my afternoon's work paid off—none of them made a fuss. I climbed to the loft and made my way to the big portal at the end, where hay and straw were lifted in. The rustlings of the mice were louder than my footsteps. The guard at the other side of the building would never hear a thing.

The big loft doors were latched shut. I opened the left one a crack to give me a view of the keep—still dark, except for the tower windows. I closed that door and opened the other to peek at the outer walls. The guard stood on the parapet, a bit above me, almost twenty feet away, looking over the countryside. I shrank back, but I left the door open. I needed to observe him for a while.

I watched for over an hour. Listening to their quiet calls, I learned that there were four guards on the walls at night. The guard on the stable side walked up and down his stretch of parapet every ten minutes, and was usually out of sight of my end of the stable for at least a minute—longer if he stopped to chat with the guard at the stable door.

I also learned that the guards' attention was fixed on the killing ground, and the forest and fields beyond it, which was good.

The lights in the tower windows shone steadily,

which was bad. Wasn't the woman ever going to sleep? Given the excitement I'd seen in her face this afternoon, perhaps not, but I had a lot to do in that keep tonight! *Go to bed, lady.*

I resolved to give her another hour, but soon my patience came to an end.

I waited until the guard walked out of sight, then I slithered out the portal and hung by my hands. The hardest part was hanging by one hand while I reached up to close the door as much as I could. It would still be open a crack, but it had been open a crack for some time now and the guard hadn't noticed.

It was only a five-foot drop to the cobbles, but that's a long way in stockings. I landed rolling, as best I could, and then rolled back to put the stable between me and the guard on the wall. Now that it had begun, my stomach shook with the combined fear and excitement that was the reason I quit burglary . . . and also the reason I regretted quitting, just a little.

I must be out of my mind to be doing this. It was definitely time to get clear of Sir Michael . . . after I saved him.

The guard's steps paused. He stayed where he was for five slow counts, so I risked a peek. He was behind the stable, no other guards in sight.

I took a deep breath, scuttled silently for the privy,

and darted inside, ignoring the familiar stink. No one shouted. I put on my boots and then (when else would I have a chance?) used the facilities. When I left I let the door slam behind me, not too loud, not too soft, just another servant. I walked toward the keep without looking at the wall. I could feel the guard's eyes on my back, and a drop of sweat rolled down my spine. But no alarm sounded.

I approached the kitchen door. If it was locked I'd kick it and swear, as if someone had barred it behind me. Then I'd probably die, if the guard had the wits to wonder why I set off around the keep instead of waking someone to let me in.

My hand trembled as I reached for the latch, but it lifted easily and the door swung open. Nobody bolts a door they're planning on using in the middle of the night when they go to the privy.

I slipped into the kitchen and was greeted by a cacophony of snores. The low flames popping in the fireplace revealed more than twenty sleeping forms. The better servants would have rooms . . . on the top floor? Above the kitchen? Imagining the noise a couple of maidservants would make if they woke and saw me peering into their room, I wished I knew.

I removed my boots and tucked them into my belt again before walking to the door that led into the rest of the house. As I passed the cellar stairs I hesitated—if there were dungeons in this keep (and there probably were) they'd be down there. But in most old keeps the dungeons have been made into wine storage, or filled with vegetable bins or firewood. Servants went down to the cellars all the time, and I couldn't see the men and women I'd met at dinner nodding and wishing the prisoner a cheery good morning on their way past—not without gossiping about it. I hadn't heard a peep about Sir Michael in Cory Port in all the days I'd sold wrinkle cream there.

Of course, if he was dead the servants wouldn't be likely to know about it.

No. She wouldn't dare. Not yet. He wasn't dead, but he probably wasn't in the cellars either. *So where was he?*

Not in the kitchen, that was certain. I tiptoed on, breathing easier when I had closed the door behind me.

Outside the kitchen I walked down a long hall, opening doors as I passed them. On my left was a laundry, a chain of storerooms, and a small dining hall—one that would seat only twenty guests in comfort.

A service door on the right led to the great hall. Moonlight streamed through the narrow windows, and an unseen draft stirred the hanging banners. It felt very empty, especially when you noticed that the dais at the far end held no great carved chair. I remembered the thing falling into the murky water of the *Albatross*'s bilge, and felt a twinge of guilt. For what, I couldn't say—certainly not for Lady Ceciel's loss.

Halfway down the hall, corridors stretched to the left and right, and I paused again. Michael wouldn't be in any room on the ground floor—too public. But then, I didn't think he'd be tucked in an upstairs guest room either; it was just the better chance of the two. What if she had him in a cave in the woods or some such thing?

The thought struck me so forcibly I stopped in mid-step. Now *that* made sense. Outside the keep, away from the servants—all she'd have to do was send a guard to feed him . . . and I could find him by following the guard! When they threw me out tomorrow, I'd hide the donkey cart, double back and watch to see who went where! It would be much easier to break him out of some isolated shack than the keep itself. I could go back to the stable and forget this whole risky idiocy . . . and if I was wrong, I'd never get inside again.

Don't assume people are going to do the intelligent thing. Jack Bannister's cynical voice rang in my memory. Even smart people do stupid things. That's how con artists make money.

Jack was the one who taught me about crime, about people, and in the end, about life. He'd been a cheat, a liar, and a son of a bitch, and there were times when his final lesson still hurt—but he was usually right. I was here; I might as well search the place.

I was two thirds up the stairs when I heard footsteps coming down the gallery toward me. Step-click, step-click. *Hackle!*

My stockinged feet thumped on the stone as I raced down the stairs, skidded around the newel post, and shot for the door under the stairway. I had assumed it was a storeroom—and for once I was right. Shifting in carefully amid stacks of buckets and brooms, I left the door open a crack and watched Hackle stump down the hall. He carried a lamp and looked perfectly at ease, if a little grim. The click of his peg leg was almost lost in the drumming of my own blood in my ears. This kind of fear was the reason I *quit* burglary.

I bet his bedroom wasn't on this floor, either. That settled the question of where to start searching—if Hackle was tramping around, I wanted to be as far away as possible. And it wouldn't hurt to make certain that Lady Ceciel really was involved in her workshop.

The route up to the third floor was familiar from my visit this morning. The hall that led to the lady's tower was dark—had the lamps been lit, I might have missed the dim glow that fanned out from under a door halfway down the hall. A brighter glow flared beneath the door of the tower room, but I knew the tower windows had been the only ones alight on this side of the building. So she'd moved a lamp into another room . . . or that room had no windows.

There were a thousand explanations, I told myself as I crept down the hall, but my heart leapt with foolish hope. A hope that grew when I reached the door and saw a thick bolt—on the *outside*. But why was the bolt open? Because someone currently inside wanted to be able to get out. I looked for the hinges—but the door opened inward. I hesitated a moment before lying down to look through the crack beneath, since it left my head perfectly positioned for a kick, if someone opened the door unexpectedly.

The stone floor was hard and cold. I could see very little: the hem of a woman's skirt, and the backs of a pair of flat-heeled shoes—the sort worn by women who spend a lot of time standing. Beyond the lady I saw nothing but furniture legs, but I knew it was Lady Ceciel because I heard her voice.

". . . for the lateness of the hour, but it took most of the day to finish this batch. It's quite a complicated process."

Who was she talking to? I looked past her skirts as

well as I could, but I saw no other feet. Please, let it be Michael! The furniture creaked.

"I'm sorry about the discomfort," the lady went on, actually sounding sorry. "But as you've learned, it will pass. In two hours the potion will have metabolized, and I'll return to free you. I need to finish some work, anyway."

She was dosing someone—a prisoner! Please, let it be one of the simple ones, not— No such luck. Michael's voice replied, rough, weary, familiar.

"I hate you." It should have sounded childish, but the flat sincerity of it froze my blood.

"You won't," said the lady. "When I'm finished, you'll . . ."

I stood up, missing the rest of her speech. Whatever was going on in there, I had to stop it. The door opened in and she was facing away from it—I'd never have a better chance.

CHAPTER 16

Michael

I tried to summon the strength to reply to Lady Ceciel's lunatic ramblings, but I'm not sure why I bothered. Over the last few days I'd tried every form of argument, bribe, and plea. Nothing had worked.

I had taken several doses of her accursed potion now, but the cold serpent that coiled through my gut had had no effect, except to add to my nausea. *No effect*, I told myself firmly. My wrists were raw from struggling against the ropes that bound them to the bedstead. My throat was raw from the funnel. I felt sick, and very tired, and my eyes were beginning to play tricks on me. I hated her. I was about to say it again when the door flew open with a force that would have knocked her down had she been standing closer. As it was the door struck her wide skirts, spinning her around, face to face with Fisk.

Fisk!

His face was a mask of determination, and the lady's eyes opened so wide I could see white around the rims. She drew a breath to scream, but Fisk moved faster than I'd ever seen him, leaping forward, shoving her shoulders, kicking for her ankles. They fell together with Fisk on top, and Lady Ceciel's head struck the floor hard enough to crack her skull, if the thick knot of hair at the back of her head hadn't cushioned it.

Even so, the blow stunned her for a moment, which was all Fisk needed. When she opened her mouth to scream he stuffed in a handkerchief; her teeth snapped down so fast he almost lost his fingers. He clapped a hand over her mouth to keep her from spitting out the gag, and she began to struggle. She also started screaming behind the gag—making an astonishing amount of noise.

Fisk kicked the door closed and clamped one of her wrists behind his knee. Then he grabbed the hand that was clawing at his eyes and pinned it. Only then did he stop to look up at me. "You might lend a . . . oh."

I was sitting up, in the uncomfortable crouch that was all I could manage with my wrists bound to the bed. I was also, I realized, gaping at him like an idiot.

He looked thinner and tired . . . and blond. I'd never been so glad to see anyone in my life.

"Fisk!"

"I guess you can't lend a hand. Any suggestions?"

"Fisk." My eyes filled, and I blinked them clear.

Lady Ceciel squirmed beneath him, twisting the wrist tucked under his knee. In a moment she'd free it.

"Wake up, Michael! What's the matter? You knew I was coming."

I drew a deep, shuddering breath, struggling to clear the fog from my mind. "Of course I did."

I have always been a terrible liar.

My heart twisted at the hurt that dawned in his eyes. But anything I said would make it worse, and we had other things to worry about. The lady's squirming grew more urgent, and more effective, with every passing second.

Fisk grimaced and returned to practical matters. "Can you throw me one of those blankets with your feet? I want something around her head if she starts yelling."

Why hadn't I trusted him? And if I failed so significantly, how could I expect him to trust me?

"Michael, wake up! Come on, Mike, throw me a blanket!"

Mike. He was trustworthy, but he could also be very

annoying. I fumbled in the bedclothes with my feet, and finally managed to pick up a blanket and pitch it within his reach. My ankle chain rattled, and Fisk's lips tightened at the sound.

He had to let go of Lady Ceciel's mouth to grab the blanket. Thankfully he got it wrapped around her head before she started screaming. She'd be free of the gag shortly, but I knew how thick these walls were. Once his hands were free, it took Fisk only a moment to roll Lady Ceciel over and tie her wrists with a cord he pulled from his pocket. 'Tis nice to have a squire who is well prepared. The knowledge that I had been rescued made my spirits soar, despite the tight knot of pain growing in my belly.

Fisk tore the hem off one of Lady Ceciel's petticoats to bind the gag back in place. She got off an earsplitting shriek when he unwrapped the blanket, and Fisk swore when she bit his fingers.

He bound her ankles, struggled to his feet, and glared down at her. She glared back in silence.

"I wish she hadn't yelped," Fisk muttered.

"I don't think it makes much difference. Nobody ever responded when *I* screamed. Cut me loose, Fisk!"

He hurried to the bed. "I'll have to untie you. They took my knife." My struggles had tightened the ropes, and he swore again as they resisted his tugging fingers.

"How under two moons did you get here, Fisk? Did the sheriff—" The pain in my stomach intensified, in the sudden way that was common with that damnable potion; I doubled over, breath hissing between my teeth.

"Are you all right?" Fisk pulled the rope off one of my wrists and reached for the other, concern and urgency warring in his expression. We hadn't time for this.

My other wrist came free and I staggered over to a corner, where I rid myself of Lady Ceciel's potion.

In the midst of my spasms I felt Fisk's clasp on my shoulders. I would have thanked him had I been able to speak.

When the heaving stopped, Fisk helped me stumble back to the bed. I was shaking as I sank onto the rumpled blankets, but my mind began to clear. If my practical, craven squire had come here on his own, incredible as it seemed, then we needed to get out fast. Fisk must have a plan, but he simply stood there, looking down at me.

"So now what?" I asked.

Relief flashed in his eyes, and I realized how groggy I must have been before. "Now I get you out of this." He examined the lock on my shackle, and pulled a pick from his boot.

I started to laugh and he looked up, startled.

"I knew you could pick locks. Never mind. What next?"

Fisk's gaze dropped. "I was hoping you'd have an idea."

'Twas like being hit in the head with a brick. "*What?* You came all the way in here with no plan for getting out?"

He abandoned the lock to scowl at me. "It was a little difficult, Mike, when I didn't know what the defenses were, or where you were, or in what condition. My plan was to get in, find you, and then make plans once I had some information."

"I'm sorry." I'd have been sorrier if he wasn't calling me Mike. "But of all the ridiculous—"

"Look, could we discuss my stupidity later?"

I drew in a breath and let it go. "What are the defenses?"

"A problem." Fisk returned to picking the lock as he spoke. "There are four guards on the walls, and probably one on the gate—I didn't have a chance to find out. There are horses in the stable, but a guard on the stable door. None of them will let us out without Lady Ceciel's permission. . . . Maybe if we took her hostage . . . I can get a knife in the kitchen . . ."

It sounded feasible until we looked at Lady Ceciel.

She sneered at us. She would not make a good hostage.

"Not a chance," I told Fisk. "She'll fight us off and make a break for it."

Fisk grimaced in agreement, then his face lit. "Michael! Do you know how—"

The door swung open.

For several seconds Hackle and Fisk just stood there, staring. Then Hackle turned toward the hall, drawing breath to shout, and Fisk leapt across the room and catapulted into him.

On a peg leg Hackle couldn't keep his balance—he and Fisk careened across the hallway, into the opposite wall. But unlike Lady Ceciel, Hackle wasn't stunned. He drew another breath, and Fisk clamped both hands around his throat.

I jumped from the bed and stumbled halfway across the floor before the chain yanked my ankle and almost sent me sprawling. Recovering my balance, I spun in place, desperately estimating the distance. The hall was wide—even if I dragged the bed across the room, I couldn't reach them.

Hackle clawed at Fisk's wrists for a few, futile moments—then he did the smarter thing and reached for Fisk's eyes. Fisk ducked, burying his face against the nearest shelter, which happened to be Hackle's chest. I heard Hackle haul a ragged breath past Fisk's hands. His face had a purple cast, but if he was still getting air, 'twould be a long time before he passed out. I had to get loose—now!

I flung myself onto the bed, braced my hands, and kicked the post with both feet, as hard as I could. The blow jarred my legs from toe to hip, but the give I'd worked into the post over the last few days kept me from breaking bones. I kicked again and again. The post locked into place, and pain rang in my heels, but I didn't stop.

Hackle gave up trying to reach Fisk's eyes and grabbed his hair, trying to drag his head back. I swear I saw Fisk's scalp leave his skull. He made a muffled sound of pain, but he held his place, nearly invulnerable, except . . .

The same thought occurred to Hackle. He let go of Fisk's hair and reached for his hands, feeling carefully, gripping the little finger and bending it back. One hand came away from Hackle's throat and air rasped into Hackle's lungs. He still couldn't shout, but it wouldn't be long.

Fisk would be captured.

Lady Ceciel would win.

Bracing my back and arms, I put everything I had into the next kick. My bones vibrated, but there was no pain—because the wood began to crack. I kicked again, even harder, and was rewarded with a sweet snapping sound as the bedpost broke. My hands shook as I twisted it apart and slid the chain free.

Hackle saw what I was doing. He clawed at Fisk's hand in such a frenzy that his nails drew blood, but Fisk held on.

The shattered bedpost made a wonderful club.

I sprinted out of the cell and struck Hackle's temple, trying to hit him hard, but not enough to crack his skull, for I wasn't prepared to do murder . . . not quite. I must have judged it fairly well; his eyes rolled up, and he slid down the wall, taking Fisk with him. Hackle was still breathing, but he'd have a monster of a headache when he woke—a thought that gave me considerable satisfaction.

Fisk stared up at me. "You *broke* that?" 'Twas a sensible question—the thing was four inches thick.

"I've been working it loose for days." I tossed it back into the cell and reached for Hackle's feet. "Give me a hand."

"I'm not cut out for burglary," Fisk moaned.

The loudest sound, as we dragged Hackle back into the cell, was the rattle of my chain on the floor.

Lady Ceciel's eyes widened above the gag when she saw her steward's limp form.

"He's alive," I told her, checking as I spoke to be sure 'twas true. "Just stunned." Her eyes closed in relief.

I didn't care.

Fisk stripped blankets off the damaged bed and we hauled Hackle onto it, tying his wrists and his good foot to the remaining posts. His eyelids were fluttering, so we gagged him as well. Then it took several minutes of scrounging over the floor to find the lock pick Fisk had dropped.

I sat on the floor and Fisk lifted my shackled ankle. He still looked stunned, but his hands were steady.

"Right back where we started." My lips twitched. "You were saying?"

"Huh?" Fisk looked up, puzzled.

"When Hackle interrupted. You were about to ask me something."

"What? Oh. Yes! Michael, do you know how to brew aquilas?"

I stiffened. "No one in my family has *ever* used that vile stuff. We wed our women honestly—we don't seduce them with drugs!"

"I didn't ask if you'd used it," Fisk said, fishing inside the lock. "I asked if you knew how to make it. Come on, Mike, nobles are supposed to pass that recipe from father to son."

"My father didn't! I told you, no one—"

"But you know the formula, don't you?"

"Yes," I admitted. "I learned it at university."

Fisk's jaw dropped. "They teach you to make aquilas at *university*? I thought it was illegal!"

"Of course it is," I snapped. "They don't teach you—the students write it with chalk on the inside of privy doors. You couldn't help but read it. Though the formulas differ a bit."

We turned again to Lady Ceciel. Her eyes glittered with fury, but I thought I saw the beginning of fear.

Fisk's eyes were bright with hope. "The real question is, does it work?"

"How should I know? I've never used it." But I'd heard tales. My hopes began to rise as well . . . but to make aquilas? To use it against a woman? My father would never forgive me.

"But you could make it?"

Could I forgive myself? I thought of Janny, of my misery over the last few weeks, of the oddly luminous potions, twisting in my intestines, and became so lost in thought that Fisk had to repeat his question.

"Could you make it?"

I took a deep breath. "Yes, I think I could. Some ingredients were the same in all the formulas. But I—"

"This is no time for scruples, Mike." The shackle

clicked open and Fisk pulled it wide. I reclaimed my
ankle and rubbed it, erasing the feel of captivity more
than any pain. "It's our only chance to get out of here."

I owed it to Fisk to get him out. I owed a debt to
Janny, and the others as well. I met Lady Ceciel's defi-
ant gaze and the past few days filled the space
between us, destroying my remorse.

"You're right. I'll do it."

Fisk took a few seconds to put his boots back on—if all
the noise we'd made hadn't alerted anyone yet, we had
nothing to fear from boot steps. I wasn't afraid of making noise. I wasn't afraid of anything. We left Hackle in
the cell—door neatly bolted. He was coming around,
but he looked like his head ached too badly for him to
do much. I was glad for that—a bitter gladness that felt
heavier than grief.

Lady Ceciel we brought with us. Or rather Fisk
brought her, having first retied her ankles with a short
hobble so she could walk but not kick or run.

I let him handle her—not because I didn't want to
touch her, but because I had never in my life wanted
to hurt someone the way I wanted to hurt Lady Ceciel.
The cold fear of what I might do, given the chance,
occupied my mind as we hurried down the corridor to
her herbarium.

Then we opened the door, and I beheld a sight so horrifying it made all my previous fears hollow. It wasn't half a dozen guardsmen, or a monster, or a mutilated corpse. Just a room full of bottles and herbs—but some of them glowed with their own light, the light of magica, made visible, in a way no normal person could see.

She had changed me.

CHAPTER 17

Fisk

Michael froze in the doorway. The rigid set of his shoulders made my neck prickle.

"What is it?" I tightened my grip on Lady Ceciel and peered around him. Lamps mounted on the walls cast their light over shelves of bottles, pots, and arcane paraphernalia. There was a cheery fire in the hearth, and a stuffed raven perched on one of the roof beams, its outstretched wings forever frozen in place. The room was empty of any threat that I could see, but Michael didn't move.

He seemed more focused than when I first found him, but he wore a cold expression that made him a stranger . . . a stranger I didn't particularly want to know.

"What's wrong?" It came out sharper than I meant it to.

"Nothing." Michael took a deep breath and stepped into the room. "There's nothing wrong."

Looking at the sheen of sweat on his face, I wasn't inclined to believe that, but he was speaking and moving again, so I decided to leave well enough alone.

I tied the lady to a table leg and then checked the windows. The parapet was lower than the tower, so a guard looking up would see nothing but a few feet of ceiling, unless someone stood in the window and looked out.

I told Michael that, and he nodded absently. He was wandering up and down the herb rack, choosing the jars he needed. Suddenly he froze again, looking at a half-empty bottle. I was about to go to him when he shook himself, and went on picking out ingredients.

He carried them over to one of the tables, and I hurried to clear a space for him, but even when I finished, he just stood there, his arms full of jars, staring at a thick pile of notes.

When he looked at me his face was pale again, his eyes dark with anger and pain.

"You brew, I'll burn," I told him.

I burned every scrap of paper in that room in the big fireplace, ignoring the tears rolling down Lady Ceciel's face.

Michael appeared to be intent on his work, but his

face grew more human, more himself, with every page I laid in the flames.

When the papers had been reduced to ash, I poured the potions out of their bottles and onto the floor, till they ran over our feet in shimmering floods. I hesitated when I came to the bottle that had frightened Michael. It looked like all the others—the label held a list of ingredients and the directions—two doses daily. The writing was in a different hand than on most of the bottles, but there were several labels with different writing. I looked at Michael and caught him staring at the bottle in my grasp.

"Well?" I asked.

His expression changed again. "Dump it."

So I did.

I told Michael to gather up everything he needed, and went back to the cell to grab some blankets. Then I folded all the glassware into them and smashed it. Lady Ceciel flinched at every crunch.

By the time I finished, the herbarium had been demolished—even the dried herbs, which I'd not dared to burn lest the scent alert the guards, had been ruined by the moisture on the floor. Michael was eyeing a pot of murky liquid dubiously. "It needs to cool."

"Will it work?"

"Hanged if I know."

We looked at the lady again. She sneered at us.

"She won't drink it," I said. "She'll spit it out, or dump it on the floor."

A smile I didn't like at all touched Michael's mouth. "Wait a minute."

He went out, returning only a moment later, which meant the object he carried must have come from his cell. It was a funnel, made of reddish wood with a curved spout, and my stomach lurched as I realized its function. Michael set it on the table, holding Lady Ceciel's eyes with his own.

"Cut her free, Fisk, and stand behind her with your hands around her throat."

I did as I was told, trying to conceal that my hands were trembling again.

Michael picked up the potion. "I'm going to ungag you now. If you try to scream, Fisk will throttle you unconscious, and we'll pour the stuff down you. If you drop it on the floor, I'll brew another batch—and next time we won't give you a choice."

Lady Ceciel's throat rippled beneath my hands as she swallowed.

Michael's eyes were alive with mockery, and I knew he was quoting her when he said, "We can do this the hard way or the easy way—the choice is yours."

If he was bluffing, he was better at it than I'd ever

suspected, and worry tightened like wire around my heart. I wasn't surprised when Lady Ceciel took the jug and drained it.

We tied her hands and gagged her again, and then destroyed the equipment and herbs Michael had used. The last thing Michael did was put the funnel on the fire. The red glow illuminated his thoughtful expression, and some of the tension eased out of his shoulders.

I turned to Lady Ceciel. She no longer glowered defiantly, but she didn't look beaten either. She looked . . . relaxed?

"You think it's working?" I asked Michael.

"One way to find out. Lady Ceciel, if I remove your gag, will you promise not to scream?"

She made encouraging sounds.

"Nod if you won't scream."

She nodded.

Michael untied the gag and pulled it out of her mouth. I was ready to grab her throat, but she didn't scream. She looked pleasant and amiable, an expression I'd never seen on her face. I was willing to bet the guards had never seen it either.

I met Michael's dubious look. "It's a dark night. Maybe they won't notice."

He frowned. "How are we going to explain this, Fisk? Even if she agrees, they're going to wonder why she's letting us go in the middle of the night. You *are* going to let us go, aren't you, Lady Ceciel?"

"Yes, of course." She smiled.

"So we'll think of some excuse." I began to pace. "Say . . . say I offered to show her some arcane herbal something or other. Something that requires blood sacrifice by moonlight."

"Nothing to do with herbalism requires blood sacrifice, by moonlight or otherwise," said Michael.

"You may know that, but I'll bet the guards don't. Especially the way she practices herbalism. And that gets all of us out. You can take her back to Lord Dorian and repay your debt."

Michael frowned. "It gets you and her out—where do I fit in?"

"You're the sacrifice," I told him. "Lady Ceciel, would your guards believe you'd practice human sacrifice?"

She looked confused. "Yes, of course."

Sir Michael snorted. "You won't get any information from her—not without a lot of patience. But it might work, Fisk."

"It might not." The more I saw of Lady Ceciel's vacuous expression, the crazier our plan sounded.

"Have you got a better idea?"

I shook my head.

"Then we'll try it."

Only a lunatic would have agreed to this lunatic plan . . . so I shouldn't have been surprised.

I had to tie up Sir Michael, and we both agreed that he should be bound tightly, since the guards would notice if they checked the ropes. He didn't like the idea of being gagged, but I told him it would look suspicious otherwise. Actually I didn't think that mattered in terms of the guards, but he was such a rotten liar I didn't dare leave his tongue free.

Managing Lady Ceciel would be hard enough. This wasn't going to work.

We were halfway down the hall before I remembered I should turn out the lamps in the herbarium, and we had to go back. The second time we passed the cell door, Michael stopped and thumped his elbow against it. He looked at me commandingly.

"All right, but we really don't have time for this." Despite my grumbling I was rather relieved. I liked the crazy Sir Michael better than the ruthless one.

I entered the cell. Hackle's eyes were closed, his face slack, but he roused when I touched his shoulder, and after a moment his eyes focused. He scowled at me. His pupils were the same size.

"He's fine," I announced, bolting the door behind me.

I had to lead the way, for Sir Michael didn't know

the keep's layout, and Lady Ceciel did nothing but smile and nod. We were almost down the main stair when I remembered something else.

"Lady Ceciel, where's your bedroom?"

"Yes?" She smiled.

Michael turned on the step, brows raised.

"They'll never believe she's going out at night, in early Oakan, without a cloak. M'lady, where's your room?"

"Oh, yes." She smiled.

Michael snorted with laughter. I glared at him.

"Can you point to it?"

"Yes, of course."

"Point to your room. Point to your bedroom, Lady Ceciel."

After a moment she pointed back up the stairs; no surprise. In the gallery I asked her to point again, and she directed us down the hall.

We crept down the corridor in silence. I still didn't know where the upper servants slept, but ladies' maids frequently slept near them. We might be able to fool the guards, but a personal servant? Not a chance.

We were acting too fast, not thinking things through, not planning enough. But if I stopped to think, my nerve would fail.

My employer, curse him, appeared to be enjoying himself.

We reached the end of the corridor. "Where's your bedroom? Point to your bedroom, Lady Ceciel."

She pointed back the way we'd come. Michael choked. I was glad he was gagged.

"Lady Ceciel, when we pass your bedroom door, point to it. Can you do that?"

"Yes, of course."

Michael choked again. I swore.

We went back down the corridor, and Lady Ceciel stopped at a door not far from the gallery.

"This is it." She smiled.

I went in first, checking quickly for a maid. None, thank goodness. I hustled Lady Ceciel inside, and Michael followed.

It took only seconds to take a cloak from the wardrobe and wrap it around her shoulders. I pulled the hood over her head, shadowing her silly expression. A definite improvement.

We were about to leave when the jewel box on her dressing table caught my eye. I looked at Sir Michael. He glared at me.

"Mno," he said, as distinctly as he could.

"Look, we're going to have to leave all our money with the donkey cart. She'd be more than recompensed."

"Mno!"

"Not to mention all the gear we'll have to replace. And our clothes. And weapons." I flipped up the jewel box lid. It was empty. "Curse it."

Michael snorted.

"That reminds me. Lady Ceciel, why did you sell the tapestries and your jewels?"

She looked confused. "Yes, of course."

I moaned.

I extracted the story from her, bit by bit, as we went down the stairs to the entry hall.

She'd sold the tapestries for money.

She'd given the money to Lord Gerald.

Lord Gerald had agreed to let her be baron, and not have to marry anyone.

That a liege would put a multiple murderess in charge of a barony and a smallish town surprised even me. "Ruthless bastard," I muttered.

Sir Michael was frowning.

"Yes, of course." Lady Ceciel smiled.

I dashed into the dining hall for a sword from one of the wall displays, and we emerged from the keep a perfect picture of prisoner and captors—Sir Michael walking in front of us at sword point, and Lady Ceciel clinging to my arm.

The Creature Moon was still rising. Unbelievable as it seemed, I'd been in the keep only a few hours. A wind had come up; it ran cool fingers through my hair, and ruffled Lady Ceciel's hood. I hoped fresh air didn't diminish the drug's effect. I hoped the drug didn't affect her so strongly that she fell down the steps. I hoped Michael could manage, with his hands bound behind him.

This wasn't going to work.

I shut the great door behind us and turned to face the guards. The guard on the parapet stared at us. There was a gate guard, and he stared at us, too, his hand on his sword hilt.

This wasn't going to . . . *Hang it!*

"Ho, fellow." It was my best fake noble accent. "Fetch out some horses for your mistress, myself, and this carrion. We've crafty business in the wood tonight."

The guard looked dubious, as well he might. It took all my concentration to maneuver Lady Ceciel down the steep stair without skewering Michael.

When we reached the bottom, the gate guard was standing there. His sword wasn't drawn, but you could tell he was ready to go for it. "M'lady, is—"

"Are you deaf, fellow? I asked for horses. I'll take that big gray I saw in the stables this afternoon. The lady will take her favorite riding horse, and we'll mount this man on the smallest horse you have—and I don't mean my donkey. He'd slow us up too much."

"Lady, do you want me to get the horses?"

"Yes, of course." She smiled.

I patted her hand, and babbled about the power of sacrifice by moonlight.

The guard looked even more dubious, but he could see I didn't have a knife at her ribs, and she was clutching my sword arm. She could certainly have hindered me long enough for him to run me through.

He called up to the parapet guard, to pass word to fetch the horses. Then he turned back to watch us . . . intently . . . with most of his attention on Lady Ceciel's face. Not good.

"I hope you remembered to bring a sharp knife, lady. And a needle and thread for the stitches. After all, we only have to sacrifice the fellow's fertility—pity to kill him."

Michael spun to face me with a startled squeak. I lifted the sword with a flourish, *really* glad he was gagged.

"Oh yes," said Lady Ceciel vaguely.

The guard decided he didn't want to know more and retreated to the gate, leaving me to babble about the Green Moon drawing the fertility up into the leaves and other such nonsense. Lady Ceciel nodded, and Michael stared at us in frozen silence.

Chanticleer's neigh sent Michael spinning around, but

Chant's neigh was loud enough to turn heads over half the barony. The big gray was prancing with excitement.

"He hasn't had much exercise lately," the rumpled-looking groom apologized. "Are you sure you want him, sir?"

"He'll do well enough." I took the reins and hauled his head away from Sir Michael, whom he was sniffing with great enthusiasm. Michael ignored him, but a sheen of tears brightened his eyes. I was *very* glad he was gagged.

The guards threw Michael up on Tipple, who was, as I knew from my earlier wanderings, the smallest horse in the stable. They tied Tipple's lead rope to Chanticleer's saddle, then they tied Michael's feet to the stirrups.

The lady's favorite riding horse was a sprightly bay mare. I stepped forward to help her to the saddle, but the gate guard intervened.

"I'll take care of it, sir." As he hefted her onto the mare's back, out of reach of my sword, I heard him ask, "Lady, do you want some of us to go with you? Is everything all right?"

"Yes, of course," said Lady Ceciel, but she sounded confused.

The guard looked confused, too.

"What she means, fellow, is that the mysteries of the craft are not for the eyes of the uninitiated, and she requires no escort but her humble instructor." I sheathed my sword and sneered at him. My heart thumped sickly. "Isn't that right, m'lady?"

"Oh, yes."

The guard stood back. He was still suspicious, but there wasn't much he could do about it . . . I hoped.

I swung into Chanticleer's saddle and he pranced restively, wondering, no doubt, why his master was riding Tipple.

"Let's be gone, shall we, Lady Ceciel?"

She smiled.

"Open the gate, fellow." I turned away, chatting with Lady Ceciel as if I was certain of his obedience.

Those creaking hinges were the sweetest sound I ever heard. We clattered out of the keep and onto the road, accompanied by a stream of nervous babble from me, with Lady Ceciel smiling and nodding.

The road wandered down the hill in front of us, open as the sky. No one shouted for us to stop, and if they did we could run for it. We were free. It had worked. I didn't believe it.

"I don't believe it," I muttered.

"Yes, of course," said Lady Ceciel.

Michael choked on a laugh.

We were free.

CHAPTER 18

Michael

I rode down the hill from the keep with my hands bound behind me, my feet bound to the stirrups, Tipple's lead rope bound to Chant's saddle—expecting an arrow in the back at any moment!—and my heart sang with freedom.

Fisk was still lecturing on imaginary herbalism— nervous reflex, I suppose, for we were out of earshot of the guards. How did he make his face look so thin? With that pale hair, and those mincing mannerisms, I wouldn't have recognized him if I'd met him on the street! Not to mention that awful accent.

He was undoubtedly a brilliant con man. And though he might deny it, he had proved a better squire. I remembered the hurt in his eyes when he saw that I'd lost faith in him. I'd spent a lot of time worrying about gaining Fisk's trust, but I'd given no thought to offering him mine—and until I did, was I worthy of his trust? The truth was that, in my doubt and fear, I had failed him. Mayhap this was something we both had to earn. But could trust grow under obligation, or in captivity?

Shortly after we reached the bottom of the hill Fisk turned the horses into the trees, bidding Lady Ceciel to follow, which—"Yes, of course"—she did. Amazing stuff, that aquilas. But much as I disliked her, I found my stomach turning at the mindlessly pliant expression on her face. Or mayhap my nausea was the last of my reaction to her potion—gods curse her!

In the darkness, the magica plants and trees glowed as if lit from within. I could see them hundreds of feet away. To be able to sense magic with touch was not uncommon—the one truly magical Gift granted to men—but no one I'd ever heard of could *see* it. The knowledge that her potion had changed me, even if, as I prayed, 'twas only temporary, dampened my elation. 'Twas hard to forgive, but I couldn't forget her fury at my suggestion that she'd harmed the simple ones. She hadn't been half as insulted when I accused her of killing her husband . . . and now I thought I knew why.

As soon as we were out of sight of the keep, Fisk cut me loose. My first act of freedom was to throw my arms around Chant's neck and apologize for not having greeted him properly. As I did so, I realized that Fisk must have known our horses were in the stable, and he hadn't told me. Ah well, mayhap he forgot it in the press of events. Mayhap not. I was in no position to upbraid anyone for lack of trust.

Fisk swiftly transferred Lady Ceciel from the mare to Tipple, binding her hands to the saddle pommel. He held up the crumpled strip of cloth he'd pulled from my mouth and glanced at me in question, but I shook my head—why gag her? We'd be long gone before the drug wore off.

Fisk mounted her mare and we rode into the forest. The moons gave enough light for us to pick our way through the trees at a nearly normal pace. This was too slow for Fisk, who kept looking over his shoulder, but I had no real fear of pursuit until the boy who brought my breakfast found Hackle in my place. By that time we'd have so great a start, they'd never catch us.

At first I was content to take in the beauty of the night, the crisp rustle of leaves beneath the horse's hooves, and the wheeling wonder of moons and stars. But as Fisk slowly relaxed, I persuaded him to give me an account of his activities over the last few weeks.

'Twas shaming to learn how faithfully he had striven for me.

In an attempt to repay that loyalty, I told him

something of what had happened to me, but 'twas difficult to discuss and emerged as more of a patchy summation than a true account. Fisk did not press for details, and I was grateful. As I listened to his account, and gave my own, questions arose to plague me. Some were things I had asked myself from the start, and some were new, but all were linked, like the chain that had bound my ankle during those weary, frightened days. As I considered them, the anchor post that held the chain became clear. The question of what to do about it had me riding in silence for a long time.

At sunrise I found a clearing and drew Chant to a stop. Fisk pulled the mare up beside me.

"Get her off Tipple, Fisk. We need to talk."

He did as I asked. The tree trunks cast long shadows in the slanting light, and birds chirped. Now that we'd stopped riding I was cold, but the sun would warm us soon enough.

Lady Ceciel looked cold as she stood there, eyeing me with a hostility that made it clear the drug had worn off. Strands of dark hair had pulled loose from the knot at the back of her head, and her skirt was rumpled and stained from the flood of potions over the herbarium floor.

That was something else I owed Fisk. The destruction

of that accursed place had cleansed my heart in a way that even the woman's death could not have done. Mayhap it hurt her worse, too. She stood defiantly, head lifted, and spoke first.

"You can take me to trial, but they won't convict. I am baron now, in my own right, and I can't be tried without the presence of my liege. In a few weeks I'll be home again, restoring my herbarium. This gains you nothing. You might as well—" She stopped, color flooding her cheeks.

I smiled grimly. "Might as well let you go? That argument didn't weigh with you, when you held *me* prisoner."

Her eyes flashed. "You were unredeemed! I had a legal right to do what I did. I—"

"Legal, yes, but right?"

It silenced her only a moment. "I paid for the right to rule that keep—to do my research in peace. I won't give it up. Take me to trial and do your worst! I'll still win."

"Yes," I said softly. "And no. I've decided to let you go, Lady Ceciel."

"What!"

I think Fisk's shriek was the louder of the two. 'Twas he who went on, "Are you out of your mind? She's killed dozens of simple ones, her own husband, tried to turn you into some sort of malformed, magic thing . . . and you're letting her *go*?"

"Yes. You're wrong, Fisk—not about me, but the rest of it. We should have seen it earlier—the clues were all there."

"Like dozens of graves full of mutilated bodies! Like—"

"Fisk, how long do simple ones live?"

He frowned. "Not long. The ones who have magic, never past adolescence. But—"

"How old were the simple ones you saw among the servants?"

"Adolescents," he admitted. "Or older children. But—"

"So they probably died of natural causes, just as she told me. You said yourself, if she had anything to hide she'd have tried to conceal their graves. And I have a hard time believing that Mistress Agnes, who must have known what her sister was doing, would continue to send her victims. Or that her servants, or even Hackle, would permit her to kill them. Such villains are possible, I fear, but not dozens in one place. 'Tis simply not credible. 'Tis also incredible that Lord Gerald would give her the barony if she'd done such a thing."

"But she did dose them! Against their will!"

"Sometimes," I agreed. "But she also took them in, and saved them from starvation and abuse. Their lives may have been better and longer in her keeping than they'd have been in the world. She did dose them, but I don't believe she killed them, Fisk, any more than she'd have killed us. She could have, since we're both indebted. All she had to do was send her guards into Cory Port to slay us, instead of cudgel-crewers. But she didn't. I believe her."

Lady Ceciel smiled nastily.

Fisk scowled. "I'd be more inclined to believe it if she hadn't killed her husband."

"But she didn't. That was the final clue. That's what makes it all fit!"

"Then who did poison him? With *magica*. In *repeated* doses."

"He killed himself."

"That's an awfully expensive method to commit suicide . . . Mike." Fisk's voice was so sarcastic I had to smile. "Not to mention drawn out, painful, and chancy. People who kill themselves slit their wrists, or jump off bridges, or—"

"He wasn't trying to kill himself, he was trying to cure his infertility. Isn't that right, Lady Ceciel?"

She stood in silence for a moment, staring not at me, but into the past. "That was our marriage bargain."

"Sir Herbert told you he was infertile," I continued, when she said nothing more. "So he didn't care that you weren't Gifted. But if his infertility became known, he'd have been scorned and pitied. Lord Gerald might have appointed an heir to share in governing the barony. So you agreed to say that you were infertile; in exchange, you gained wealth, rank—"

"I gained the freedom to pursue my research," she broke in. "To find a way to Gift the Giftless! To give magic to normal men. You won't stop me, Sir Michael. I kept my part of the bargain. All those years, his brother telling him to put me aside, the neighbors snickering . . . No one else ever guessed. How did you? I never told you anything about Herbert and me."

"But you did. When I asked you why you didn't take the potions, you said it contained an ingredient that no woman who might bear children should take. That puzzled me, but it wasn't until I saw the potion bottle in the herbarium, with another's writing on the label, that I understood. I know the effects of some of those ingredients. You kept it to analyze?"

A whisper of sadness passed over her face. "I was curious," she admitted. "It shouldn't have killed him. And Herbert . . . Well, I owed him something."

"Yes. You kept your bargain with Sir Herbert, despite the risk of being sentenced for his murder.

Would you have kept your silence to the end, Lady Ceciel?"

"Gods no! I'm not that foolish. If it had come to a trial, I'd have told the judicars the whole story. It can be proved, you know. Herbert went to every herbalist for leagues around, trying to find a cure. The faker that poisoned him fled, but the rest would testify. Lord Gerald checked it out very carefully before granting me the barony—in spite of the 'tax' I paid for passage of the title." Her voice grated on the last words, but she went on almost cheerfully. "No, I liked Herbert, and we respected each other. Enough that I sent his body home for burial without explaining how he died. I'd hoped to let him keep his secret to the end. But I wouldn't have died for him. He wouldn't expect me to. And as it happened, I didn't have to confess . . . I was rescued."

Her lips twitched at the memory.

Fisk swore, but I began to see the humor of it.

"You're really going to let me go?" she asked.

"Yes and no," I replied. "I know you believe what you're doing is beneficial, but you've no right to test your theories on others without their consent. And you've no right to use the simple ones as your victims whether they consent or not. Man must look after man, for we have no gods to watch over us."

"But I saved them! They—"

"You saved them only to use them for your own ends. I'm going to report what you've done to Lord Dorian, who will pass it on to the High Liege—and he won't permit this to continue. He'll speak to Lord Gerald, to your neighbors, mayhap place watchers in your household. You may retain the barony, but you will never again be allowed to experiment on human beings."

She whitened at the truth of it. "You can't do this! He'll make it impossible for me!" Her gaze darted about, seeking inspiration, and settled on Fisk. "There must be something you want? I have wealth, Sir Michael, I can . . ."

The expression on my face answered her before she finished.

"How much?" asked Fisk, in a tone of considerable interest.

"He's joking," I told her firmly, wishing I was certain.

She gazed at me defiantly. "There must be something. Something you want as desperately as I want this. If you tell me what it is, perhaps . . ."

"There is something I want," I said. "But I've already figured out how to get it." And the joy of it warmed my heart. "If you start walking now, you should hit the coast road by midafternoon."

"But—"

"We'll be going in another direction. I've no desire to be pursued, so you'll forgive me if I don't reveal which one."

I also had no desire to be ambushed. I made a mental note to approach Lord Dorian with caution, for she wasn't above setting a trap, and this time her men might have orders to kill.

"But what about Ginger? You can't just steal my horse!"

"You stole ours," said Fisk, "when you had us cudgel-crewed."

With a horse, she might get back in time to send men after us. On the other hand, she might truly care for the beast. "Once I've spoken to Lord Dorian, we'll send her to Mistress Agnes."

"But I have to have a horse! What if I encounter bandits?"

"Or a wild boar," said Fisk. "Or cudgel-crewers. They'd be lucky to get out of your hands alive."

She looked at his grim face. She looked at me. I don't know what she saw, but her chin lifted stubbornly.

"Very well. But I'll succeed someday—despite all you've done! I'm right, Sir Michael. You, of all people, know it."

Her eyes were full of fanatical fire. She would try again, unless I stopped her. And suddenly I knew that I *could* stop her, that I was the only one who could. Mayhap that was what gave me the strength to say easily, "What do you mean 'You, of all people'?"

"You know what I mean." She gazed at me hungrily. "I saw you looking at the potions in my herbarium and the way your eyes fix on certain plants and trees. Any man with a sensing Gift can *feel* magic, but you can see it! I've—"

"My lady," I said, "I don't know what you're talking about."

"You're lying." But the quiver in her voice revealed the first crack in her confidence.

Fisk snorted. "In two weeks you should have gotten to know him better than that. *He* never lies."

She had come to know me, and that knowledge was reflected in her face.

"All right. Meet my eyes, Sir Michael, and tell me that you've noticed no effect from my potions."

I met her eyes. "I've noticed no effect from your potions. Well, except for nausea. I'm sorry, Lady Ceciel. Mayhap you had some effect on the simple ones because they already had magic, but it hasn't changed me."

Watching the dream crumble in her eyes, I found I did pity her. 'Twas passion to prove herself that led her into evil, not cruelty. And 'tis no light thing, to face the death of dreams. I, of all people, knew that, for I'd been trying to do it ever since Father had passed his sentence. Now my dream was within my grasp. Oh yes, I understood Ceciel.

"You're lying!" she cried. But she didn't believe it. Her face twisted.

"I'm sorry," I said gently.

"I'm not," said Fisk.

I doubt she heard him. She spun away from us, stumbling off into the woods, and I felt a stab of remorse—despite all the pain she'd caused me and the others. She'd done them good as well as harm. Now she had nothing.

I felt surprisingly little remorse for the lie I'd told. My father wouldn't approve, but mayhap 'twas time to try living for my own approval.

As a child, I remember thinking that learning to tell the truth, even when it cost you, was the end of childhood. Mayhap learning to lie, when needful, is the beginning of adulthood . . . or mayhap I'd simply been too long in Fisk's company.

Fisk watched Lady Ceciel hurry away, his expression a blend of disappointment and relief.

"You're out of your mind," he said pleasantly.

"Why? She's innocent, and she can prove it.

Dragging her back to trial would be a waste of time. And 'twould be wrong."

"It would also have gotten your debt repaid! All you had to do was take her back—if she could prove her innocence she'd be acquitted! As it is, Mike, you're going to have a cursed hard time convincing your father to pronounce you redeemed. In fact, he can't— he set the terms publicly, in the old speech. You're going to be unredeemed! Permanently!"

"True." I gazed at his worried, furious face. He cared about me, but I had no illusions that Fisk had been reformed by our brief adventures. He was an excellent con man—reforming him would take years, if ever. But my own captivity had taught me that real trust, or friendship, is impossible between prisoner and jailer. If Fisk did harm in the world, 'twas his problem, not mine. I would miss the scoundrel, curse it. I drew a deep breath.

"Today seems to be my day for letting people go. I declare thee redeemed, Fisk."

"What!" The astonishment on his face was comical, but for once I had no desire to laugh.

"I declare thee redeemed. Your debt to me is paid— several times over. You can take Tipple, if you like."

As I spoke I slid from Chant's back, put the halter and rope on Lady Ceciel's mare, and adjusted her bridle for

Tipple. Fisk gazed at me in silence as I worked.

"There you go." I handed him Tipple's reins and remounted. "You were a good squire, Fisk. I'll miss you."

Fisk glared. "You *are* an idiot. At least make me pay for her. I have nine gold roundels and you're broke, remember?"

Actually I hadn't. I blinked.

Fisk moaned.

"Pay me what you will," I told him.

I turned Chant and set off toward the north. A longer way home, but Lady Ceciel's men would be less likely to intercept me . . . and soon Tipple's hoof-beats trotted up behind.

"But why didn't you take Ceciel back? You'd have fulfilled your father's conditions to the letter, if not in spirit."

"True," I said.

"You'd have been redeemed! You'd have gotten your honor back. You'd have been . . ." His jaw dropped.

"Made Rupert's steward," I finished. I'd been wondering when he'd figure it out.

"You devious son of a . . . I didn't think you had it in you! You're out of your mind! This is permanent! They'll tattoo your wrists!"

"True," I repeated.

"Your father will cast you off without a backward glance!"

"True."

"No job to fall back on. No more rescues from jail."

"True."

"If we can't scrounge a living at knight errantry, we'll starve! Even the beggar's guild won't take a permanently unredeemed man. No one will hire you."

"We?"

"I can't leave you on your own," Fisk ranted. "You'll probably be in jail again by the end of the week! You need a keeper more than anyone I've ever met. *Mike.*"

I winced, but 'twas better than "Noble Sir." And as my squire once told me, sometimes you have to settle for what you can get.

"That may be," I said. "But you'll get me out. Besides, I like a little adventure."

Life stretched before me, filled with freedom, and the shadows cast across my path hindered me no more than a chain that was no longer there.

HILARI BELL recently retired from a career as a librarian to pursue writing full-time. Her favorite books are fantasy, science fiction, and mystery. Not surprisingly, these are the kinds of books she writes very well herself, often combining genres when it serves her story. Her growing list of titles includes THE PROPHECY, THE WIZARD TEST, GOBLIN WOOD, and A MATTER OF PROFIT. Perhaps a starred review of THE WIZARD TEST in *KLIATT* describes Hilari's unique talent best: "Politics and intrigue, honor and friendship, are Bell's real subjects, and her novels are thought provoking as well as exciting reads." Hilari lives in her hometown of Denver, Colorado.